BEFORE THE FALL

CENTENARY EDITION

ORNA ROSS

REVIEWS

BIBLIOFEMME.COM: "An incredible debut that will have the reader absolutely enthralled."

SUNDAY INDEPENDENT: "The sort of book you could happily curl up with...A hauntingly captivating read."

IRISH INDEPENDENT: "An impressive canvas... a captivating read...an achievement."

EVENING HERALD: "A haunting tale...a gripping story."

SUNDAY TRIBUNE: "Epic sweep...ambitious scope... an intelligent book."

EMIGRANT ONLINE: "A riveting story...vividly brought to life."

AMAZON.CO.UK: "It made me laugh, it made me cry, it made me think. It's beautifully written. I highly recommend it."

BEFORE THE FALL

VOLUME II OF IRISH TRILOGY

PART I
BREAK

1995

*M*idsummer is past. The days are getting shorter again. Sometimes, it feels like I've never lived anywhere but this tiny shed, in this tiny village, on the edge of the ocean. My busy days in San Francisco — so full of to-dos and appointments — used to seep past without me, but here, my life is stripped down to six basic activities: sleeping and eating, writing and reading, running and relaxing. Time is mine again.

Life likes to take it easy, it seems, and the only way to be properly alive is to slow your pace to match.

So I find myself less bored than when I was busy, and less lonely than I've been for years, though I've never spent so much time alone. Solitude soothes me, along with the fresh air, the sound of the sea, and the past that I'm excavating with my pen. All are helping me to heal. I didn't know that was what I was doing when I came here, but I know it now, and I tell myself that's why I've stayed on, why I haven't yet left as planned.

I'm reading an election leaflet of Gran's from 1923 when a voice from the door interrupts. "Jo Devereux, sometimes I think you're mad."

I jump. Then I see who it is. Irritation, instant and involuntary, coils in me.

I don't want to stop writing, certainly not to listen to my sister's views on my lack of reason. Yes, it is Maeve, come all the way down to Mucknamore from Dublin to visit me. She stands at the door of my shed, neat and slim in linen shorts and Ralph Lauren polo shirt, her car keyring looped over one finger.

Living here as I have been since May, centred on the secrets I've been finding in my mother's family papers, I've long ceased to notice the dilapidation. Now, following my sister's eyes, I see what she sees. Flaking walls. A concrete floor. An unmade bed on one side of the room. Debris piled into the opposite corner.

"What brings you here?" I ask.

"Lovely welcome, I must say. Can I come in?"

I hesitate, conscious of my shape and that I never did get round to telling her.

It wasn't intentional. What I had planned was to go to Dublin, to see her there, and explain. I never thought I'd still be here in this shed so many weeks on.

There's nothing for it now except to get up from my chair and step out from behind the table.

Her eyes fall on my body, swoop in on my abdomen, then swing back upwards to my face. "What —?"

She is stunned, her face so very shocked that I find myself laughing, that nervous laughter she always brings up in me when I've done the wrong thing.

"Oh my God!" she gasps. "I don't believe it. Oh my God!"

"Let's go round the back," I say, voice airy, as if I am a society hostess suggesting tea on the lawn. "That's the nicest place to sit."

I take my rug from the end of the rumpled bed and, while she's swallowing her surprise, I lead her to the grassy patch where Rory and I have been sitting most long evenings of this long, strange summer. It's private out here, between the shed and the edge of the little cliff, and the sea is singing a soothing song today, as if it's on a go-slow, not really wanting to turn the waves over.

"You should have rung Hilde to tell me you were coming," I say, flicking the rug out over the grass. "I'd have arranged to meet you somewhere a bit more comfortable."

"I've been expecting to hear from you every day, Jo. You've been down here for weeks and not so much as a phone call. But," she breathes, "never mind all that...What about this?" She leans across as if to touch me, then changes her mind. "Look at you. My God."

I gesture her to sit on the rug. "Would you like something?" I remember to ask when I'm down. "A drink? I only have orange juice."

"Orange juice would be nice." She puts a hand on my arm to stop me trying to push back up. "I'll get it."

"It's just inside the door, in the corner. The coolest spot."

She comes back with two plastic glasses and hands me one. "That's quite a mountain of manuscript you've got in there."

"I know. It keeps growing on me."

"Am I allowed read it?"

I shake my head. 'Not yet."

"When?"

"Soon. I have to type it up, and it needs a lot of tidying."

She opens her mouth to say something, but closes it again.

"Sorry the juice is warm," I say, when the silence stretches too long. "No fridge, obviously."

"I really thought I was beyond being shocked by you, Jo, but you've done it again. Why didn't you tell me?"

"I didn't tell anybody." Well, nobody except Rory.

"Not even the father?"

"No. Especially not the father."

She dips her head down to her plastic cup, trying to stop the disparagement that's rearing up inside her. She is thin, I notice, too thin; her hipbones jut against her shorts.

"What about you?" I ask her. "How have you been?"

"Fine. Fine. Nothing compared to this."

"Are you sure?"

Her face creases. "Oh, up and down, I suppose." Then she tilts her head towards the house. "Two shocks in a row. What they've done to Mammy's house, to the shop...It's so different, isn't it?"

"Unrecognisable."

Our mother had died just as she closed the sale of her house to Hilde and Stefan Zimmerman, an efficient German couple who'd pre-organised planning permissions. They'd arrived to live here within a week of her funeral. Work had begun immediately and was well advanced already.

"I wish it could have been kept as it was for a while," Maeve says. "It would have been nice to get used to Mammy being gone first, before we had to deal with this too."

"It's been easier for me, I suppose, being here. Seeing it change day by day."

"I still can't believe I'll never see her again. Can you? I think of things I want to tell her before I remember she's not here. And it hits me all over again."

"Time helps," I say.

"Is it helping you?"

"It's not the same for me, you know that. I hadn't seen her for almost twenty years."

"Still, she was your mother."

I try again. "I do know the feeling you're talking about and how awful it is. Time really does help."

"Your friend Richard?"

I nod, gratified that she remembers.

"Well, then, I wish time would just hurry up and do its thing."

We both fall into a silence, looking out over the sea.

How have I let this shed become my home-away-from-all-homes? That's the question my sister's arrival has thrown into relief.

I was supposed to depart for Dublin a week ago. Yet still I sit, day after day, at my makeshift desk, sifting through sentence after sentence bequeathed to me by my mother and grandmother, telling myself I need to be here to do it when I know I'm really here for Rory.

Though I told him I was leaving. Though I wrote it down to show him, to show myself, that I really meant it and though every word I wrote was right and true. If Rory's marriage was indeed so wrong for him, if our love — the first love — was what he wanted, then that had to be formally acknowledged. Properly done. Slip-sliding into an affair was not an option.

So, I wrote him. I was leaving. I was going to Dublin where my sister would help me organise an obstetrician. I would have my baby there and, as soon as possible afterwards, I was going to fly back to San Francisco to make a new home as a single mom.

My letter set him free. "We missed our time, my love," it said and I can still feel how good it felt to write that, to break the will-we-won't-we game we'd been playing since I came back here at the beginning of summer.

If his wife and family were not what he wanted — if what he wanted was me — then he was going to have to find a way to tell them and do what he should have done the first time, twenty years ago, when it was all less complicated. Come after me.

I didn't quite say all that in my letter, but it was implied. "When we were young, I so wanted you to follow me," I said. "I wanted that long, long, long after there ceased to be any possibility that you might."

Hint hint, Rory. Over to you.

When Maeve arrived fifteen minutes ago, I'd been typing out documents. A letter to Peg from her friend Molly, a letter to Norah from Peg that was never sent, and an election leaflet that

seems poignant to me, that seems to carry in it all the yearning
that my grandmother passed down the years.

Dear Voter,

*We were told the Treaty with the British Empire would bring
peace. If so, what is WAR?*

We were told it would bring freedom. What, then, is SLAVERY?

We were told it would bring order. Then what is CHAOS?

*They said this Treaty would fill Irish pockets. It has filled only
Irish PRISONS and GRAVES. If the British Government is going to
keep fighting and destroying us, we prefer that she should use her own
English troops — as she does in the North of Ireland — and not our
own misguided pretend-politicians.*

*People of Ireland, come back to us. Our country's future is now in
your hands.*

*A REPUBLIC is the only basis on which we can build a proud and
prosperous national life. Use this coming election to vote NO to this
terrible Treaty. Then we can ALL share TOGETHER in the final
victory over the British Empire.*

Come back to us.

Vote for those who will yet SAVE THE NATION.

Vote Anti-Treaty.

It gets me every time, this leaflet put together by my
grandmother and great-grandmother. It's those words: "Come
back to us." Come Back.

People don't, do they?

We can't.

That's what I was trying to say to Rory, in my letter. Trying
to reclaim what we had, to start over, to get it right this time,
wasn't possible. No matter how much we wished it was.

So why am I still here?

"So tell me," Maeve asks, echoing my thoughts. "Why are you still down here? What have you been doing with yourself?"

"You saw that heap of papers in there. Reading and writing, mostly. Lying low."

"Is there anything of interest in those papers of Mammy's? Are they all rubbish?"

"Oh, no, they're not rubbish."

"Really? Tell me."

"I think you better wait until I've put it together."

She sits up, intrigued by something in my voice. "What on earth have you found?"

"All sorts of things."

"Deep dark secrets?" she grins.

"Yes, as a matter of fact."

"Things Mammy didn't tell us?"

"You're forgetting, Maeve, Mrs D. never told me anything."

That stops her smile. "Oh no, Jo, you're not going to write something Mammy wouldn't want known? Please tell me you're not."

I spread my hands and examine my fingernails.

"Jo!"

Above us a gull screams, slides across the air towards the sea. How much did Mrs D. know? That is the question. In her letter, she said she didn't read Norah's "scribblings" or all of Gran's diaries. I have read everything now, some of them many times, and still I'm not certain. Sometimes I find one thing in their words, especially Norah's. Sometimes another.

But what I hear in almost every sentence is the sound of their words shrinking from what they're saying, even as they say it. That's what speaks loudest to me across the years.

Maeve is annoyed with me again. "It's not your story, Jo, to do what you like with."

"Hey, calm down. I'll tell you in a while."

She looks sceptical.

"I will, Maeve, I promise. I just want to get it straight myself first."

"So you're not going against Mammy's wishes?"

I shrug. "Nothing I write can hurt her now. And if she really didn't want me to know — or write — about something, all she had to do was take it out of the suitcase."

"Maybe she wanted you — us — to know, but not the whole goddamn world."

I shake my head, though she's right, of course. That's possible.

Maeve takes off her sunglasses, blinks at me in the sunshine. "Jo, if you publish something she wouldn't like just to settle some score of your own, you'll be sorry later."

I don't think that's what I'm doing. I think I want to tell my family's story because if a story is to be told, it must be told as whole as we can tell it, not picking and choosing the bits that make us look good, as Mrs D. liked to do.

If I am to make anything meaningful of my life — and what else has this whole strange summer been about, if not that? — then I cannot let myself add one more drop to my family's unfathomable well of silence.

I know Maeve will never allow me all that, so I shrug and say instead, "There is no score."

She blinks even harder at this. I see her trying to calm herself, trying to find tactful, persuasive words to convince me. Just at that moment, you ripple inside me, then settle, like you are snuggling down.

I put my hand to where I feel you. Maeve notes the movement and, despite herself, smiles an indulgent smile. "Where are you going to have it?"

"I don't know."

"What does your doctor say?"

"I haven't seen a doctor."

"What? You're...how many months pregnant?"

"About six."

"Six months pregnant and you haven't seen a doctor?"

Here we go. I close my eyes, take a breath, wait for the next onslaught.

"That's just downright irresponsible."

This is why I haven't told her. Do all big sisters think they have this right to reprimand like this? It seems we don't have a single safe place to rest, Maeve and I, no matter how hard we both try.

"I'm sorry, Jo, but that's what it is."

"Correct me if I'm wrong, Maeve, but I thought this was my pregnancy?"

"When you're pregnant, Jo, you have more than yourself to consider."

"Yeah, well, I don't happen to think pregnancy is an illness. And I don't see why I need some doctor I've never met before to tell me I'm fine. I know I'm fine."

"But at your age especially..."

"Is this why you came, Maeve? To deliver a series of sermons?"

That works. "Oh God." She sighs and sags, like a pricked balloon. "How do you do this to me, Jo? Coming down in the car, I swore I wasn't going to criticise no matter what I found. But I never ever expected to find...this."

She's right, she can't help it any more than I can. Here we are, thirty-eight and forty years old, and as testy with each other as ever. We'll always be the same. The best time we ever had together was when she visited me in San Francisco, when we were on my territory, but here in Ireland, I'm her inadequate little sister again. Here, she'll always take liberties.

I try to appease her. "As a matter of fact, I am going to see a doctor soon."

"I'm glad," she says, trying to match my conciliatory tone. "Do."

"I will, I will."

I lie back, close my eyes to the sun. Should I tell her about Rory? What would I say?

That two days ago, I came out here, the day's work not so much done as abandoned for the evening, and found him sitting, his back to the shed, looking out to sea, waiting. He'd heard that I hadn't left after all and had come straight to me.

I knew that moment of seeing him there was one of the most important in our whole relationship. As important as the day when we were two children first spying each other across the village divide that separated our relatives. As important as the first time we spoke to each other properly, at a wedding, under the noses of our people. As important as the first night we slept together, twenty years ago, in his flat in Dublin. And yes, as important as the night soon after when I told him we were pregnant, and he responded so inadequately.

I hovered in the doorway of my shed, afraid to go forward. What would I say? Tell him to leave, to go back to his wife? Ask him to...Well, it doesn't matter now what I thought or considered saying, because all I did was go across and slip into sitting beside him.

We sat together for a long, long time, quietly watching the waves, afraid to speak. And ever since, it's been just as it was before, with him coming round each evening at sundown and us sitting, late into the night, talking, talking, talking.

It can't go on, I know. It has to stop, and soon.

While I'm trying to find words that might be able to explain some of this to my sister, she says, "You said 'her'? The baby's a girl?"

"That's how I find myself thinking. Of 'she', of 'her.'"

"So you don't know for sure?"

"No, how could I? But right from the start, I've had the feeling it's going to be a girl."

And it's true. "She," "her": these are the words I used when talking about you to my sister — or to Hilde or Rory — but most of the time we're not with others. Most of the time we're alone together and the word I use is "you".

You are changing me, making more of me: swelling my breasts and my girth, expanding my heart and my lungs, ripening and plumping my genitals, filling and darkening my nipples, increasing the volume of my blood.

You have splashed my skin with colour, drawn a bold line of brown down my belly. Greased and furry, somersaulting and thumb-sucking inside me, getting firmer in the world: you rely on me. Soon you will be what they call viable, able to breathe on your own.

Still I can see how you will draw on me, body, heart and soul, for the rest of my days. For the first time, I see how a mother birthed every bird and animal and person on the planet. Everything, everywhere, has been mothered into being: how had I never noticed that before? I think of all the churches holding up their God the Fathers, the men who have insisted that children carry their names through the generations and, instead of my usual anger, I feel pity.

You've unpicked the me I used to be. I am going to join the band of mothers, those people who let themselves fade in the light of their offspring, those people — like my sister — that I used to slightly disdain. Now, as I sit here with her, as I look back up the tunnel of time at our mother's life, and our grandmother's, and our great-grandmother's, what I disdain is that earlier, unknowing me.

"Did you know this place used to be called Bastardstown?" I ask Maeve.

This was a secret of Coolanagh sands that I came across while doing library research. Coolanagh, Mucknamore, Inisheen: these names for our village, and the topography around it, came from the Irish language, but outsiders gave the area this different, ugly, English name, because it was famous as the place to go if you had a baby you didn't want, or were unable, to keep.

Infanticide. Thanks to its unique play of sands and tides, Coolanagh was where reluctant mothers came, according to legend — truth's abiding sister — to do their agonizing deed.

The book I read about it was schlock. It told its grisly stories, some of them going back centuries, without pausing once to consider the lives of those women, of why they were unable to rise to the demands of motherhood. To the man who wrote it — M.K. Trevalyan — they were ciphers, travesties of pure-and-holy womanhood: mad, bad and murderous.

Maeve shivers. "Bastardstown. God, I haven't heard it called that in years."

But she doesn't want to talk about that. While she embarks upon another long stream of sisterly advice, I look out to Coolanagh. It looks so innocent out there, on yet another beautiful summer day. The tide is so far out that the sands stretch almost as far as the island.

What age was I when Gran first brought me out that causeway to tell me her story about these sands having swallowed an entire town? The height of her hip, anyway. Auntie Norah was with us and the three of us stood on the tallest dune and I felt like we were on the high deck of a ship, sailing through an ocean of sand.

Gran's palm was rough, I remember, like the skin on a rock, but hers was the hand I most loved to hold. I can feel the damp of her swimming costume against my cheek as I leaned my face against it. Beneath the fabric was her soft old flesh and underneath that again, her tough hip bone.

She pointed in a diagonal from where we stood, towards the island.

"Look across now at that stretch of sand," she said to me.
"There behind the barbed wire. Tell me what you see."

Hearing this, Auntie Norah took a few steps away from us.
Gran looked back but, unusually, didn't follow. Instead, she
pulled me in closer, gripped me tighter. "Do you notice anything
strange about what you're seeing?" she asked again. "Come on,
pet. Look a little harder."

I stretched my eyes for her.

"Can't you make out that double row of sand-hills near the
edge and that long, straight dip running in between?"

All I could see was an undulating blanket of sand that looked
flatter and flatter the further away you looked. The tide was way
out that day, just as it is now.

"I wish we could walk across to it," Gran said. "If we could
walk the length of it, you'd feel what I'm saying to you."

But we couldn't walk across Coolanagh sands. Young as I
was, I already knew that.

"What would you say if I told you that what you're looking at
is the rooftops of a sunken town?"

I turned my face up to hers, tried to read it.

"Yes, a sunken town. Under those bumps there, the ones that
are so regular, all in a row. See? That's from the houses down
below. And across there...that dip between them — " she pulled
my hand up, pointed my finger — "that's the long main street."

She began to talk in her story voice. "Fadó, fadó – a long
time ago – a big town stood on that spot I'm showing to you
now. A city it was called, though smaller in them days than any
of our cities now, but with its own charter to prove it. It was one
of the largest sea ports in all of Ireland, and so rich that it used
to send not one, but two, Members of Parliament to the
government in London. I'm talking hundreds of years ago now,
not long after the English first came to Ireland.

"What the poor people who lived in this city didn't know was
that their town was built on sinking sand. From the first day

those buildings went up, the sands were sucking at them — slowly, slowly drawing them down. So slowly that at first they didn't notice, but day by day it went on, until they came to know what was happening and to realise that they'd all have to leave.

"So they did. Still the city kept on sinking, until nothing was left of it above the ground only those bumps and hollows that you see before you."

At that, Auntie Norah, who must have been listening behind us, made an explosive sound, something like the harrumph of a horse. She started to walk away, back along the causeway towards home.

Let her go, the inside of my head pleaded to Gran, but already we were turning after her. "It's all right, Norah," Gran called. "Wait now, don't be going on." We broke into a run, my arm pulled along, Gran calling after her back: "Ah, Norah, where's the harm in a bit of an old yarn?"

In the library, researching facts about quicksand, I was astounded to learn that Gran was right. There was once a bustling seaport town on this spot, five centuries ago. And it was sand that caused its demise. The inlet silted up and couldn't be navigated and that was the end of the trade on which the town depended. It declined and died and, eventually, disappeared. All of it, every building, into complete oblivion, until there was almost no trace of evidence that it ever existed.

Everything else she told me about Coolanagh, though, was wrong. Quicksand does not suck, it is not bottomless, it does not have a life of its own. It is a phenomenon, not a substance; any sand can become "quick" given the right conditions.

On Coolanagh, those conditions are a stream flowing off the island onto the sands, the stream in which I once pretended to see fairies to please a bunch of mean Mucknamore schoolgirls. That, and a layer of rock underlying the sand that slows drainage, keeps the sand grains in permanent liquid suspension.

As to the danger, the books I read were divided. One said it was impossible for an upright human to sink below the surface of such sand. The density of human body mass is less than that of any sand–water suspension and so they'd never get down far enough. Yet people have died on Coolanagh. On the island, there's a cross which commemorates three people — a man and two women, who died out there in 1879 — as well as "all who fell victim to these sands". And there was Dan, of course, in 1923, the real source of my enquiry. They would have died, this book claimed, through trying to escape. It was their wriggling and writhing that would have pulled them face down into suffocation.

Another book disagreed. It held that a human body falling into deep quicksand behaves as it would on falling into deep water, plunging down below the surface then rising back up again. Except in quicksand, the higher density elongates the down-and-backup motion, so that the lungs run out of breath before the body re-emerges from the depths.

On the tidal sands of Coolanagh, there was a third possibility: the sea. A victim who survived an initial immersion in sand, who succeeded in re sisting the urge to struggle, would remain stuck in the sand until the arrival of help, or the return of the next tide. Whichever came soonest.

Since reading that book on Bastardstown, my head is full of lonely women and their lost babies, and thinking again of them now, it comes to me. That's why I'm still here.

As Maeve and I run out of conversation, as we get up and she prepares to leave, I'm only half with her. Talking to her about you has brought it all together.

I see it now. I'm being held here by the loss that Rory and I never discussed.

He and I were doomed before we got started: we knew it back then and the family papers have shown me why. But none of that excuses how we behaved. Or accounts for what we ourselves destroyed, what we added to the loss. And the shame. And the silence.

We've talked about everything else, he and I. Everything I've discovered about his family and mine. All the events of our lives since we met and before. Everything, except how we came to fail each other so very badly that I ended up taking that boat to London, without him.

1923

*K*nock, knock, knock! *Knock, knock, knock!* The sound had been going on for a while, Peg realised, as her sleeping ears woke to it. As it sank in that what she was hearing was somebody banging on the front door, like they were trying to rouse the entire county, she heard a voice calling. Her mother's, calling from across the hallway, from what used to be Barney's room, querulous in her weakness. "Peg? JJ? Peg?"

This was how they'd slept since Barney died: herself, her father and mother in three separate bedrooms, all doors open, in case Máire took a turn or needed anything in the night.

"It's all right, Mammy," she answered, already out of bed and shoving her feet into her slippers. "I'm coming."

Knock, knock, knock! again. Free Staters, no doubt, on another raid. Holy God, they'd been round twice already this month. They'd find nothing; they must surely know that by now. Nothing only the pleasure of persecuting true Republicans, a sport that never seemed to grow weary for them.

"I'm coming," she called to the front door as she hurried down the stairs, fast as she could without falling. Only when she opened the door, it wasn't soldiers on the step, but her neighbour, Mrs White, Lama's mother, and in a state.

All dishevelled, tears drying on her cheeks, with Tipsy Delaney beside her.

"I'm sorry, Peg," she said. "I'm sorry now to rouse you in the night like this, with you having the childer to teach in the morning."

"What is it? What's wrong? Come in."

"I didn't know where else to go. Tipsy suggested here."

No doubt he did. "That's all right, Mrs White. Come in, come in both of you." She ushered them into the hall. "What's happened?"

Her coat was on over her night clothes, and her hair was thrown up, falling out of its clips. In her hand, she was holding what looked like a letter.

"Is it...?" Peg stopped, not wanting to say her friend's nickname – Lama, so-called for his habit of saying "Lamb of God" every few minutes – to his mother. For a panicked moment, she found herself having a blank about the proper name of this boy she'd known her whole life long, who'd become a close friend in the experiences they'd shared over the past years, first in the War of Independence, and even more through being on the same side in this follow-up war.

This "War of the Brothers", as it was coming to be called. Only it wasn't only brothers divided. It was sisters, and friends, and parents from their children, and husbands from their wives.

John! she remembered, the name jumping to her mind. And with it her friend's face, long and angular and teeth forever stretched into a smile, like the wooden face on a rocking horse. A flood of feeling for him rushed in with the image, hot and soft.

When you shared a killing with somebody, as she had with Lama last October, it drew you close like nothing else. Even if the killing was something you knew you'd spend the rest of your days regretting, you were bonded to all involved.

And all the more so to Lama, with Barney, the third of the trio who'd done the deed, gone from them.

Killed in reprisal.

And now...? Was she in danger?

"It's bad," said Tipsy, his tongue, as always, a little too large in his mouth. Anyone looking at him would think he was smiling, but Peg knew better.

"Yes," wailed Mrs White, bursting into a fresh round of tears as she pushed the letter into her hands. "Yes Peg, it's John. It's the worst."

Dear Mother and Father,

I am very sorry to have to be writing what I know will be sad and shocking news for you. The Free State army has, without judge or jury, decided our fate. Tomorrow morning, at dawn, I am to be shot for my part in Ireland's fight for freedom.

This is a hard letter to have to write. But, if it were not for knowing how it will grieve you and Mattie and Janey and the little ones to receive it, I would not regret this way of leaving the world. I am proud to have served Ireland and I hope you, knowing I died to save the Republic, will be proud too.

I have seen a good priest, Father Carty from Kyle, and have made my peace with God. He who knows all has forgiven all and I, too, forgive the men who do this to us. Irish soldiers doing English work: they know not what they do.

I, and the three boys who will die with me, go to God in peace, knowing our blood — like that of Pearse and Connolly in 1916 — will bring new soldiers to Ireland's cause. For our cause is the cause of right and God is on our side.

So if you can, do not grieve me, Mother dear, or Father. We will meet again in Heaven.

May the Lord have mercy on us all.
Your loving son,
John.

JJ came downstairs, sent by Máire to see what the fuss was about and Peg, heart thumping as she read the letter a second time, sent him out to the byre to rouse George, the pony, and hitch up the trap. She sat Mrs White down in the parlour with Tipsy while she ran back upstairs to explain all to her mother. As always, Máire was roused out of awareness of her illness by Free State perfidy.

"You're right to go in," she said, when she heard what Peg intended. "Where there's life, there's hope."

"I pray we're not too late. And that they'll listen to reason. Surely even Free State soldiers won't sink so low."

"They've done it in other counties."

"But here in Wexford, Mammy. These are the selfsame boys who fought with us against the English. They surely won't do down one of their own."

"Take Tipsy in with you," said Máire. "They'll take more notice of a man, even poor Tipsy, than of a girl."

Would they? Peg wasn't so sure but the company would do no harm.

"Oh, I wish I could go myself, I'd give them what's what."

"We'll do our best, Mammy."

"I know you will, lovey. I didn't mean that. I just wish I was more use."

"You did enough, Mammy. You did more than anyone. We'd have no-one on the side of the Republic around here at all were it not for you. You rest yourself and we'll be back before you know it. With good news, I hope."

Peg kissed her cheek, as she always did now, whenever she

took leave of her, and looked back for a moment at the door. Her poor mother, so reduced in size, and face so changed, it was hard to believe it was her and not an old aunt or relative in her bed.

No time for any of that now. Peg took the stairs down two steps at a time, and led Mrs White and Tipsy out of the parlour, into a night of high, tight stars, and a sliver of moon. Calm and clear and dry. That, at least, was a blessing. The night air was cooling on the heat of her thoughts.

As they climbed aboard the trap, she handed Tipsy the reins, so she could keep Mrs White company.

Peg had never gone into town by night. This was a new road to her. The trees and ditches were shadows of black on black, turned inside out in their night clothes. She didn't recognise any of them. For a while, she tried to keep Mrs White distracted by small talk, but then let them both settle into their thoughts. Oh, but that letter of Lama's. It had sounded so final. Would they even be in time? It was thirteen miles into Wexford: the journey would take them the bones of an hour, more maybe in the dark.

And of course the never-ending questions about Dan O'Donovan came slithering to the surface. Would he be there, in the jail? If he was, what was she going to say to him? Would he be moved to help? It was a measure of how things had changed between them that she hadn't a clue of the answer to that.

Surely he couldn't possibly be involved in this, the execution of his old comrade? If he was, then he was capable of anything now. And that, of course, was the real question, the one that rose in her still, hour after hour, driving her into a torment that let go of her only while she slept — and sometimes not even then. Had Dan fired the shot that killed their Barney, his onetime best friend? Was he capable of such a thing? And was that the real reason he was keeping her and Norah apart?

He had assured her not, told her the kindest thing she could do for Norah was to leave her alone, insisted that Norah had expressly asked not to be contacted by the Parle family. And while he was before her, handsome and bulky and seemingly sincere, she'd believed him. His flashing eyes, the fervour of his words, his sorrow about Barney all but convinced her.

All but. But. But.

Words come easy to some but it's actions that tell the real story. If his reported doings were to be believed, only a fool could trust him. Organising round-ups; stalking about the county making raids and arrests galore; putting Lama, Molly, Des Fortune and other good friends behind bars: all that she knew to be true, but could maybe be explained by politics and conviction. She mightn't like that he thought different from the rest of them, and was willing to go against them, but it was a long leap from there to the other thing she suspected.

And now, this. Lama, his friend and hers, to be shot at dawn. Executed — a word that was never made to fit any of them. If it was true, and Dan had any part in it, then she had her answer.

Trusty George clip-clopped on. Somewhere along the way, Peg fell into a place between waking and sleep. She was half-dreaming — Barney was chasing Norah down the strand with Dan running after them and Peg was looking on from the top of the cliff, helpless — when the sound of hooves and wheels hitting a harder surface jolted her awake.

A good road. They were coming into the town.

How did anybody live in a town at all, she wondered, as the houses started to cluster together and road turned to street. It was so unnatural. She wouldn't be able to breathe if her house didn't have field around it and the sea in its sights. She put her face up to gulp some air and saw that light was cracking a thin, faint line across the horizon.

Dawn.

At dawn, I am to be shot for my part in Ireland's fight for freedom.

Oh pray God, not. Not.

The buildings huddled, stern in the darkness, saying nothing.

At the bottom of Hill Street she said, "Pull over the side here, Tipsy," and he did as bid. "Mrs White, you stay here and look after George. Tipsy and I will go see what we can find out."

The older woman's frightened eyes were so like her son's. How had Peg never noticed that before? She handed her the reins.

The sound of their boots rang loud in the empty streets as they ran towards the jail.

"What should we say when we get there?" she asked, knowing as soon as the words were out that Tipsy wouldn't have any ideas to offer. "Should we ask for Dan, do you think?"

All she got back was a shrug.

At the jail, there was nobody about: just the big oak door, closed, and the thick stone around it.

"There's nobody here," Tipsy said, specialising as always in stating the obvious, but she, too, had expected somebody outside. A sentry. Someone.

Tipsy knocked on the door. Nothing.

They knocked together, hard as they could, but the slab of wood swallowed the thin sound of their knuckles.

What now? She sat on a stone ledge, trying to straighten out the snarl of her feelings, to decide. How had she ended up here, outside a jail in the middle of the night, with Tipsy Delaney? Her brother dead, her best friend gone from her? Had she brought it on herself?

Was it that she liked being a freedom fighter more than was good for her? That she wanted her own way too much, as Dan said? Was he right? She saw that in her mother sometimes. Did she suffer from the same trait herself without knowing? Would she ever find in her thoughts a key that would open the door to peace?

Everything around them was slowly revealing its lineaments as the sun rose, but no such emerging light for her. As she sat, watching shadows become shapes, a barrage of rifle fire suddenly sounded from inside the jail. She and Tipsy jumped up together. This fusillade was followed by four single shots at short intervals. The echo of it pounded in their ears and reverberated over the town, on the quiet of early morning.

She ran over to the door and banged on it again, but it was such a weak, ineffectual sound, compared to what had just assaulted their ears. Oh sweet divine Jesus, what was she to do? She laid her forehead against the door and, from the other side, heard footsteps slowly approaching, then the sound of whistling. Whistling!

She stepped back. There was the sound of a bolt being pulled and the door started to move.

A soldier came out, with a hammer and nails in one hand, a notice in the other.

He was surprised to see herself and Tipsy — to see anyone — standing there. The three of them stared at each other for a long, uncertain minute, then he squinted at Peg.

"Miss Parle, isn't it? The schoolmistress from Mucknamore?"

She nodded. He looked familiar. Was he an O'Donnell? She wasn't sure enough to say. "Is it bad news for us?"

He turned, unable to cope with the question, and pinned the notice he had in his hand onto the door. She and Tipsy went close in, to read:

By order of the Government of the Irish Free State, the following men were executed by firing squad on this day, March 13th, 1923: John Creane of Clonerane, Taghmon; Patrick Hogan of William Street, Wexford; James Parle, of Clover Valley, Taghmon; John White of Mucknamore.

At that very moment, Mrs White came running up. "Did you hear that shooting, Peg? Tipsy! Did you hear it?"

Then she saw the soldier, the notice, the hammer in his hand.

"Oh my God! No. He's not...?" She sounded as shocked as if it was the first she'd heard of the possibility. "He's not, he's not, he's not, he's not."

Peg went to put a hand on her shoulder, but Mrs White shrugged it off as if Peg herself had done the killing, and dropped into the well of pain that was breaking open in her, hands to her face.

The soldier slipped back inside the door as fast as he could, away from the unbearable sound of her wailing, away from the unbearable sight. The latest in Ireland's long line of mothers bereaved.

Dear Dan,

I have been asked to write to you by Mucknamore Company, the organisation that you may recall first fostered your involvement with the Irish Republic.

You must know that the illegal body over which you and your associates now preside has — since the signing of your Treaty with England — declared unholy war on the soldiers of the true Republic.

We, on our side, have at all times adhered to the recognised rules of warfare. In the early days of this conflict, we took hundreds of your forces prisoner, but accorded them all rights of prisoners-of-war and better. We treated them as fellow citizens and former comrades-in-arms. Your soldiers have often been released by us, although captured with arms on each occasion.

But those of the Irish Republican Army (not long ago, your own army) that you have imprisoned, you have treated barbarously. When helpless, you have tortured and wounded them.

We have definite proof that many of your officers have been guilty of the most brutal crimes and have reduced your soldiers to a state of savagery on occasions.

And, now, you have committed murder. Your sham government pretends to try IRA prisoners before make-believe courts. After such mock ceremonials, you have done to death four of your former colleagues. We hereby give you due notice that unless your "Free State" army recognises the rules of warfare in future, we shall have to adopt very drastic measures to protect our Republican forces.

Irish Republican Army,

Mucknamore Company, South Wexford Brigade.

Dear Dan,

I won't send this one, but I need to write it. Did you get my earlier letter? I'm supposing you did, but how will I know, when you made no answer and we never speak any more? I was told what to write — did you realise that as you read it?

Dear Dan, my dear Dan, here's what I'd really say to you, if I could. I know why you took the turn you've taken and I understand. I do, truly. I know how it felt for you to be the outsider here in Mucknamore, with the wariness felt towards you and your family when you arrived here from Cork. You who had always been so liked and admired. I know it was hard for you. I know how you worried about what you'd do with yourself since the farm was for Thomas, and the priesthood definitely not for you.

And I can see how this gives it all to you, all solved. A soldier in the new army — a lieutenant, no less. A fancy title and uniform and boots and pay to match: all a young man could ask for.

But Dan, no good can come of it, you must know this. The one true way is the way of The Republic. Though that way is thorny now, denying it will do you no good in the end.

Dan, there are so many ways a person can fail to think enough of himself. The likes of you doesn't need a uniform and a shiny salary, especially one paid for with English money.

Oh Dan, don't you know that there are good people who see and know your worth without such trappings?

Oh Dan, won't you come back to us?

Please.

I –

Dear Molly,

Thanks for your letter and your kind words of sympathy. It means so much to hear from those who knew Barney well and truly mourn his loss with us.

Thank you too for the compliments about the ballad and Mammy's pamphlet. It was Mr Connolly, the printer, who said we should put that it was written "By A Comrade" instead of people knowing it was by two women (his mother and sister). He said it would sell better that way, and maybe he was right, because it has sold well – he is going to do a second printing. We just hope we did our boy justice in it.

All the talk here, as you can imagine, has been of the Free State executions. We were so shocked, as I'm sure you were too. The night after it happened, we organised a crowd to gather around the jail to recite the Rosary, and afterwards we marched to St Peter's Square, where we held a protest. The Staters broke us up, of course, firing shots over the head of the crowd. But they won't find it as easy as all that to scatter us.

More and more people are coming onto our side, sickened by their actions. Our main aim now is to make governance of the country impossible by disrupting the railways and destroying public buildings and services. Proper soldiering would, of course, be preferable, but this is all we can do for now, with no money, no arms, no ammunition and no jails.

It's that, or stand idly by while they wreck our Republic, end to end.

We are also to make private "Big Houses" – owned by unionists –

a target. The bigger the property, the more likely to receive our attentions. Joe Hickey calls their fine paintings and books and furnishings immoral. "Wealth built on the sweat and starvation of the native Irish," he says. And he's not wrong, but it gives me a queer feeling to think of any private house being burnt out. And to imagine books and paintings that took generations to gather, being destroyed.

What do you think, Molly?

I'm glad to hear conditions are not too bad for you there in Kilmainham. It must be hard to be locked up, even with the company of the other girls. It's very quiet around here without yourself and Norah. I'm in danger of going loo-lah, I sometimes think, from being too much on my own.

Not that I should complain, Molly. I do know, of course, that it's much worse for you, locked away without trial, indefinitely. I'm not really comparing. Don't mind me.

The children in school are a great comfort. When I have doubts, I look to their little faces, and think about their future, and know we work so they may grow up in a new Ireland. An Ireland no longer enslaved.

God bless their innocence. It has saved me more than once in these dark days.

And God bless you, my friend, and may He soon bring about your release.

Yours truly,

Peg

Dear Norah,

This is the letter I wish I was sending, instead of the one I just wrote to Molly that's sitting there on the table before me, all stamped and ready for the post.

I am so tired, Norah, and I'm so lonely.

There. I've said it. I needed to say it. I miss Molly, yes, and all the

*others imprisoned. And Lama I can't think of without a hole opening
in my heart. But it's nothing to how much I miss Barney and you and
— yes, let me write this also, for I can, as I'll not be sending this
anywhere but the back of my diary — I miss your brother too.*

More than anything, how things used to be between us all.

*If you were here, Norah, I could talk to you about all this, instead
of the half-truths and platitudes I have to feed Molly and Mammy
and everyone else. I would tell you how a decade has settled on my
father's poor shoulders and bewilderment taken over his eyes.*

*We could discuss how Mammy squashes any scruples and won't
hear of any uncertainty or doubt, and how that can't be good for her,
not with her facing her Maker any one of these days.*

*I'd tell you how each of us in this house lives with the fragility in
the other two, making us over-careful of one another — and so
separate in our sorrow.*

*If you were here, Norah, I wouldn't constantly be thrown back on
— of all people — Tipsy Delaney, the only one, besides myself, left
alive and not imprisoned. He comes down to the shop most evenings
now and we always end up talking about the old days, before the split,
when we were all together, fighting the English. How simple it seemed
then, how happy we were. It was only months ago, yet so far from us,
it might as well be decades.*

*Tipsy and I sound ancient when we get going, harking back, back,
back, like exiles in America, lamenting all the fine things we've lost,
things we took for granted when we had them.*

*If you were here, I'd tell you how sometimes I am sickened by our
own side's attitudinising. How I'm tormented by all the opposing
opinions I carry inside me, fighting against each other.*

*The latest I heard is that four Stater officers are to be shot dead as
a reprisal for the executions in Wexford Jail. Is this right or wrong? Or
is there some other category for an event like this?*

*There was a time you could take a question like that to Mass or to
your priest, but the church is a disgrace now, the way it has turned
against us to side with the "Free State".*

Tipsy says I should stop looking for answers, get used to living inside a question-mark. It was a strange thing to say, but the things he says sometimes make a strange kind of sense. It's funny, we all think Tipsy such a fool, yet he's the only one of us to have come out of this business intact.

He was on the run with the boys in the best days, when the people were still with us and, somehow, without letting anyone down, he seemed to miss out on the most troubling actions, like the Donore raid that still has me waking up in sweats.

Oh, Norah, I'll never forget that bomb dropping in a big, slow arc off Donore Bridge, landing in that lorry and blasting those four soldiers out of this life. Over and again it plays out in my mind, especially when I'm in bed. The sight of it falling from Barney's hands, dropping down and bursting into blast on contact. Then that soldier, who was somehow thrown clear, getting up and trying to run, and Barney and the boys finishing him off from the bridge.

I find myself sometimes with my eyes squeezed closed and my hands over my ears. How stupid, when it's inside myself that the sight and the sounds are sealed.

Tipsy has no such guilt on his conscience. And somehow he's escaped jail too. He just wandered back home when the going got rough and took back up the work on the little farm where he lives with his mother. The soldiers don't ever bother them, while we're persecuted, not able to turn around without them bursting in and pulling the place apart, with no regard for the illness in this house, or our bereavement. Worse than savages, all humanity absent.

Here's something else I'd have to tell you, Norah. Two nights ago, in reprisal for Dan's involvement with the executions, our boys went up to your house, and ordered out your parents and the children, and sprinkled your house with petrol, setting it alight. When I heard of the planned action, I didn't know what side I was on.

Of course, I was right glad when prompt action by a neighbour saved the house, with only slight damage to the front parlour. And nobody was hurt. Nobody was ever going to be hurt; that wasn't the intention. They were ordered out. The intention was to send a message, loud and clear, to your brother.

What side would you have been on, Norah? It was your house, your people, but you'd grown so far from them in the freedom fright, or you'd seemed to. Only Dan said otherwise. Did you really tell him you wanted nothing more to do with our family? I could understand, Norah, given all that happened, if you did — but did you? Did you?

If you were here, I'd get some answers to these questions that plague me night and day. We would sort it, I know, complicated as it is, if we were only one in front of the other. You wouldn't blunder in on top of me, trying to flatten my opinions with yours. We might differ but you'd be reasonable. We'd fathom it out.

I thank you now, as I should have before, for all the times we were able to do that together, Norah. I never knew what a precious thing it was until it was taken from me.

I miss you for it. And I thank you for it. That is what I'd so like to say to you, if I only knew where you were.

1981

I'm told there are those whose lives exceed their expectations. Is this really true? For me, imagining and anticipation are always the high point of any experience. So it was here, now. London life had not turned out as I imagined at the age of eighteen.

In my early days here, I used to wander about the city on my days off, looking at the pigeons strutting about on their wine-coloured legs, wondering where they'd flown in from, admiring their sense of ownership. Two years on I seldom go into the centre where the pigeons gather and, if I do, I almost always find myself staring into the river, twelve times the width of the Liffey, but the same murky colour. The same as all city rivers, carrying so many centuries of human debris that they become unable to reflect the sky.

My home in London is near Brent Cross, in a dark and dank basement flat in a dark, dank and indefinable suburb. Its single opaque window faces the garden above, tinging the light -— such as it is — green. Mrs Fairbairn, my landlady, resents her dependence on paying tenants and, aside from visiting us once a week for her money, does her best to pretend we're not here.

I cannot ignore her in return as her dog, Bruno, thumps his tail on my ceiling all through the hours that I am here.

But I am not often here. By day, I work in Montgomery's of Hillingdon, a huge paper products distributor. I am the voice at the end of a phone-line, the person the customers get to shout at when their serviettes, kitchen towels or toilet rolls don't arrive on time, or are the wrong size, or the wrong colour. I take the insults that spill into my ear, the accusations of our company's incompetence, and hand the customers polite apologies in return.

If you cared about the bad and hoped for the best, you couldn't do my job, but it's easy for me. I expect the planning department or distribution to bungle, although I always pretend to be surprised. I despise them for caring so much. It's only toilet rolls, I want to say.

They'll be with you tomorrow, I think, as I'm offering the formulaic words that muffle true thoughts: "I'm so sorry. Yes, I understand. Let me see what I can do for you." Or the next day. Or next week. Who cares?

I'm dead to everything in that office, except the clock circling its hands, slowly, slowly, round the minutes. Morning break, then lunch, then afternoon break and, finally, half-past five when I can cover my typewriter, lock my desk drawer and walk out of the office, out of the building, out though the gate, to a few hours of life.

Evening life. Real life. It usually begins in the Rose and Crown, with some of my new friends, Mark and Sandra or Joe and Frank, Sadie and Melo or Anita, Kim and Natalie, snuggling into soft seats where we'll light up our insides with alcohol, as darkness begins to press in against the windows. All you need to join the group is a willingness to laugh, to tease each other and belittle our bosses.

Or at least that's where we begin. By end of the night, the

mood has usually shifted, changed by some secret that's come surfing out on the alcohol. Sandra crying about how she always wanted children and now it's too late. Frank confessing to a bullying father. Natalie talking about the stresses of a Down's syndrome brother.

I share too, but nothing too heavy. When I'm asked why I came here, I talk about unemployment in Ireland, the need for work. I can no more say the A word after doing the deed than I could before. No, I tell them about the convent and the village and other things that are ordinary in Ireland but exotic to them. Nobody realises I'm only handing over the bits that don't matter.

On weekend nights, we follow our drinking bouts with a nightclub, an Eden of wet kisses and grinding hips. I meet men there, lots of them. No one like Rory, but I know now that Rory was not what I thought. He hasn't come, he hasn't even written. And now I know he won't.

So I go with others, expecting nothing of the encounter but desire. Their desire, not mine. Admiration is what I am after, and I collect it from any source, even from those who are too eager. That's the way I prefer to keep them, keen and slightly beneath me, taking what they offer, flitting on to the next.

The key to it all is vodka, clicking me open and surprising me with what pops out. I wait for the moment of intoxication when the sober world gets shrugged off like a dull outfit and resplendent me emerges, arrayed in flashes and sparkles. It usually comes halfway through my fourth drink, sometimes earlier. For a while, then, the whole world seems contained in whatever warm and noisy place we are in and I am suffused with love — there is no other word — for my drinking friends and myself.

It never lasts. Soon it slides into confusion and dejection and sometimes, if I've had too much to drink too many nights in a row, I can miss it altogether, go directly from self-consciousness to self-pity without any exuberance in between. Yet that perfect interval is the promise that alcohol always seems to hold out. That's what I drink for.

That, and the licence it gives me to be bad. Whenever I start to sing or shout or flirt or laugh too loud, Natalie teases me: "So you are Irish, after all." As if they ever thought of me as anything else. One of the guys in the office even calls me that. "Hey Oirish!" he says, by way of hello.

Even my own name is different here. Jo Deveroh, I am called now, the "x" that Wexford people always sound made silent. "Dever-ex?" my friends hooted, when I first introduced myself. "Dever-ex! Ha-ha-ha."

I have learned to say it their way.

I am the outsider in London, so my ways are not just different, they are wrong, and in nothing more than this: my way of speaking. I have never been talkative but now, when sober, I speak only when I must. I slow my sentences, enunciate more clearly, skip around the snare of the English "th", a sound that unsettles the swing of my own words in my own mouth. I swallow Irish jokes, though I know they arise from the very ignorance they mock.

Every immigrant is awkward as they grapple with new ways, but the English don't think of us as immigrants, or Ireland as another country. They label our lack of fluency, our way with their language, as stupidity. Few of them know, or care, about the history that rammed their language into our ancestors, a language so foreign to us that — two whole centuries on — the rhythm of a sentence on an Irish tongue still makes an English "th" impossible.

To them, we're not different enough to be alien; we're just inferior versions of them. And of course there's part of me that agrees.

Most, but not all. Kathleen in marketing, who also happens

to be the best looking girl in Montgomery's, chooses to have an Irish passport. Not just because it's cheaper, she tells me. Though born and bred in Bolton, she spent every childhood summer with her grandparents in Donegal. "I feel Irish," she says, her hand to her chest, her eyes shiny, almost damp. And I smile, disarmed.

Sometimes, on the tube or the bus or walking down the street, my ear will pick up on soft, hissy 't's at the end of words, or the thudding 'th's at the start and I'll turn and talk to these strangers, about what part of Ireland each of us is from, and how long we've each been over, and whether we'd like to go back. There seem to be only two variations — either they yearn to return or, like me, they'd never even consider it.

Exiles or escapees.

Coincidences crop up often with these strangers — shared times or places or acquaintances. I laugh at Londoners who expect me to know everyone from home, but now I find myself doing the same. Ireland seems very small from here.

Dear Jo,

I got your address and telephone number from Deirdre Mernagh. Don't be cross — I bullied it out of her by telling her there was a crisis at home (there isn't). I was going to ring, but I thought it might be better to write first.

I hope you're keeping well. Deirdre tells me things have worked out for you over there. That's good anyway, although it's a pity about your degree. I heard a bit about what went on the night you left, but I don't really understand. Mammy is very upset about it all, but I suppose you know that. Don't worry, I'm not taking sides.

It's just that she'd love to hear from you. We all would. Maybe you might think about coming home at Christmas? Whatever happened, it shouldn't be allowed to drag on.

Granny Peg is not that well. She took a bit of a turn a few weeks ago and has been told she has a heart condition. She's on tablets now and is supposed to give up the fags, but you know yourself.

Mammy is well and Auntie Norah is the same, no change.

I am still working at the school in Terenure where I did my teacher training. I teach fifth class this year, they're a nice bunch so I'm having a fairly easy time of it. Also, I have met a nice fella. He's called Donal and he's an accountant. I've been going with him for six months and I suppose you could say it's getting serious. He goes to England a lot on business so you never know, I might go with him sometime and meet up with you.

Well, that's it for now, Jo. Don't lose touch altogether, you hear?

I'll give you a ring in a while.

Mind yourself.

Love,

Maeve

One late November evening, I return to our table in the Rose and Crown and know, from the unnatural way my friends are talking as I sit down, that the subject has been changed. They'd been discussing me.

Natalie tells me it wasn't me they were talking about but "the bombs."

The IRA explosions that have been going off all over England, the most recent — the third this year — killing twenty-one people and injuring hundreds in Birmingham.

London and Guildford have also suffered. The Guildford bomb went off in a pub too, and that's what my friends had been considering while I was in the Ladies. Imagining what it must have been like for those people. Wondering how we'd react, if one exploded there and then in our pub.

A conversation they felt they couldn't have in front of me.

Northern Ireland. The residue of England's centuries-old

"Irish problem", the quandary that leaves the everyday English person squinting, helplessly, into inexplicable darkness. The Fighting Irish. Irrational, truculent, violent, doomed by fanatical sectarianism, who could be expected to understand them?

Who can make them see reason?

This is how my English friends play it, but they're not truly convinced. They know their country is not blameless, but they feel defensive. What has it to do with them? Ancient history. Can we please let bygones be and move on?

I don't explain to Natalie how it is not as bygone as we all wish it was. Instead, I spell out how I'm from Wexford, which is the other end of the country. How I have no sympathy with the IRA and no longer care whether Ireland unites or not. How I am glad to be here in London, even when I feel awkward and different, how it keeps me attentive, stretches me. How I'm not the same as the people of the huddling communities in Kilburn and Cricklewood, who came over in the 1950s and immediately set up their own mini-Irelands over here.

She's not listening. They have put me in the Irish camp. Irish is what I am, whether I claim it or not.

It's been months. Still nothing from Rory. I know now I have to drop the possibility that there ever will be.

I am promoted in work. Customer Service Manager. Mr Green, my boss, tells me my prospects are excellent, if I play my cards right. Work hard, but more important, be seen to be keen. Take a class by night: the subject doesn't matter, the piece of paper is the thing. The higher-ups are on the lookout for career girls. "We have to improve our 'gender quota'," he says, holding the words out and away from him.

My new job often keeps me busy and, often, late in the office. As soon as I can get away, I do, and join my gang down the pub. They thought my new status might affect our drinking dynamic, but I won't let it. I am the last one standing most nights, so they'll know where my allegiance lies.

Between work and socialising, I am rarely at home, except to sleep myself back to recovery. Dirty dishes accumulate in my sink until furred. Magazines, cups, glasses, papers surround my bed, like fallout from a blast. My clothes get picked up from the floor, laundered as I need them, but never find their way back into the wardrobe. Some days I have to turn my knickers inside out because I have none clean and no time to get to a shop before work. Time and money keep calling at me to pay attention, but I am gone, off and away.

Then, suddenly, unexpectedly, I meet Jack. Jack Ward. A teacher. Not just that, a teacher of disabled kids. An unlikely boyfriend for me in every way, so different to any of the others. Jack has none of Rory's flamboyance, but he lets me be and — for the first time in my life — I don't try to impress, don't do what I think will win approval. I carry on drinking as I have always done and in his company I am raucous, shouting and singing and swearing. None of it fazes him. He smiles through it all, goes home when he feels like going, stays and sings along if that's his mood.

Jack takes pleasure in everything – walks in the park, Sunday mornings with the newspapers, nights out to the cinema – but the me he likes best is the one who comes out when we're home, snuggled up, three-quarters way down a bottle of red wine. He is uncomplicated in bed, easy to delight. Kind, gentle, good-looking and more clever than I allow, he sneaks into my life with his openness, his ease with the world.

It seems audacious. Surely it will rebound on him?

Jack rarely meets me straight after work with my friends, though he easily could, his school being just one tube station from The Rose and Crown. He likes to shower his working day away, to change his clothes, to have something to eat before he goes out, instead of making do with crisps and salted nuts until we go to the takeaway after closing time. He rarely comes clubbing with us either, though he loves to dance. He prefers it when it's just the two of us, he says without rancour, without the least pressure on me.

Sometimes it annoys me that he is so agreeable. He has such confidence in himself, in me. He is like me in my old days with Rory, thinking love was enough. Asking for trouble

PART II
REFLUX

1923

North Dublin Union

Dear Peg,

You'll have noticed the change of address above. So much has happened since I last wrote, I hardly know where to start.

I have to say that we felt not altogether unfortunate to be in Kilmainham Jail for Easter weekend. The seventh anniversary of the 1916 Rising felt like a good day to take our Oath of Allegiance again to the Republic and to be one of three hundred Republican girls housed there, where those brave heroes were executed.

Now, a few weeks later, what a contrast!

It began when we were told that we were to be moved from Kilmainham to North Dublin Union, a former workhouse. We were none too keen on this idea, as Kilmainham, with its noble association, suited us far better. Also, Mrs O'Callaghan and Miss MacSwiney were still on their hunger strike (nineteen days by then) and we were very anxious about the effect of such a move on them. So we sent our decision to the governor: no prisoner would consent to leave until the hunger strikers were released.

Our best strategic position seemed to be the top gallery, as it is caged in with iron bars running around the horseshoe-shaped building. So we took up our posts. The place was in darkness, except for one lit window beside a gateway, behind which figures of soldiers and wardresses hurried back and forth. Our officers gave the instructions: we were to resist, but not attack; we were not to come to one another's rescue; no missiles were to be thrown; and, above all, for the sake of the patient in her cell, no one was to cry out. Then we knelt and said the Rosary and, after that, we sang some of Miss MacSwiney's favourite songs.

Suddenly, the gate opened and the men rushed in, across the compound and up the stairs. The attack was violent, but disorganised. Brigid O'Mullane and Rita Farrelly, the first seized, were crushed and bruised between men pressing up the stairs, dragging them down. Our commander, Mrs Gordon, was next. It was hard not to go to her rescue as she clung to the iron bars, the men beating her hands with their clenched fists. When that failed to make her loosen her hold, they struck her twice in the chest, then one took her head and beat it against the iron bars. I think she was unconscious after that. I saw her dragged by the soldiers down the stairs.

The men were determined. Some twisted the girls' arms, some bent back their thumbs. Some were kicked by a particular CID man who was fond of using his feet. One was disabled by a blow on the ankle with a revolver. Annie McKeown, one of the smallest and youngest, was pulled downstairs and kicked in the head. One girl had her finger bitten off, Lena O'Doherty was struck on the mouth, one man thrust a finger down Moira Broderick's throat. Lily Dunn and May O'Toole fainted. They do not know where they were struck.

My own turn came too. After I had been dragged from the railings, a great hand closed on my face, blinding and stifling me, and thrust me back down to the ground, among trampling feet. After that, I remember being carried by two or three men and flung down in the surgery to be searched. Mrs Wilson and Mrs Gordon were there, their faces bleeding. One of the female searchers was screaming at them like a drunkard on a Saturday night; she struck Mrs Gordon in the face.

They removed watches, fountain pens and brooches. Our orders not to hite back were well obeyed.

The wardresses were bringing us cups of water and they were crying, and some of the soldiers too looked wretched, but the prison doctor – and a few other soldiers – looked on, smirking, smoking cigarettes. The doctor seemed to have come along for the entertainment; he did nothing to help any of the injured girls.

After another long struggle, we were thrown into the lorries, one by one, and driven away.

Peg, you have to let the world know of this disgrace. I don't know whether word has reached the newspapers or not; we're so much more isolated in this place than we were in Kilmainham. Please also tell the world that Republican women are housed in a place that is filthy and freezing, with no privacy or facilities for washing or bathing. The sentries can, and do, look into our wards on the ground floor. We've asked to have the lower window panes frosted or painted but no, so we have to hang clothes over them to get in or out of bed. We're experiencing every kind of discomfort: hunger, cold and dirt. And, though only a few yards from one of the most populated districts of Dublin, cut off from everything.

We have had no news since of Miss MacSwiney. We hear rumour of peace moves outside, but never see a paper. Please fill me in on everything you know when you write. I haven't heard from Norah this long time: tell her she's not to forget me. The person who gives you this letter will tell you how to get mail through untampered.

Please also tell your mammy and daddy I was asking for them and that I keep Barney in my prayers.

I was thinking of you and the family at Easter time.

You will write soon, won't you, to

Your friend,

Molly

Mucknamore,

> *26th June, 1923*

> *Dear Molly,*

> *Thank you for your recent letter: what shocking news. Yet nothing should shock us anymore.*

> *What do you think of the ceasefire? I don't know what to make of it. I agree with Mr de Valera that further sacrifice would be in vain but I don't understand what's going to happen next. It can't be over. What was worthy of bloodshed a month ago now can't be unworthy now, surely to God.*

> *And surely to God they're not going to tell us that those who died did so in vain, or that women subjected to the assaults you'd experienced are to pretend it never happened.*

> *Be assured that the few bits of weaponry we have left here in Mucknamore went into a safe dump. I suppose we can add to them as time goes on. We'll be keeping quiet for a while, though. Areas never before visited now swarm with troops and they're bringing in a new Public Order Bill.*

> *So, ceasefire or not, it's clear they don't intend to soften. Flogging as a punishment for arson or robbery — did you ever hear the like?*

> *And I don't think the ceasefire makes it one bit more likely that you, or any of the prisoners, will be let out.*

> *They'd be afraid to have too many of us on the loose, in case we might go to the weapon dumps and start the fight again. Which is exactly what would happen, of course.*

> *Still, it's against any notion of democracy to incarcerate thousands of people without trial or prospect of release. And now we're to have this election. Run by a State we don't believe in, yet we're to field candidates to give the people the opportunity to show they support us. But if we win, they won't take their seats. They can't take part in a government they don't believe in.*

> *It's one of those jokes that makes nobody laugh.*

> *But I'll support the work, of course, and do what is asked of me.*

Mammy and I have been writing a bulletin to distribute, house to house. See what you think of this:

Dear Voter,

They said this Treaty would fill Irish pockets. It has filled only Irish PRISONS and GRAVES. On behalf of the King and Commons, the Irish "Free State" government has — in fourteen months — murdered, executed, tortured and imprisoned more Irishmen than were killed by the English during six years of terror (1916–1922).

There's more about the SLAVERY and CHAOS created by the Treaty — and then it asks them to come back to us and VOTE AGAINST IT.

Mammy helped me with it. We think it will stir the Irish people in the right direction. What do you think? It would be great to have your opinion.

At least this time we women, and the young men under thirty, will be allowed our vote. Small mercies, but we may as well be thankful for them, because it doesn't look like we'll be having any big ones coming our way anytime soon.

Your friend,

Peg

Oulart, Co. Wexford, 29th September, 1923

Dear Miss Parle,

You don't know me. I am writing on behalf of a friend of yours, Miss Norah O'Donovan. She has asked me to tell you that the reason you haven't heard from her is because she is in the asylum in Enniscorthy. She has been there since May of this year, looked after by the Holy Sisters of Mary where she was held before, but she remains enclosed.

She is in good health and manages all right most of the time, but it can be hard. She is inclined to be a loner and that is not allowed in the asylum, not unless you are sent into confinement.

She also asked me to say that she has written to you many times. It was her firm belief that you never got those letters. We know the asylum holds on to letters if they do not want them sent.

I believe a visit from you would cheer her greatly.

Write to me at the address above if you want more information.

Yours sincerely,

Mary Clooney

1995

*R*ory comes with me to Enniscorthy, takes a day off to drive me to the hospital. He's back again, visiting every night, and I can't help but let him. And when he heard what I was intending to do today, he insisted on coming along, though I could easily have taken a cab. That big building up on the hill always fascinated him, he said, and he'd love to take a look inside.

And after all, Norah was his aunt too.

"It's hard to believe that she used to be good-looking," I say to him, as we set off. "Peg is always talking in her diaries about how beautiful she was."

"I only remember her as an old woman."

"She had deteriorated by then. She had been through so much."

He changes gear, his hand brushing against my thigh. It feels strange to be out with him in the world beyond the two square yards of grass outside my shed. At night, we are careful to keep further apart.

It's so physical, the attraction I feel for Rory: whatever it is that makes one body attract to another, we have it. Always had, since I was ten years old and looking at him across the gap put in place by our relatives.

And I know he feels it too, though he's better than me at hiding all he feels under that jokey façade he's made his.

That part of me, which I thought was numbed forever, is thawing. I know he's not the only reason I feel good these days, but this quivering delight that runs through me all the way down my limbs and into my fingers and toes: that's him.

As we drive through Wexford, he shows me his office, with its view over the harbour: Rory A. O'Donovan, Solicitor. Conveyancing. Family Law. Company & Commercial.

"Rory A.? A.?" I burst out laughing. "Not Aloysius? I had forgotten all about that. Rory Al-oo-ISH-us O'Donovan, Gentleman At Law." I drag out the syllables, as we did when teasing him about that name years ago. "I can't believe you use that."

"I had no choice. They throw you out of legal-land if you don't," he says. "You have to sound important. One name doesn't cut it." He's smiling, but there's an edge under the insouciance. His sense of being in the wrong life.

I feel sorry I brought it up. Then the part of me that wants him to acknowledge its wrongness is glad. He's brought his camera; he will photograph what we find in Enniscorthy. At least I can be glad about that.

Each night now, he fills my sleep. Him and tiny babies, that's all I seem to dream about these days, as if my subconscious mind is funnelling in. Two nights ago, it was that the baby was born and I was running along the beach, with her snug in a sling against my chest. I looked down to smile at her and found the sling was empty. She was gone. Panicked, I retraced my sand footprints, but no matter how hard I looked I couldn't find her.

I have dreamt of breaking her leg while changing her clothes, of dropping her on her head, of her floating out to sea. Once I dreamt she slipped down behind the skirting board in my San Francisco apartment: I was calling everybody in a frenzy, all unknowing that she was there, at my feet, her cries too tiny to be heard. As I shouted down the phone to Maeve, my baby came back, settled into my lap. But another tiny baby was still there, behind the skirting board, crying, crying, crying, while everybody else went around, all unknowing.

It is almost twenty years to the day that I travelled to London with Dee. That's what I'm carrying in me as Rory points through the windscreen at the café where he enjoys his morning latte and Irish Times, and at the pub where he meets his friends after work on a Friday. For the first time since we were students, wrapped around each other, I'm getting a sense of his everyday life.

This carries in it all the longing of the years apart, especially the early years and my time in London. We've never mourned what we made happen back then. I need to mourn it. I need him to mourn it.

Now does not feel like the time to talk about all of that, but if not now, when? We can't go on like this, I say to myself, once again. Yet whatever is next, I'm not urging it on as I would have before. I do know that the time is coming when we must either tilt forward or retreat forever.

For now, I feel safer here on the unknowing edge. And anyway, today is Norah's day.

A mile or so from Enniscorthy town, the building comes into view: a massive, neo-Gothic, red-brick concoction, utterly incongruent with the landscape and other buildings around. In the convent, we used to joke about this place, like we joked about everything we feared. We'd circle our fingers round our temples or turn our eyeballs inwards towards our noses.

The size is staggering and its looming presence at the top of the hill always draws comments from visitors. "What is it?" they ask, awed by its wings and towers and turrets, its two hundred windows glowering down at the road and railway below.

Today, the stigma is supposed to have gone. We've been taught to say "mental illness", not lunacy; "patients", not inmates. Walls have been knocked down, gates opened, people released into the community, but it's still a place apart, moated by green fields and trees, the nearest house a distance away, and the shame that soured the word "asylum" lives on.

Rory's car purrs in through the gates and up the short avenue. The building is tamed as we approach from the side, losing the scale of its vast dimensions. Up close, it's the smaller details that catch your attention: the weeds cracking through the tarmac, the shutters blacking out so many windows, the paint flaking off pillars near the door. Two men sit at the entrance, one beside each pillar, so still they might be statues. One of them is shrivelled with age, perhaps old enough to have been in here with Norah back in the 1920s. Only their eyes move as they watch us park, get out of the car, and approach.

Their staring makes me more conscious of how we must look to them. Like a couple, a man and his pregnant wife. I am acutely aware of my belly, thrust forward, and I want to take Rory's arm and lean against him, to be supported through what is to come. I resist and we walk between the two men with a gap of air between us.

The younger man says, "Good morning," but in a blank way that makes me wonder whether I imagined it.

"Hello," Rory and I say together, our voices too loud.

Inside, we are welcomed by Miss Bell, the administrator, who allocates us one of the many empty rooms with a desk and two chairs and shows us the cupboard where the hospital records are stored. She is sorry about the confused nature of the files. Nobody really knows what is where. A work experience girl tried to get the papers in order two summers ago, but she never finished the task and that was the last time anybody touched them. Miss Bell wishes they were more ordered; she wishes she could be of more help; she wishes us the very best of luck in our search.

The cupboard smells of dust and over-boiled cabbage, stale and unpleasant. We soon find that Miss Bell was wrong, that only the files from the 1960s onwards were poorly kept, sheaves of loose papers escaping their binders. Norah was admitted further back, when records were painstakingly transcribed into big hard-backed registers, gold-embossed with the title: 'Wexford District Lunatic Asylum for the Insane', each person's name and details carefully lined up with those above and below. It is Rory who, mid-morning, finds the one we want: Casebook 1923. He hands it over to me like a prize. I receive it with solemnity and, blowing dust off its edges, lay it down on the desk.

He moves across and stands beside me — too close — but I let him, liking the nearness of him and that we are doing this together. We each run a finger down the careful column of names, leaning into the words, and we find her easily: May 25th, 1923: Miss Norah O'Donovan, Mucknamore.

He takes out his camera, to photograph the dry, yellowing page with its sloping list of names. I am unprepared for the feelings that rush through me when I see her name: something inside me, in the pit of me, starts to tremble. Each word that describes her shines on the page, clear and cold and distinct as a star, a bright echo of something that once flamed, a long, long time ago.

When he's finished, he takes my hand and I hold his, as we read together.

Patient No: 1496.
   Name: Norah O'Donovan.
   Address: Mucknamore, Co. Wexford.
   Age: Twenty years.
   Marital Status: Single.

Religion: Roman Catholic.

Education: Reads and writes.

Previous Occupation: Home Duties.

Category of Insanity: Puerperal Mania.

Cause of Insanity: Childbirth.

May 19th, 1923

Admitted from the Holy Sisters of Mary Convent, New Ross, where she gave birth three weeks ago. She had a troublesome labour, with forceps delivery leading to a severe puerperal rupture. This rupture extends to the rectum and has turned septic.

Patient resisted coming to asylum, having to be dragged up the front steps kicking and struggling wildly. The Convent reported that she seemed all right in mind when she was first admitted there, being quiet and obedient and willing to work in the laundry. Since she gave birth, however, the nuns are unable to control her. Won't sleep or eat, weeps and wails through the night, disturbing others. Threatened to kill one nun; also, to do away with herself.

Patient placed in D Ward and given a bath. Her wound was cleaned and a poultice applied. She submitted quietly to the bath and other attentions and afterwards took some warm milk.

30g Veronal administered.

May 20th, 1923

Patient slept the night and seemed in better spirits this morning. She is a well-spoken and highly-educated young woman, and at first seemed very rational. Says she is not insane, that the convent put her here because they could not cure her birth wound or help her cope with the pain. It was pain that kept her awake at night, crying out loud, and nobody would do anything to help her.

Her family had placed her with the Holy Sisters of Mary when they learned of her condition. When asked if they would be willing to take her back should she be discharged, the patient became agitated.

*She began to cry and shout: she shouldn't be here at all, she did
nothing wrong, we have no right to keep her, she would not stay. She
exhausted herself with crying and abusing and I left her to the care of
attendants.*

She is not so sound in mind as she appears at first.

June 25th, 1923

*Patient tried to escape today. Left by front gate somehow
unobserved, but was brought back by two local labourers. Very hyped
and threatening on her return. Said she had plenty of help outside if
she wanted to call on it, that we were as bad as the nuns and we had
no authority to keep her here. 30g Veronal administered.*

June 26th, 1923

*Had long interview with her this morning which started well, but
degenerated. Very impudent and resistive still. She refuses to work,
saying she doesn't see why she should be expected to provide labour for
nothing. Also complains that she never has a minute alone the whole
day long, with attendants and patients coming and going. The food is
disgusting, she claims. She can't sleep at night with the noise in the
dormitory and the heat and the smell. She refused to stay in bed,
throwing her arms about, pacing up and down and shouting in a loud
voice. 30g Veronal administered.*

August 10th, 1923

*Patient has built herself a sort of shelter from sticks and old
sacking in the field beside the avenue hedge. She sits in this little hut
most of the day, talking to herself or feverishly writing, indulging*

delusions of a persecutory nature. Those who accuse her of wrongdoing are lying: she is a good girl and the bad things that happened to her were not her fault, God sees all and God would forgive all.

She abuses us as she sits there, saying she should never have been brought here.

Attendant Lizzie Cloake gives her paper for her writings and, when it runs out, patient harasses Lizzie and the other attendants, or even doctors — anyone who might be able to procure pen and ink for her. As it is not harmful to herself or others, the behaviour is permitted. She is less inclined to abuse the attendants or other patients once she has her pen and paper.

August 24th, 1923

Since last note the patient has conducted herself well, being quieter and generally obedient — though still refusing to work. Spends her days outside in her hut, writing and talking to herself, coming in only to sleep and for meals. While waiting for the meals, she paces up and down the corridor, refusing to talk to anybody.

September 12th, 1923

Attendants today tried to get patient to give up her hut as the weather grows colder, but she resisted.

September 24th, 1923

The patient is now confined to divisions. It is too cold for her to spend all day outdoors. Also, she was becoming very untidy and collecting a large store of rubbish in her hut. She has taken her confinement very badly, becoming troublesome again.

September 25th, 1923

Patient caused a disturbance at breakfast when she accused another patient, Frances Sills, of putting a dead cockroach in her porridge and attendant Lizzie Cloake of laughing and turning a blind eye. Then, at dinnertime, she put an earthworm onto Mrs Sills' dinner plate and a struggle ensued, with them hitting and scratching each other. Patient would not let go of Mrs Sills' hair and had to be forcibly restrained by attendants and removed from the dining room. The incident led to some patients becoming greatly distressed. It was mid-afternoon before order was restored. Patient placed in seclusion overnight. 30g Veronal administered.

September 27th, 1923

Patient out of seclusion today. She emerged quiet and withdrawn. Interview attempted, but now she refuses to speak when spoken to.

October 1st, 1923

Patient's behaviour has improved, though still not communicating. She is withdrawn and passive, ignoring all around her. Still refusing to speak and to work, but considerably less troublesome than before.

1984

*W*hen Jack asks me to, I leave Mrs Fairbairn and
join him in his two-bed maisonette. We have a
"moving-in-together" party and people buy us sauce bowls and
matching towels and I buy an apron and a recipe book and
spend a few evenings cooking for us, a housewifely turnabout
he finds highly amusing. He comes up behind me while I am
cooking, puts a glass of wine into my hand, slides his arm
around me under my apron. We go to the launderette together
and sit watching our underwear and shirts revolving around
each other's.

I give my Sundays, Mondays and most Tuesdays to him, but
the other nights still belong to the pub. He comes with me less
and less often. When I arrive home late, he turns to me in the
dark and often we make love, his body hot against my cold skin.
I act drunk and outrageous, to make him chuckle into the dark.
Next morning when my head is thumping with pain and I am
groaning, "Never again," he is still chuckling, still indulgent. He
makes me tea and puts his hand on my forehead while I wonder
whether I love him or not.

I meet his family, the father and mother and sister who all

think he's wonderful. The dad is Jack, with thirty years on; the two women are kind, if puzzled by his choice. I am not what they expected, not — frankly — what they would have hoped for him, but if I make him happy...
When I tell him this, he laughs it off. "They loved you," he says, refusing to see.

And even if they didn't, we do not need their approval. We have our friends, and we have each other.

We spend Christmas away: one year in Scotland, the next in southern Italy. Our Montgomery's group gets smaller as time passes on and individuals break away. The core of us remain: Natalie, Frank, Sally and me. We believe we are connected to each other, but our real bond is to the alcohol and it's tightening all the time.

Sometimes, I have blackouts. I don't tell Jack about this. I don't tell anybody, not even Sal or Natalie, though we love to rehash the shocking or silly things drink makes us do. Everything that happens during an alcohol-induced blackout is irretrievable, I read. It cannot be revived by any of the methods that recover lost memories, like truth drugs or hypnosis. Something about that frightens me. I do magazine quizzes that all tell me what I already know: I should give up, or at least cut down. I resolve to give up drinking doubles, drinking so often, drinking before six, but can never make the resolutions stick.

Ah, what the hell becomes my most used phrase, as I tilt back another glass.

At work, I start to miss targets and deadlines. I gargle with Listerine in the morning, suck peppermints and chew gum all day, spray Gold Spot into my mouth before going out for the evening, but still I stink. People sniff me out and I hate them for it.

I begin to lie, something I have never done. I don't know why. Jack, of all people, can handle the truth, but I never come home late now without a story prepared. He hates lies, but pretends to believe mine. I don't know when it started — maybe at the very beginning — but silence is now piling up around our apartment, masking what we're not saying.

Maeve arrives to London for a weekend to show off Donal, her fiancé. They want to take Jack and me to dinner to celebrate. "Donal's treat. He insists."

She sits enfolded within his arm, sending little glances to her ring. When the waiter arrives, they order each other's food.

"It's more interesting," says Maeve when I ask why they each don't order their own like anyone else. "It's nice to be surprised."

"We know each other's tastes," says Fiancé.

And they shower each other with smiles. I discreetly make a vomiting gesture to Jack. He and Donal talk about work, suss out each other's place on the career pecking order, while Maeve fills me in on the news from "home". All goes fine for a while, where we are almost what we seem to be: two happy couples enjoying each other's company.

During a lull, she leans across her plate of mussels to Jack. "Have you ever been to Ireland before, Jack?"

"No."

"You'll love it. You'll have to get Jo to take you to the West. It's much more scenic over there."

Jack looks at me. "I'm not sure if —"

I cut in: "We've no plans to go to Ireland, Maeve."

"But Jack, you'll surely come to the wedding. We'd love you to come."

"On his own? I don't think he'd fancy that. Would you, Jack?"

"Jo!" Maeve declares, taken aback. "Come on! You didn't really mean what you said about not coming. I didn't think you —"

"Maeve, I told you." I had too, earlier in the evening, when they came to the flat for drinks. I made sure to tell her, in advance of her asking, and had tried to explain why, but of course she hadn't taken me seriously.

"But —"

"I can't, Maeve. Please accept that."

Fiancé says: "Maeve was hoping you'd be her bridesmaid, Jo."

"I'm sorry," I reply. I lift the champagne bottle to pour us all a refill, but find I am the only one whose glass is empty. Replacing the bottle in the ice bucket, I catch a long look sloping between Maeve and Jack and — horrified — I realise my sister has been there already with him. They have discussed me.

Rage makes me tremble. I cannot believe this of Jack.

After that, the night is a disaster. I get drunk while Maeve lectures: why am I being so unwelcoming to Donal? It's so selfish to greet him into our family like this. As for Mammy and Granny Peg, I have broken their hearts. The wedding is the ideal opportunity to put everything behind us. All I can do is throw it back in their faces.

Donal and Jack look at the wreckage. Jack's face is impassive.

"What's it like to be perfect, Maeve?" I ask, at some point. "Does it never get tiring?"

Feeling something on my face, I put up my hand. I stare at my damp fingers in surprise. I am crying. But I never cry any more, not since I left Mucknamore.

"Nobody asked you to come here," I snap at my sister. "Why don't you just go home and leave us alone?"

So it is Maeve's old friend, Anita Shiels, who is her bridesmaid. I receive some photographs in the post: an older Mrs D., heavier but somehow more frail, trying to look composed; Gran and Auntie Norah just the same, Auntie Norah away somewhere in her head, Gran holding her arm.

Jack is withdrawing his love. I can feel it pulling away, like the tide going out, leaving me beached. Nothing is said. I eat breakfast on a stool opposite, The Guardian divided between us. I watch television from a separate armchair, the couch we used to share staring at us from across the room. I lie in bed beside him, not touching, my head blistered with thoughts.

Sometimes, when I am drunk, I insult him, trying to goad him towards a reaction. He looks at me like I'm a crazy intruder and he's wondering how I got in. When I sober up, I get frightened and try to blot out whatever I've done with sex. We do it furiously, long sessions that leave me physically drained but dissatisfied. I am losing the ability to tell pleasure from pain. Or am I? Do I even care? Jack is not Rory. Rory knew me, every inch: skin and bone and sinew. I would not be able to keep my thoughts sealed off from Rory. He would not be so indulgent, so accepting, so careless. Rory wouldn't hide behind the paper. He would confront the situation. He would make me think, make me laugh, make me change.

Rory O'Donovan. I swore when I was too young to know what it meant that I would love him forever. I said he was the only man for me and that, it seems, is how it turned out.

Or was it the swearing that had made it so?

*V*isitors, Dr Kennedy told Peg, were generally received in the day room by the friend or relative they had come to see, but in this first instance he would wish to be present when Peg and Norah met.

"Her behaviour is unpredictable," he said, index finger prodding the big brown casebook on his desk. "You can never be sure with her."

He began to read to himself again from the heavy book, silently frowning at it as if the words held a personal insult. Peg sat, hands fastened to the handbag on her lap into which she'd packed food and books and a lovely rose-perfumed hand cream for Norah.

At the window, a fly trapped between the blind and the pane was thudding itself wildly off the glass, but the doctor read on, oblivious. His pen-stand held a careful row of identical pens, shiny and sharp. Beside it was a pile of clean sheets of paper, edge to edge, awaiting his words. Peg wished he'd give her a better idea of what to expect. She wished he would tell her what was in that book that made him look so affronted. She wished he had better manners.

"Doctor, are you able to tell me what's wrong with her?"

He answered her without taking his eyes from the book. "Mania. A form of mania."

She tried again. "But can you explain to me what that means, Doctor? In Norah's particular case?"

This time he looked up. "I could only have such a discussion with a member of the inmate's immediate family."

"It's just...It was such a surprise to us, Doctor."

"She showed no signs of her weakness before?"

"No," said Peg, though the memory of a night in the grocery, when she and Norah were working on election leaflets, rose unbidden in her mind. That night, Norah had beaten herself about the head with her hands, decrying her family situation. "Nothing. Not a thing."

He picked up his pen, made a note in the casebook, the scratch of his nib loud in the solemn room.

"So can you?" Peg asked, when it looked like he wasn't going to speak again.

He looked at her over his spectacles.

She began to get frustrated. "Can you tell me what's the matter with her, how she came to be here, whether she's going to be all right?"

"Haven't I just said, Miss Parle, that such a discussion was possible only with family?"

"Norah was my best friend, Doctor. She was engaged to marry my brother, only...only he died. We are very close, closer than many sisters."

"Nonetheless..."

"I want to help her, and so do my parents. We're all so fond of Norah."

"No doubt, Miss Parle. I do not doubt you. But you will appreciate the nature of our work here. It would be most unorthodox to discuss such matters with anybody who turned up wanting to know."

Peg nodded, putting on a reasonable face. She didn't want to get on the wrong side of him. "Do her family know that she's here, Doctor?"

"Most certainly. All the proper parties were informed, by the Holy Sisters as well as ourselves."

"Yet she's had no visitors up until now?"

He hesitated, realising the point to which she'd steered him. "She hasn't, has she? As soon as I knew where she was, I came, Doctor, but they won't. You see? It's those who care most for Norah who must look out for her now."

"You know them, the O'Donovan family?"

"I do."

"Her father is a farmer, I have been told, of some substance. Is this correct?"

"They have about thirty acres."

"Good land?"

What had that to do with anything? "Yes, good enough. A bit waterlogged b'times maybe."

His lips pursed. He made another note, this time on one of his clean, separate pieces of paper. "Is there insanity elsewhere in the family, do you know? Any other relatives?"

"I don't know, Doctor. The O'Donovans are not from Wexford. They moved here from Cork some years ago."

He took off his spectacles, rubbed the inner corners of his eyes with finger and thumb. Two red pressure marks marked each side of his nose. He asked: "Would your friendship extend towards ensuring that her keep was paid for here?"

So that was it.

Mr O'Donovan mustn't be paying for Norah's upkeep. It was a constant complaint of the asylum, that many of those who could well afford to pay didn't. The governors were always writing in the local paper about it.

"Certainly, Doctor. Of course. That would only be right."

He clasped his hands together on top of the open casebook,

white hands with blue veins raised to tracks along the skin, and let another long silence lapse, so long she began to wonder if he would ever speak again. When he did, his tone had changed, become conciliatory. Confiding, nearly.

"What you need to understand, Miss Parle, is that insanity is a dissolution: a regression to a lower nature. In this respect, your friend is a classic case. For years, she goes about her business, a seemingly respectable young girl, until the underlying insanity manifests itself and her true nature is revealed."

He circled one thumb around each other, paused a moment. "You know, I presume, the chain of events that led to her committal here?"

Did he mean what she thought he meant? Peg opened her mouth but shut it again, unsure of what to say. She could feel herself starting to blush. The doctor, also embarrassed, hemmed a small cough. "You will pardon me if I speak frankly. It is essential to your understanding of the case. You are aware of the circumstances that brought her first to the Holy Sisters?"

Peg bowed her head.

"This, as I say, is a classic example of female insanity. In your friend's case, after her gestation and delivery, the balance of her circulation was greatly disturbed."

Peg didn't know where to put her eyes.

"This made her liable to disorder from the application of any exciting cause. Something as simple as a cold affecting the head, a violent noise or the want of sleep distresses a puerperal patient before her milk comes in, and if there is any underlying weakness there, such an impetus is readily converted to the head and may produce either hysteria or insanity."

What was he talking about? He had lost her completely.

She didn't understand the medics, but the whole thing sounded unlikely. Whatever was afflicting Norah, it was nothing to do with head colds or loud noises. The girl had good reason for any mental strain she might be suffering. In the last year, she'd gone against the politics of her family, to the open ire of her father; broken with her closest brother; lost her sweetheart in a shootout; learned that it might have been that same brother who killed him; and found herself in the worst trouble a girl can get into — with the father of the child deceased — and so must have had to ask whether that was the reason her brother might have done it.

Who *wouldn't* be having a breakdown?

"Insanity of lactation is only one such disorder that may affect a woman. We suspect that this is the cause of your friend's condition, but we cannot be sure. Ovarian madness is also a possibility. We have given her the general diagnosis of puerperal mania."

He looked at her as if he expected her to say something.

"Are you saying, Doctor, that women are more inclined to insanity than men?"

"Oh, yes. Yes, indeed. The female reproductive organs are frequently the seat of disease or abnormal function. And men, even when predisposed to insanity through heredity or other factors, have superior powers of resistance that can overcome their latent tendencies."

"But I thought there were more men in the asylum than women."

His eyes opening wide behind his glasses. Oh, why had she gone and said that? Now he thought she was being smart with him. "Maybe there are other reasons for that, Doctor?" she said, in her most compliant voice, the one she kept for Father John and the master at school.

"Indeed. These things are never as simple as they seem."

His eyes still held her, uncertain.

"How is Norah now, Doctor?"

He looked down at the big casebook. "She has improved somewhat. When she was admitted here by the Holy Sisters, she had forsaken all vestiges of self-control and become a prisoner of her passions. Here, she has learned to exercise self-restraint. For some time now, we have witnessed an improvement. However, we would not consider her cured. No. Far from it, indeed. She does no work, for example. She does not mix with the other patients. She is subject to delusions" — here he glanced again at the case notes – "yes, delusions of persecution."

It was all wrong, Peg thought, turning Norah's life into a package to be wrapped up in fancy words that parcelled her off from the rest of us.

"Is she well enough to go home, Doctor?"

"Miss Parle, I do not think you understand what I am explaining to you. At the moment, Miss O'Donovan is moving from acute mania to a more chronic stage that looks like it may settle into one of the many forms of melancholia. I think it unlikely that we shall witness any real improvement for some time. Perhaps never."

"But maybe at home...?"

He shook his head. "I'm sorry, I could not recommend such a course of action."

"I can't believe it, I really can't. Norah was as sane as myself the last time I saw her."

"It may have appeared so to the untrained eye, Miss Parle, but I assure you, insanity does not occur in people who are of sound mental faculties. It does not — like smallpox, for example — attack indifferently the weak and the strong. It will only raise itself in those whose mental constitution was originally defective. Your friend's immorality...and her insanity were both symptoms of an underlying flaw. Now do you —? Oh my..."

The door crashed open, interrupting his flow. Though Norah's arrival was expected, they both jumped off their seats.

"My goodness," Dr Kennedy said, crinkling with disapproval.

Norah was standing in the door frame, breathless, holding on to the handle, her chest rising and falling, looking as if she might fly off again. A sheen of sweat glowed on her forehead. An attendant came running up behind, panting. "I'm sorry, Doctor. I couldn't hold her..."

The doctor waved her away her with the hand of a man who doesn't have time for excuses. "Come in, Miss O'Donovan," he said, curt as he could. "You have a visitor."

It made Peg want to laugh, or it would have, if the sight of Norah clinging to the door handle wasn't so alarming. Lunatics of every order paced this place and the doctor was getting himself in a stitch over how somebody entered a room. Pretending he thought sanity a matter of manners, of keeping your desk tidy and your record book straight.

Norah was transfixed in the doorway. Everything that had happened since she and Peg had last seen each other was flooding the space between them. Awareness of the gap between what she had been and what she had become was leaving her stranded.

Peg took a step towards her, but Dr Kennedy stopped her: "No, Miss Parle, please."

To Norah, he repeated his order: "Come in, I said."

Peg longed to meet her halfway, but under the doctor's eye, she waited. Waited and watched her friend walk towards her, walking as she never walked before, like it hurt her to make contact with the ground. So it was true, she had lost her sanity. Oh God, dear God, would she be able to get it back?

When Norah was almost at the chair, she slumped down. For a moment, Peg thought she had fainted, then realised she was kneeling, and reaching for Peg's hand, and then her other hand.

Peg tried to help her back up onto her feet, but Norah wouldn't let her. Instead, she brought Peg's hands to her lips and kissed them. "Thank you," she said, into Peg's skirts, trying not to let the doctor hear her. "Thank you, thank you..."

"Oh my God," Peg said. "Don't do that, Norah. Please. Don't be doing that."

. . .

"No, Peg!" Máire pulled herself up on her pillow. "Holy Mother of God, what are you thinking of? To even ask such a thing!"

Hold on, Peg orders herself in her mind. You knew she wouldn't say yes straight off. Take your time, best words out. "Mammy, it's not right, is it, that she should be left to rot in that place? That she should have to bear it all alone?"

"I know it's hard on the girl, I'm not saying it isn't. But don't you think we've had enough trouble ourselves?"

This was the first word Peg ever heard her mother say that was anywhere close to self-pity. She was having one of her weak mornings: unable to get out of bed. The good days were becoming fewer, the bad days getting worse. The blood in her sputum had changed in colour from a dark, venous red to bright crimson, and she had passed from the world of the healthy to the separate, shunned world of the tubercular.

Peg sometimes felt she was locked up in that world with her. The house had to be swept and disinfected daily and kept well ventilated. Her eating and drinking vessels and cutlery had to be kept apart; her utensils and bedclothes cleaned separately from everyone else's. They had lost custom in the shop. And nobody ever came all the way into the house to visit any more, except loyal Lil Hayes.

After all Máire had done for the community, and the country, since the first rising in 1916, she was now left alone to her disease.

"You better get started on that porridge before it gets cold," Peg said. "It's made on milk, the way you like it."

Máire picked up her spoon, sliced through the thin skin that coated the surface of the cereal, swirled it round in the milk, releasing steam. Peg could see the effort of will it took for her to lift the spoon, open her mouth, swallow the food. After a couple of spoonfuls, she paused. "Even supposing," she held her spoon aloft. "Even supposing we were to do such a thing —"

"Yes?" Peg felt her head spin.

"Could we not set her up in Dublin or somewhere?"

"That wouldn't work. The asylum would only let her go to us if we were to take charge of her care. Anyway, she wouldn't be able to look after herself in Dublin. She's not what she was."

Máire made a face. "Another person to look after, that's all you need."

"I don't think it would be like that always," said Peg. "I don't believe that old doctor. She'd get better herself if she were out of that place, I'm sure of it. If she were..." Peg paused. This was the tricky bit. Dear Mary, Mother of God. Mother of all that is holy. Help me here now. Give me the strength to say it. "If...if she were to be reunited with her child..."

"Dear God in Heaven! That's not what she wants, is it?"

"It is."

"Are you sure?"

"She's told me. You can talk to her same as ever, you know. She's troubled, but she's no fool."

"You haven't encouraged her in this madness, I hope?"

"Is it madness, Mammy?"

"Pure, utter, complete, unadulterated madness. And there's some excuse for her to talk lunacy, she's in an asylum. But you...You have to help her, Peg, to see the errors of her thinking. To help her reconcile to the inevitable." Máire sighed, put her spoon back in the bowl with the half-eaten porridge. "Will that do for today?"

"Mammy, you haven't even had half."

"I'm sorry, a ghrá. Not this morning. Maybe later on."

She pushed the tray away. Peg took it from her, put it over on the dresser. Guilt pricked her: it was encouraging her mother to eat she should be, not arguing with her and springing surprises that would put anybody off their food.

"Come back over here, Peg, and sit on the bed where I can see your face," Máire said. "Good girl, that's it. That's better."

She took a breath. Peg could see her reaching for the strength to talk through all she wanted to say.

"I don't want to say no to you, Peg. I know you are trying to do right and that's what I've always taught you to do...But think about it. Really think about it."

When Peg said nothing, Máire went on. "Think about the O'Donovans. They'll be furious, so they will, and they'd be within their rights. We already have Barney and all that business between us. Do we want to further it into an unholy row that will make it irrevocable?" She stopped, reached again for breath, holding up her hand to stop Peg saying anything. "No...wait..."

The rise and fall of her chest hurt Peg to watch, but she knew better than to suggest they might leave it, talk about it later. If Máire had something to say, she would be heard.

"Then...What about Norah herself?' Máire asked, strength marshalled. "Do you think she could settle in here, could be happy in herself, knowing that her mammy and daddy were a small walk away and so upset? Knowing what the whole place would be thinking and saying about her? Is it fair to do that to her after all she's been through?"

Peg let her head fall. Her mother was raising the very questions that had most worried herself when she considered the plan.

"I'm sorry, Peg," Máire said, in a voice that declared the argument over. "I know what good friends you were, but if her family won't help her, we can't. It wouldn't be right to go against her family."

She broke into the coughing fit she'd been staving off and her face took on the unmistakable mask of her disease. On the peak of her cheeks, two bright red spots appeared, as if dabbed on. Her eyes turned glassy and perspiration broke across her forehead. Peg handed her the bowl, stood by while she coughed and spat. Once, not long ago, she used to find this nearly too distressing a job to do; now she was so accustomed to it, she stood holding the bowl while her attention wandered off into the distance. She understood what her mother was saying.

Oh, but the feel of Norah's lips scorching into her hands...

After Máire recovered, Peg covered the bowl with its special clip-on top and put it outside the door. She walked across to the window, where the pale morning sun fell onto her arms.

She asked gently, "Mammy, why should we bother about the O'Donovans? If they object, what do we care?"

It was not something they discussed, Peg and her mother: Dan's part in Barney's death. The subject was too raw. What could be said that wouldn't widen the wound? Each morning still, Peg tumbled out of the comfort of sleep into the heavy weight of consciousness. How could he? was still the question that drove her out of bed as soon as her eyes fell open and that stayed with her all through the business of the day. She no longer had any doubt but that he did it. He'd stood in front of her and lied so completely about Norah that she now knew all he said to be false.

Her mother didn't answer. So Peg said the other thing, the thing she had held back, the thing she'd hoped she wouldn't have to say. "After all, Mammy, it is Barney's baby."

Her mother put her hands over her ears. "Holy God, child! Hush!"

"It's Holy God's own truth I'm saying." She sensed a weakness, and pressed on. "Are we going to let Barney's child be brought up by some strangers from God knows where? Or leave her — yes, her, she is a little girl — leave her to grow up in an orphanage?"

"Stop that talk: we all know what happens. There's no need for that kind of talk."

Peg looked out the window. She was getting to know the view from this room as well as she knew the one from her own on the other side of the house. Everything that made this room Barney's was gone. Since her mother had moved in, that had been swallowed up by the paraphernalia of sickness. Medicines and peppermint drops on the bed table and facecloths and handkerchiefs to cool down or mop up. Bed-bottles and a good fire going all day. The window open for ventilation, no matter how cold. Porridge and soups and beef tea.

"Oh, Peg, I don't know...All my life I've done what I thought was right and I have to say that it hasn't got me very far. And now I'm dying —"

"Ah, Mammy!"

"It's the truth, isn't it, God's own truth, like you said. If that's what we are to have here this morning, then let that be said, along with the rest. I can't say it to your father, you know that, so let me say it to you."

Peg went back over to the bed, sat beside her.

"It's only a matter of time for me," Máire continued. "So here I am. I've lost one child and I'm leaving the other behind with an ageing father and an ailing business. If I thought what you wanted was the best thing for all involved, I'd say go ahead, and the O'Donovans and all the tattlers of the village could go to the devil. But is it, Peg? Is it?"

Peg hung her head. How could she know the answer to that?

"I can't read the future, Mammy. All I know in this moment is that leaving her there might make everyone feel easier — but I can't believe it's right."

Máire lay back. The clock ticked loud in the room, reminding Peg to get up and wind it. When she was finished, she sat back down in the bedside chair. After another silence, Máire spoke. "The child could have been adopted already by somebody else. Have you thought of that?"

"She hasn't been."

"You've checked?"

"I've checked."

Another silence. Then: "But Peg...Tipsy Delaney?"

"Tipsy will do it. I know it's not many men would but —"

"That's not what I meant. I know he'll do it, the poor eejit would jump onto Coolanagh sands if you asked him." She smiled a dead smile. "No, it's you I'm thinking of."

"I'll be all right."

"No." She turned in the bed to take hold of Peg's wrist. "You're not listening to me, girl."

"I am, Mammy, and I understand what you're saying. It's not like I haven't thought it through. I know what it means and I'm happy to go ahead."

"You can't know what a marriage is like until you're in it. And think of this: supposing Norah doesn't get better? Supposing she's a hopeless case and she ends up back inside? You'll be left tied to..."

She let the sentence trail, worn out maybe, or maybe just afraid to put a word on the man who might become her son-in-law.

"The child has to have a father and a mother," Peg said. "They won't give it to us otherwise. Tipsy is the only man who'd do it."

"Oh, Peg..." Máire lay back, weary.

"Never mind Tipsy. What about Daddy?"

Máire closed her eyes. "You don't need to worry about that," she said, her voice fading into her exhaustion. "You can leave your father to me."

CASEBOOK: *Wexford District Lunatic Asylum for the Insane*
    Patient No: *1496:*
    October 24th, 1923: *Patient Discharged. Not Improved.*

1984

By the time Jack asks me to leave, I expect it, but still, it seems sudden. It doesn't seem right that we can pass through all the stages and arrive at the end without even a decent quarrel. Heaven knows, I've tried to break through with snarls and insults and drunken diatribes. All he ever says is, "I'm happy to talk about it, Jo, when you're calm."

When I'm calmer, though, I'm frightened. Fearful of being alone. So I wheedle or joke or outright humiliate myself, begging him to reconsider, making promises we both know I can't keep, even though I know breaking up is right for me as much as him. Jack always does the right thing.

So we keep going, until the evening he comes home and firmly tells me I have to be gone by the end of the month. The end of the month. His face is set against me, craggy lines around his mouth shutting me out.

"We haven't tried hard enough," I say. "We haven't talked. We should talk."

He shakes his head. "Too late," he says. Two words only, as if they are rationed.

I gabble: "I'll stop drinking, Jack...I know that's the problem. If that's what you want..."

Again, that shake of his head.

I throw myself on his mercy. "I have nowhere to go."

He says nothing, as if he is the one who is helpless.

I am starting to cry. "I gave up everything for you, you bastard. Where the hell am I supposed to go?"

"I'm sorry, Jo."

He doesn't sound it or look it, but underneath my blustering tears, I know he is. His sorrow is an axe, slicing me off.

I move in with Natalie, who owns a flat in Camden Town, and has a box bedroom she never bothered to fill after her last flatmate moved out. The decor is dire and I keep promising myself I will paint the walls and the cheap melamine furniture, but I can't seem to get round to it. I'm too busy — out a lot — home only in time to cry myself to sleep.

Crying is what I do now, especially after a few drinks. I tell everybody who will listen that Jack has broken my heart. This half-truth gives me permission to wallow in sorrow, and to try to drown thoughts I don't want to be having. Natalie and I drink in the pub near the flat now, instead of The Rose and Crown. It's handier. We can just walk home instead of having to negotiate the Tube after closing time. And anyway, the old gang has broken up. People have moved on: to relationships, marriages, mortgages.

Natalie and I have fun in the pub, but at home we bicker, like an old married couple. She is small-minded about money and motives, and not very bright. Often I wonder how I ended up with her. I miss Dee, my old friend from school, and resolve again that I will write to her, a letter that I will finish, all the way to the end of a page, or maybe even two, and put in an envelope, and stamp, and actually send.

Natalie is also a nag. She ticks me off for not keeping to the housework rota she drew up. The effort of housework is beyond me. I always intend to do it, but when we're not drinking, I wind up sitting in a corner of the couch, or on top of my duvet, staring at nothing, locked inside a struggle. Not moving, but with every coil in my brain contorted and all my muscles straining to keep still.

When you're slipping, people think you don't know, but you do. For a long time before anyone raises a whispered note of concern to you, or passes a comment across a sea of laughs from others, you've been telling yourself what's wrong, and how to put it right. Giving yourself sensible advice that you don't know how to follow.

I never drink at home, but I'm not stupid enough to believe that matters. I know what I am. I know I have to stop. And I try, I do try, and sometimes I even succeed. Every day starts with good intentions pressed into place, but many evenings, and sometimes even afternoons, find me again pouring drink down my throat.

I am a limp drunk now, occasionally boisterous, but mostly weepy and full of self-pity. I can't stand her, this interloper who intrudes into my evening, wet-eyed every time, yet still I feed her. Whisky now, Scotch — never Irish — on the rocks. One night, I wake in bed beside a stranger and have no memory of how I got there. The skin on my chest and back stings and, when I investigate, I find I am covered in scratches.

My boss calls me in. I have used up all my leave, paid and unpaid, and my sick days, certified and uncertified. I am late three mornings out of five. If I don't improve my performance, he has no choice but to let me go. So what? I say to myself after this rebuke. It's not like I like this low-grade, beneath-me job, but I have no qualifications and so no hope of a better one. It's a dilemma.

Natalie and I take to the pub to try to solve it.

At some stage in the evening, she goes home, but I go on to a club. Somebody puts me into a taxi at the end of the night. Staggering up the steps to our front door, I trip and burst my lip. Next morning, I arrive late to work again.

I am shuddering a coffee cup to my broken mouth when the boss calls me to his office, makes me sign a form. My final warning.

"Do yourself a favour," he says. "Get a grip."

He is right, I know he is right.

Get a grip. Stop.

I stop.

I'm in Natalie's kitchen, crouching on the floor, unable to move. Darkness is fondling the windowpane, which means it's late, but I have no idea how long I have sat here like this. In my right hand, I hold a kettle, full of cold water, but I have no memory of filling it. My arm hurts from holding on, but I can't let it go. My hand, my arm, everything is jammed. My body has wound down, like a clockwork toy, while my mind has gone into overspin, spewing up thought after self-lacerating thought.

I am held captive, paralysed by the parade of taunts that come swooping in, cascading one over the other to flay me. Then, somebody speaks to me from behind, over near the door.

Do it, she says.

Fear creeps along my skin. I know that voice and I know she can't be here. She's in Ireland and she wouldn't come here, and if she did she wouldn't speak those words, not out loud. Did I imagine it? It doesn't seem so. It sounds like she is in the room behind me, her voice real and solid as a voice can be. Do it, she says again.

On the table above me is the bread knife, with its row of shiny, sharp-toothed smiles all along the blade. It doesn't hurt: slash, slash the serrated edge once, twice, across the skin, faster than thought. Two burning flashes, then the thoughts fade to silky black whispers...It doesn't even hurt, that's what they say.

Just do it.

My hand jerks and opens. Cold water splashing over my jeans breaks the spell. I can move again, though not quickly, not easily. I leave the kettle on the floor where it has fallen, the lid where it has rolled away, the water gliding along the brown linoleum. On my hands and knees, I crawl away. In the bedroom, I close the door behind me, lean against it. The thudding of my heart echoes throughout my body. Even my toes and fingertips throb. I am so frightened.

I have to go: that is what I realise. If I don't get away, the voice will move in. She will feel entitled, invited by default. I have to go, and I have to go now before Natalie comes back, before I am back into the everyday world where thoughts like these slip down under the surface and pretend they're not there.

I find the backpack I brought from Jack's house and begin to fill it. It takes a huge effort, deciding what to bring. I would prefer to just walk out the door with only the clothes I am wearing, but I cannot afford that. I have very little left and am going to need everything that is mine.

Into the bag they go: clothes, records, books, anything I can fit. When I am packed, I sit down at the kitchen table to write Natalie a note. I'm trying to find words when the key turns in the door. She is home early, but not — I read by the slackness of her jaw — too early to have had a few drinks.

"Whatever are you doing?" Her wide, inebriated eyes take in my rucksack, the other bags, my duvet and pillows rolled into a black sack. "What's going on?"

I put down the pen. "I have to go."

"Go? What are you talking about? Go where?"

"I have to..." My voice has the shakes. "I —"

"What about money for bills, and for rent while I find someone else? Were you going without paying?"

"Natalie —"Aghast, I realise I can't speak. If I do, I'll break.

"Where are you going?"

I shrug. I cannot look at her drunken face, and her swollen, fluid eyes. I crumple up the sheet of paper I have been writing on.

"You're a bit down," she says. "Are you? Is that it?"

I pick up my bags.

"You could have told me, you know. You should have. Sneaking off like this..."

She doesn't get it. She hasn't a clue, about anything. The weakest part of her and the weakest part of me, that's where we connect.

"You should leave here too," I tell her.

"What are you talking about?" Her voice squeaks.

The doorbell rings. "That's my taxi."

"You can cancel it, Jo. We'll call it again in the morning if you still want to go then."

I shift my backpack up onto my shoulder, hug the big plastic bag to my chest so I can barely see over it.

"Jo. Please..."

"I can't stay, Natalie. I don't know how." I turn away and she follows, picking up my other bag and walking behind me to the hall door.

It's raining. I hand one bag to the driver, then the other. Bending my head to the weather, I run down the steps. She follows me out to the gate, insists on hugging me, her skin hot against my cheek. "I don't understand."

Drips slink down the shiny black rump of the cab and the engine grumbles impatiently. I pull out of her grasp.

"Ring me," she says, as I'm getting in. "Ring me soon."

I slump into the seat, dizzy with relief. I'm getting used to leaving, getting to recognise its imperative: shut down; face forward. I'll write to her, I tell myself. As soon as I'm settled, I'll write a long, long, letter, the longest letter ever written, and explain it all. I'll write to Dee as well. And maybe even Maeve.

The driver asks, "Where to, love?"

"Heathrow Airport," I say.

The taxi pulls away from the kerb and I turn to look back, just for a second, but I can't see anything. Already, Natalie and her house have blurred into rain and disappeared.

I let myself in by the side door as instructed by Hilde and find myself stopping in the door frame, transfixed by change. The hinged door swings shut behind me with a slap that nudges me inside. Still I stand, bath towel cradled to my chest, looking at what has happened to our home.

"Well, look at you," I say aloud. The blank, empty rooms echo my voice back to me: "Yoo-oo-oo."

A hallway with a section cornered off by a tall mahogany desk where guests will check in to the new B&B. A row of open doorways, like empty picture frames, stretches away down the corridor.

It seems vast, this premises, as I walk through room after empty room, across floor after bare wooden floor. The square-footage of the house has been doubled, but it feels four times as big: the old strangely-angled walls knocked down and re-erected somewhere more logical, the redundant nooks knocked into place. All the walls are naked, plaster-grey. The entire back wall of the building — along the dining room, bar and lounge — is glass, overlooking the sea. From here, I can see my little shed.

Its days are numbered: now that the buildings are almost finished, attention will switch to the terraces and the gardens. Soon it will be time to go.

Which is just as well.

This is my first time inside the house in daylight, since the roof went on. I wait for a new feeling to hit — nostalgia? regret? — but the house is too changed, a blank canvas that has nothing to do with me.

My sandals leave footprints in the dust as I walk up the stairs. Tubings of wire protrude from walls and ceilings, awaiting light fittings. Only the bathrooms are completely finished, tiled and plumbed, and that's where I'm headed for a long soak in piping hot water.

When Hilde came by my shed with lunch today, she found me sitting in my swimsuit at my desk. Yesterday, the small offshore breeze that has been keeping us cool dissolved and the air grew thick and humid. I sat with sweat dribbling from beneath my breasts down my bulging abdomen, hating the heat.

Hilde laughed. "Poor Jo, always the pregnant women find it difficult, the warm weather." It was then she offered me the bath. Usually I say no to Hilde's offers, but after weeks of washing from a red plastic basin I couldn't resist.

I find the bathroom at the top of the stairs where she said. She has left out towels for me, and toiletries: soap and shampoo, conditioner and bath oil, perfume and talcum powder. Kindness in a collection of bottles. The room is stuffy. I open one of the windows a little at the top, but no air comes in. Down on the beach, a mother calls her daughter in out of the sea. "Tríona, come on now," she shrieks. "I won't call you again." But she does: "Tríona! Come in, I said. Trí-í-í-íon-a!"

I turn on the taps and a gush of water drowns her out. Hilde's bath oil smells sweet, like pear juice. Under the torrent from the taps, it bubbles up, a froth of scent. I stand into the water while it's filling and my reflection appears in a big bath-end mirror. It's the first time I've seen myself in two months. I am a new me, brown face and arms and legs, a farmer's tan, and — in between — the big belly, white and round as a giant mushroom. Underneath is my pubic hair, dark and close. I face sideways to inspect myself, the miracle of engineering that I now am, front cantilevered out from an improbably flat backside. My breasts, swollen and heavy like overripe fruit, are marbled with veins. With my fingertip, I trace one of the blue coils.

I slide down in the water, supporting my bump as I go. Heat and scent prickle my skin and draw from me a long, slow, sigh. I fill the bath until the water is level with my scalp line then turn off the taps and lie still in the soft water, so different from the salt sea. Lying quiet, enjoying the cosseting, I notice a quivering at the pit of my stomach (me, not you) and realise that it's been there all day, ever since Hilde suggested this bath, lighting up my insides. An old sensation, from long ago: anticipation. I'm not sure whether I want it or not, but there it is, regardless.

I can't lie still under it. I sit up, take the sponge and begin to soap my distended body.

He comes up the path, as always, at dusk. It falls earlier now each evening, making our nights together longer. We sit on the rug outside, watching the light leak from a heavy, purple-clouded sky. Tonight, the sea is grey and flat as a floor. Coolanagh seems much closer than usual.

"A sign of rain," Rory says, when I remark on that.

"I remember," I say, reciting the old weather forecast: "Coolanagh near is rain, Coolanagh far is fine."

"And if you can't see it at all, then it's raining already."

I smile. "It's been so long since we had rain, I find it hard to even imagine."

The word "it" comes out of my mouth long and drawn, with

the 't' soft at the end, so it sounds almost like "sh". My accent is slipping back, I hear it myself, the vowels shortening and flattening, returning to what they were.

Rory has brought red wine tonight, instead of the usual beer. He tries to persuade me to join him, stopping in the middle of twisting the corkscrew to curve his eyes up to meet mine. I shake my head to the wine, but smile his long, slow, significant smile back at him.

Yes, we are all significant smiles tonight. Why now? Why "yes" tonight after all the months of "no"? His excitement is mingling with mine, doubling it up, and any feeling I used to have that my "yes" or "no" or "maybe" was the deciding factor has melted away, dissolved by an invisible force older and stronger and far more primeval than either of us.

The cork slides from the bottleneck with a faint, quiet pop. I pour myself a juice and we lift and clink our glasses together. The air is calm, eerily calm, thick and hard to breathe. The low cloud weighs down on my head and, for a moment, I feel something like fear, but I know it's only atmospheric pressure, pressing on my brain.

I tell him, "Your hair is getting long."

"Orla hates it." He imitates her voice: "'Get a haircut, would you?'"

I don't like him mimicking his wife like that. "I always preferred it long," I say.

"I know."

I decide to dispense with the preliminaries and touch his wrist with the flat of my hand. "Do you still want to fuck?"

He flinches. "Jesus, Jo."

"What? Do you?"

"You know I do."

"Why?"

"Jesus, such questions."

"If you can't even say why..."

He spreads his fingers wide, as if he's helpless. "I seem to have made such a mess of my life, Jo. I think it was because we went so wrong, you and me." The pupils in his eyes are welling wide in the dark. The brown irises have almost disappeared. "You were my first love, Jo. Part of me never got over you."

I have stopped breathing.

He goes on: "For so long, I was bitter at you for running away. I used to rehearse in my head the crushing things I'd say when you came back to me. But you never did."

"But Rory, I —"

"I know, I know. I see it differently now. Now I spend my time in my head, wondering which particular thing I said, or did, was the one that failed us."

"It wasn't only your fault," I say after a small silence, able to admit that now he's stopped blaming me.

"I know that. It was both of us and, hey, I absolve us both. We were too young, it was just the way it was. Just life. Well, now life has brought us back together. You're here and I can't pretend you're not. I want back some of what was taken from us. I know I have no right but —"

I interrupt him with a kiss. A long kiss, deep and breathless, and by the end of it his hands are up under my T-shirt, palming across clammy skin. I pull away. I want this to be slow and deliberate, nothing pushy or clumsy. I kneel up and pull my T-shirt over my head and fold it, as if we have all the time in the world. My bra is for pregnancy, more harness than lingerie, but I sit back on my heels all the same so he can get a good look at what thirty-nine-and-pregnant looks like. My eyes hold his, trying to pin him to the moment, to what we are doing. It seems a point of honour to reveal myself and I want the same from him.

He understands. Kneeling up, he unbuttons his shirt, slips it off his shoulders. I stand, take off my shorts and wait. He copies me. So we go, item for item, the garments getting smaller and smaller until we are both naked. Only then do I move back into his arms. His body is changed too, though not as much as mine: his belly is soft from beer and his pecs have drooped. Above his hips swell two handles of flesh. He is softer but his penis, standing to attention in the candlelight, is just the same.

We are naked, here, outside my outhouse, in full view if anyone should decide to climb the small cliff-face, or come in around to the back of the house and shed. But no one will. We kiss on and on. We are quiet, as always: we never spoke during the act. A small spatter of rain drops hits my skin, as Rory traces a tingling line from the hollow at the base of my throat to loop around my right breast, then gives the same attention to the other side, and follows with his hands until both are high points, sending surges of desire in every direction. I hear myself moan, I hear myself say his name, and the scent of him fills my nostrils, unchanged. I would know him by this if we met in total darkness.

He lies down, pulls me on top: the perfect position for a seven-month pregnant woman. He knows more than he used to know. A sudden shiver of wind tears the air but I ignore it, all thought swirling away into overrunning sensation. Large, separate drops of rain start to ping against my bare skin and they feel good, pinpoints of cold caress. I am close, so close. I bear down and squeeze tight and, yes, I am there. Heart, muscle, tissue, blood pounding, pounding, pounding. There, there, there.

I slump against him. It takes a time to come back into myself. He is still with me, still inside me. His turn, his rhythm now. Another gust of rain-logged wind slaps the back of my neck, then it is falling on us. Heavy Irish rain, all over the rug and the wine and our clothes and the sleeping bag, drenching everything, but we don't care. I throw my head back to feel it on my face as we go on and on, believing we'll go on forever. His breath rises and rises and at the top, just before he lets go, catches in the back of his throat. Beloved, long-lost sound.

And then, in a moment, we are back in the world, jumping to our feet to pick up things, pick up everything, quick as we can, and run for shelter from the rain now pelting down, stabbing our bare skins, plastering our hair flat on our crowns. Inside the shed, I turn on the oil lamp to find towels. I am shivering. Water streams in runnels down my neck. Above us, the rain hammers down on corrugated iron, hurting our ears. We look at each other and have to laugh.

"Is this place waterproof?" Rory yells above the din.

"I don't know," I shout back. "It's the first rain this summer. I hope so."

I hold out a towel to him and he catches my hand, pulls me in close. I feel his lips on my wet scalp.

"How are you going to get home in this?" My shed feels like a boat, tipping and rolling on an open ocean.

"Maybe I'll stay," he murmurs into my hair. He looks across in the direction of my small bed. "Would it take two?"

"Two-and-a-half, you mean," I say, rubbing my bump. "I doubt it."

"Let's try."

I get in first and he squeezes in behind me, my back to his front, his hand settled on the base of my big belly, sealed in tight, like two sheets of paper in an envelope. We are damp and our skin is chilled, but beneath is blood, rising warm.

I turn the lantern off and darkness tucks in around us. Above, the rain pounds on the roof, like it wants to be let in. The noise is deafening, but somehow, almost immediately, we plummet into sleep.

A while later, I waken. One part of me feels like I've been

asleep a long time, another suspects not. Beside my ear, Rory lets a snore on each out-breath.

We did it. In the end, after all the pushing and parrying, it just happened. And I don't regret it, do I? No, I don't think I do.

His arm lies heavy across me, strangling my waist, and his body is too close, too hot. I slide from beneath its hold. His breathing changes as he feels my absence through his sleep, then he shifts and spreads himself out across the mattress and his slow, noisy inhalation and exhalation intensifies. Only then do I notice the quiet in the shed. The rain has stopped.

I think of his wife, only a short walk away, waking to find he's not there.

And for some reason, my promise to Gran and Richard rises in my mind: I will do this well.

I can't stay there, in bed with it. My shoes are not where I usually leave them. I have to cross the dirty floor in bare feet to the table where I find what I'm looking for: my torch. Putting my hand over the lamp, I turn it on so my fingers glow transparent pink.

I look across. He hasn't budged, so I release the glow and use it to retrieve shoes and clothes. I dress in a dry pair of jeans and a warm jumper, then go to sit at my desk. I have the overwhelming urge to write about what we have done.

I write quickly, lightly, without stopping to think or amend. As I have written, so it was. Physically, more pleasing than before. When we were young together, I used to pretend it was better than it was, so grateful to be with him that I felt no lack. I no longer love like that. How do I love now?

What now?

I imagine myself writing to Sue Denim, as I often do when I find myself lost or confused. Dear Sue, Tonight I slept with my first love for the first time in twenty years. The only real love I ever had, who just so happens to be married and a father of two... How would she answer me?

Granny Peg's stacked diaries tower over my writing hand. On top of them are Auntie Norah's notebooks and all those loose pages of hers that I struggled to organise into chronological order. Rory has been taking pictures of these, and of the other papers, and the letters. He has also taken a series of me, sitting here like this, writing about them, and brought me outside the shed and made me stand just as Gran did in one of the old photographs of her wedding day, the little slit in the wall near the roof showing in the exact same place over my head.

That wedding picture is lying on my desk now. It is old and cracked and somebody has torn a small piece off its bottom right-hand corner. Wedding Day, November 14th, 1923, it says on the back, in Gran's beautiful writing, the kind of handwriting that is both legible and ornate, the kind nobody does any more. She looks out at me from this picture, her eyes unreadable, but as I stare into them by torchlight, I feel something give in my chest.

I put down my pen, go across to the bed and try to shake him awake. "Rory, get up. Rory!" I shake him harder until he feels me, until I cannot be ignored. He groans, tries to roll over. Another shake.

"What?" he grunts. "What is it?"

"You have to get up. You have to go home."

"Don't be silly," he says, eyes shut fast.

I shine the torch full in his face.

"Hey! Stop!" His hand shoots out from under the duvet, pushes the torch aside. "What are you doing?"

"Get up."

He rubs his eyes. "What's happening?" His voice is exasperated. "What's the matter?"

I retrieve his clothes, dump them on top of him in the bed. "Put these on. You need to go."

"I don't understand," he says.

I shake my head, stubborn. "Come on, get up."

I shine the light on him, searching his face. Wrinkles crag his forehead and fan out from round his sleep-starved eyes and I want to smooth them out with my thumbs. He puts his arm up across his face against the light. "Will you put that thing away?"

"Please," I turn to him. "Please, Rory, don't say anything else. Just go."

I cross back to my desk to wait for him to do it, shine the light again on Gran's photo, on the four young people dressed up for the day: bride and groom in front, the groom in military uniform, a rifle resting across his knee, face scrubbed up, looking off to the side.

Rory sighs heavily and my bed creaks under the weight of him getting out. I hear him search out his clothes, the rustles of him dressing behind me.

The bridesmaid looks in the other direction, locked inside the casing of her thoughts. Both she and the bride wear costumes in the faux-traditional Irish style, fashionable among nationalists of the time: over-the-shoulder capes held in place by Tara brooches. Their heads are bare, their hair tied into chignons at the base of their necks, the bodices of their dresses embroidered with intricate Celtic designs, like those that illuminate the ancient manuscripts held in Trinity College.

Only the bride looks straight at the camera, her gaze serious but steady. The same expression she wears in another picture, of four girls in their early twenties, tweed and gabardine coats over their Cumann na mBan uniforms, pointing their guns at the photographer. "Peg, Molly, Cat, Kathleen. February 1922," that one says on the back. It's a staged picture and it's shocking. And I'm held by this feeling that it — like all the other pictures here, and the diary entries, and the letter — is trying to tell me something.

Rory is behind me now, standing over me. He touches the back of my neck. "It's okay, Jo." His fingers are cold already.

"Is it?" I whisper.

"Yes," Rory says. "Everything is going to be okay now."

"Really?"

He pulls me in close and, for the first time in twenty years, we stand together, leaning into each other.

"Yes, really," he says. "You can stop worrying now. Just leave it all to me."

PART III
SWELL

1986

*G*race Jones purrs her hymn to her Jamaican Guy from two massive wall-mounted speakers, pained vocals underwritten by a pounding bass drum. At the head of the exercise class, an instructor faces the group and leads them through jumps and bends and stretches, shouting her commands to be heard above the music: "...and reach, two, three, four..."

At her bidding, nineteen people arch their arms over their heads and bounce into a waist stretch. She lifts her left knee, they lift theirs; she moves right, they all shift in the same direction, swinging their arms just as she does, half a second behind her in synchronized unison, like one multi-limbed organism.

She is fit, this Lycra-clad instructor: strong, supple and lean. She can run six miles in under forty minutes, bend from her waist to touch her nose to her knee with palms flat on the floor. She can bench-press eighty-eight pounds, leg-press one hundred and ten. While instructing her classes, she stretches further, jumps higher, lasts longer than those following her instructions, though this is the third class she has given in four hours.

Sometimes, the control she has over these people's movements bewilders her. She's tempted to do something silly or lewd — pretending to pick her nose or rub herself between her legs — just to see if they might copy her. She never does, though; she doesn't want to slight what they do together: the giving over of their bodies to the music, letting the beat drive them, push them further and faster, until every muscle is primed. When it goes well, it's a high like no other, and tonight is a good night. This group is one of her most advanced, well trained, responsive: she can push them hard. As the apex of the class approaches, as the faces contort with effort and the smell of sweat rises in the room and the ceiling-to-floor mirrors fog over from breath and perspiration, her shouts grow more excited: "Yes...and just eight more: eight...seven...push harder, that's it...and five...four...three...two...one...And again...ten...nine..."

A good class.

When it is over, after she has cooled them all down with slow stretching and breathing exercises, a short line of people forms, waiting to ask her questions or share their food or fitness dilemmas. Her friend Richard also waits, but over by the window doing extra hamstring stretches, as she works through the line, advising, counselling, consoling or deflecting.

When the last of them has gone, he comes across, pecks her on the mouth. "Terrific, as always." His grey vest is streaked with sweat. "Just what I needed."

"Oh?" She returns the kiss. "Stressed out again?"

He shudders, and she motions for him to turn round. She puts her hands on his shoulders, under the towel, just at the base of his neck. "Let me see." Her fingers slide over his damp skin, her thumbs kneading the bunched muscle underneath. "Work? Or Gary again?"

He lets a long, low groan, physical delight in her ministrations, combined with frustration. "You won't believe what the little B has done to me now."

She nips the flesh of his shoulder. "Ow! That hurt."

"Then don't talk about Gary like that."

"Wait till you hear, though. On Sunday — "

"Tell you what, hon..." She gives him a final manipulation of the trapezius and releases him. "Save it for dinner. Then you can give me the full treatment." Richard's stories are always part performance, and she enjoys the entertainment. "Hit those showers," she says, "and see you down at reception in twenty?"

This engagement for dinner after her Wednesday class has become a fixture for them both. She sees Richard on other nights too, and with other people, but Wednesday's tête-à-tête has become the bedrock of their friendship. There's no one in this city she'd rather spend time with. It was Richard who encouraged her career in fitness. When she started teaching aerobics classes part-time in a local hall she wanted to be more than just another Jane Fonda clone. As she experimented with new moves and methods, Richard urged her on. Whenever she hit on something uniquely her own, he loved it. "Don't be afraid, Squirrel," he used to say. "You're great at this; go for it."

So she did. She shunned the pure dance music used by other instructors in favour of songs by artists like Talking Heads, Marvyn Gaye, Grace Jones, songs with slow beats that allowed muscles and joints to be put through a fuller range of movement. She devised routines that took the body from its highest attainable point — leaping through the air — to lying prone on the floor and back up again, all in a series of controlled moves. To an onlooker, her class might look less strenuous than the more usual fast-stepping, high-impact workouts, but those who did the routine knew just how tough — and effective — it was.

Richard was right. The more experimental she became, the

more the punters loved it. She quickly got slots in the top gyms in the city and people began to book for her class in advance, sometimes weeks ahead. Instead of taking one of the full-time jobs she was offered by the gyms, she set up her own company, Rí Rá.

"In Ireland," her publicity material read, "a rí rá is a rollicking and raucous good time. That's just what you're guaranteed with a Rí Rá Workout. A pulse-pounding, dance-based aerobic routine set to an eclectic musical mix — from Classical to Celtic Rock — that will challenge every muscle in your body. In Ireland, a rí rá sometimes turns into an outright ruaille buaille. What's that? Well, why don't you come along and find out?"

It felt hypocritical to play on her Irishness this way, after years of renouncing the place, but Richard convinced her. "You are Irish," he said, "and if for some misbegotten reason the Irish are suddenly cool, you might as well take advantage."

She knows that other people consider what she does to be superficial, or worse. Another of her good friends, the defiantly large Susan, has put all the arguments to her. Susan is scathing about what she calls "body fascism" and carries every one of her one hundred and eighty pounds with pride, a testament to her resolution to "take up space".

Susan does not approve of exercise classes, and considers exercise instructors to be implicated — "up to their necks" — in a system that uses ideals of beauty as a weapon in the war against women. Susan's arguments sway her, but she knows too, to her core, that exercise saved her.

Often, she sees both sides of an argument; sometimes more than two. This used to worry her, until she read what the American bard of liberation, Walt Whitman, wrote in his 'Song of Myself':

Do I contradict myself?
Very well then I contradict myself
(I am large, I contain multitudes.)

She had the lines written up in large letters and framed, to hang on her wall.

She has men in her life, this woman. Lovers aplenty. Generally she loves them serially, one after another, but sometimes they overlap. Monogamy no longer seems to her like the only way to live. With so many people in her life, she is rarely lonely and if she — just sometimes — finds herself marooned in a moment of yearning, she is able to extricate herself. To catch herself on, as her grandmother used to say. She no longer believes in "The One".

She, of course, is me. I like her, this creation of mine, though I don't quite believe in her. Living in San Francisco has changed me: I am not the person I was when I arrived. If I had stayed where I was, or gone somewhere else, I would be different again. Knowing this makes me feel strange.

Conditional.

Richard and I sit at our table in Mani's, drinking "love bombs": alcohol-free cocktails of passion-fruit juice, wheatgerm and ginseng. We are both dry, one of the many things we have in common. This makes us mildly self-conscious — since its lawless, boomtown beginnings, San Francisco has been a hard-drinking town — but it's just beginning to be cool to be clean. Health is a burgeoning business and sober clubs are opening up.

Over the menus, Richard is making a tale out of his complaints against Gary. On Sunday afternoon, after an argument about Richard's staying out all night after a trip to the Glory Holes, his favourite bathhouse, Gary "flounced" out of their apartment and hasn't been seen since. The word on the gay grapevine is that at least one of those absent nights was spent with Reno Lewis, who just happens to be an old flame of Richard's.

"Reno Lewis," wails Richard, dropping his face into his hands. Under the dramatics, I know his dismay is real.

Real, but misplaced, it seems to me. For weeks — months —

I have listened to Richard bemoaning Gary's predilection for monogamy as if it were a vice.

"So what's the problem?" I ask. "I thought this was what you wanted."

"Reno Lewis," he groans. "Reno Lewis."

"I'm confused," I say. "Just who are you jealous of here?"

"I'm not jealous. You know I don't do jealous."

"You're doing a good impression."

"Come on, Squirrel, keep to your script. You're my buddy. You're supposed to pat my hand, tell me I've been wronged."

"I can't, you contrary old queen. For months, Gary has wanted you to be a couple and you insisted on your inalienable rights to visit the Glory Holes whenever you fancied. Now he's playing things your way and you're outraged."

"Ouch!" he winces.

"Why are you doing this, Richard? You two are so great together."

"And ouch again! Enough, Cruella."

Our waiter comes over, a new guy, dark hair in a pony tail, whiter than white teeth, very young. Richard and I exchange a look that says: nice, very nice. Richard has taught me how to admire men, how to look at them frankly, without fear. It helps when they are younger, as this one is. He takes our order and departs, the strings of his apron tied into a heart shape over his butt.

Richard sees me look and nudges me. "Eyes off, Squirrel, he's mine."

I groan out loud; he can always tell. "Aren't there any straight men left in this town?"

Richard laughs. I'll get no sympathy on that score, I know. And he's right, it is he who is in the minority, even here in San Francisco. I turn back to our conversation about Gary. "You know, Richard, you can't have everything."

"I don't want everything, O Heartless One. I only want..." He stops.

"Go on."

He looks over his shoulder. "Is this an X-rated restaurant?"

I laugh. "Come on, Richard, be serious. What is it that you want?"

"I am being serious. At least half the time —" he lowers his voice — 'I am the horniest man alive and all I want, all I think I'll ever want, is filthy, glorious, anonymous sex."

"And the other half?"

"The other half, I want what Gary and you and the rest of the goddamn world seems to think I should want: side-by-side TV dinners and hand-in-hand trips to the stores. Romance and undying love with one wonderful man."

"So-o-o-o, all you need is to find someone who understands all that and loves you anyway. Somebody who lets you be both."

"That's all, huh?"

"But, Richard, you have that. With Gary. At least, you had, if you haven't blown it. Your problem isn't that you want everything. It's that while you get one thing, you're longing for its opposite."

He picks up his napkin, and mine, stuffs one into each ear.

"I'm right, and you know it. While you're at home with Gary, you're wondering what's going on down the baths. After a few nights in the Glory Holes, you're thinking: what am I doing here when I could be home with that great guy of mine?"

He takes the napkins down. "While I'm at the Glory Holes, honey, thinking is about the only thing I'm not doing."

I giggle. "But I'm not altogether wrong, am I?"

"You're just telling me back what I already told you. I'm a condemned man. This isn't a phase: it's the story of my life."

He looks so miserable that I laugh. "Come on, aren't you the guy who told me that happiness is a decision?"

"Oh, that. I was only trying to cheer you up. You and I know better than that. Come on, could you ever be happy in Mucksville? Could I, in Telport?" Richard comes from a small town in the Midwest. For him, indeed for many of the people we know, home is a four-letter word.

"But we're not in Mucknamore or Telport any more," I say. "We're here, in one of the best towns in the world for people like us." I reach across and touch his hand. "Look, Richard, I just have to say one more thing, so you can't fool yourself that you don't know. If Gary wasn't scared of you leaving him, he would never have gone near this Reno Lewis. Gary is man enough to let you go prowling if that's what you need to do, once he can trust you to come home to him after you're done."

Our waiter friend comes across with our food. Richard throws him such heavy looks that the poor boy breaks into a blush.

"New to town?" Richard asks.

"Yeah."

"Just arrived from...?"

"Minnesota."

"Well, Minnesota, we'll have to show you around a little. What time do you get off?"

The boy looks uncertain. "Eleven."

"Great."

"Em, I'm not sure..."

"Oh, I'm sorry. Pardon me if you've got better plans."

"No, it's not...It's just..."

"Tell him, Squirrel. Tell him I don't bite."

"He doesn't bite." I say, flatly. The boy looks at me, then at Richard.

"Relax, Minnesota. This is a friendly town. I'll just take you around, introduce you to a few people."

"Okay." He flashes his perfect smile. "Yeah...why not?"

He goes off to attend someone else. Richard is jubilant. "Take that, pal Gary," he says, discreetly punching the air.

Coffee arrives via another waiter and I tell Richard my news. "I got a letter from Ireland today."

"No! Not from the immovable Mom?"

"From her representative, Sister Maeve. She's coming over here for a visit."

"This, I deduce from the droop of your chin, is not a good thing?"

"Oh, Richard, you know what she's like. She only wants to come here so she can have a good snoop around my life and tell me where I'm going wrong."

"That's what big sisters do, I guess."

"She's bringing Donal with her."

His eyebrows lift into a question.

"Her husband. A suit."

"Poor Squirrel. How long will they be here?"

"Two weeks," I wail. "What will I do with them for fourteen whole days and nights?"

"I'll help you."

"Oh...okay. Thanks."

He notices my hesitation. "Unless I'm one of the things in your life that you don't want her snooping around."

"Don't be silly, Richard. It's not you, it's them."

He shakes his head. "She's a big girl."

"Yeah, my big critical sister."

"If she wants to be critical, you can't stop her. Let her be critical."

I make a face. "Come on, what if it was your mother coming to see you?"

He shudders. "That's not too likely, praise be. She can't come because she hasn't told any of her cronies I live here. She's afraid they'll put two and two together and work out why I'm not married." He takes my hand. "Just be yourself, Squirrel. Stand tall."

"I can imagine what she'll say about teaching aerobics." I stick my nose up and imitate my sister's voice at its pickiest: "'I'm sure it's fun, Jo, but it's hardly a proper job, now is it?'"

"Let her come, let her think what she wants, then let her go home again. That's all you have to do."

Richard is the only person who understands why I left Mucknamore and never went back. Why I won't get in touch with my mother or grandmother if they won't contact me. I have told him everything. He lifts my fingers, brushes them with a kiss. "You know you're fabulous, darling. If the Mucksville contingent can't see that, it's their loss."

"Thank you." I whisper. Then, lighter: "You're right, I am fabulous."

"You are. Too, too fabulous." He looks over my shoulder. "But now," he says, "it would appear that dessert is approaching."

I follow his eyes. Our waiter is crossing to our table, white apron gone. "I got off early," he says, sliding into the chair opposite, his skin glowing with youth and promise.

I get up, leave my half of the check on the table.

"Be nice to him, okay?" I whisper into Richard's ear as I kiss him goodnight. "He's sweet."

He answers me with a horrible leer.

"Night, night," I say, to them both. "Be good."

"Honey, you know I'm the best." His chuckle follows me out into the foggy evening.

San Francisco is my city. I knew that from the moment I arrived, from my very first morning walking through Golden Gate Park, entranced by the smell of eucalyptus and sunny November skies. It was a Sunday, I remember, and the park was full of people, but it was big enough to hold us all. On my way in, I passed a circle of homeless men drinking cider around a set of bongo drums and a guitar. One of them lifted his can to me as I walked past. "You have a good one," he said, smiling, and I found myself smiling back. I couldn't help myself, he seemed so amiable. They all did, though there were eleven of them and only one of me. It was impossible to imagine passing a group of homeless men in London or Dublin and feeling so unthreatened.

I love this place, I found myself saying over and again, as I walked around it. Born out of gold and silver, built on a core of wild spending and carousing, this city that was never a small town but wild and lawless, gaudy and greedy, diverse and world famous, right from the start. In those early days I walked everywhere, getting to know my new city. The first year was difficult, hopping from job to dead-end job, apartment to dreary apartment, trapped inside a void left behind by alcohol's absence. For sanity's sake, I walked and walked — later, jogged — all around the city, up and down the unfeasible hills, through streets where music drummed out from under psychedelic blinds, through parks where grey-haired people went roller skating, through beaches where meditators worshipped the morning sun.

I revelled in the sunshine and also in the fogs that billowed in from the ocean, as if huffed through the Golden Gate by an unseen mouth. I came to love these fogs that shrouded me in a blanket of anonymity as I went, that ensured I never took the sun for granted.

I even came to love the city's faulty underpinnings: San Andreas and Hayward, San Gregorio, Greenville and Calaveras, and the earth shudders they threw up, always hinting towards the long-anticipated "Big One" that might come at any time and topple our town down on top of us, or trigger a tsunami out in the ocean, a tidal wave that would swell and swell as it swept in from the bay, rising taller than the bridges and skyscrapers it broke against, smashing them to smithereens and sweeping away the bits in its flow, like so many pebbles and twigs.

It was frightening to ponder it, especially downtown among the office towers. According to Richard, the risk of earthquake has all San Franciscans permanently on alert. With catastrophe ever imminent, better try whatever you fancy now or else die wondering. I don't fully buy the theory — I can't imagine Richard reining in his excesses, wherever he lived — but he brought me to believe in the value of vulnerability.

I hadn't been here long when I first heard the expression, "only in San Francisco." It came to be widely used afterwards — "only in Hollywood," people would say, or "only in Europe" – and usually used disparagingly, but I first heard it applied to the town I was beginning to own, and I took it as a tribute. So many things could, and did, happen only in San Francisco. This city had given the world beats and hippies, free love and flower power, multiculturalism and gay pride... Only in San Francisco, it seemed to me, was American can-do culture applied so vigorously to realms beyond the commercial.

It was on nights out with Richard that I first cracked open my inhibitions without alcohol. His frankness about matters sexual made me see how I had always stood at the border of my own desires, hesitating, playing safe, nursing my sexual disappointment while berating myself or my lover de jour. By example, Richard taught me to own my full self. By joking, he led me past fear and shame. "Forget what your mother told you about sex," he said. "Apply what she told you about olives instead."

Mrs D. never had anything to say to me about either, but I took the point: sex is an acquired taste and it takes several tries to know which particular flavours you enjoy. There are techniques and responses to learn, social as well as sexual skills to acquire. Richard showed me the way.

But it was the night he turned up at my house with his face disfigured by a gay bashing — for yes, even here in San Francisco there are bigots — that turned our affection for each other into something more. When I found him standing on my doorstep, pretending like he didn't care and brought him in to sit on my sofa and held him hard while he tried to stop his bruised face from creasing into tears, that was when I knew I loved him. With my new, San Franciscan, way of loving.

Susan I met later, and she forced herself on me. I was browsing in a bookshop when she came peering over the top of my book, two enormous brown eyes in a wide black face. "You don't want that," she said.

"Excuse me?"

"That." She pointed at the book I had in my hand: *Woman's Words, Woman's Worlds.* "You don't want it. It's just another whitey whine."

I pulled back from this intrusion, but she didn't seem to notice. "Trust me. This is the one you want." She held out another book to me. *This Bridge Called My Back,* it was called. *Writings By Radical Women of Color.*

I looked up at her. "No," I said. "I don't think so."

"Where are you from?"

"Ireland," I said, instantly regretting that I had answered. I decided to be rude and turned my back.

"I knew it," she said, coming round to my front. "I said so to myself when I saw you. But I'm reckoning on you being the right kind of Irish. That's why I'm saying to you that this here is the one you want." Again, she shoved the book towards me, and resisted as I tried to push it back. When I wouldn't take it from her hands, she carried it across to the checkout. "The lady will take this," she said, pointing across at me.

Now I was annoyed. I worked in a bar back then, a down-at-heel place where the tips were poor and given out once a week with our pay packs. That day I had less than $5 in my purse and, if I bought that book, I wouldn't eat again until payday.

Susan saw my expression and opened her purse. "Here." She handed $20 to the assistant.

"No," I protested "Stop."

"I'm making you do this, honey," Susan said, taking her change. "So don't waste no time feeling bad. But I do have a condition. You've got to call me when you've read it and tell me your opinion." She was writing down her number for me on the paper wrapping. "But you'll like it," she said, handing over the scrap of paper. "Yeah, I'm getting the feeling I know just what you like."

I caught the hint in her voice, enough to make me wonder if she meant what I later learned she did. By the time I knew for sure, I didn't recoil from the notion as I would have on that first day. By then, I knew Susan well enough to be glad that, if she had been mistaken in that, she was right about the book. And about lots of other things too.

It was a great book, just what I needed to read at that time. I had always held that any self-respecting woman had to be a feminist, and living in more than one place had taught me that each culture has its own particular ways of keeping its women under. Just as I was getting used to this idea of a pan-national, trans-historical sisterhood, the essays in this book — by Afro-, Asian-, Latin- and Native-American women — complicated that idea. The essays were eloquent, passionate and thought-provoking, and made me see how I benefited from having white skin. For the first time in my life, I saw myself as a person of relative privilege.

When I telephoned — or called, as I was learning to say — to tell Susan so, she squealed with delight. "I knew it," she cried, her voice an even deeper shade of chocolate over the telephone. "I knew you were the right kinda Irish."

I said, "I don't know what you mean by that."

"Your people come in two types, honey: those who pretend like there never was an attitude that said 'No Blacks, No Irish', the ones like to put as much distance as they can between their black brothers and sisters and their own white, lily-livered asses. Then there's the kind who've learned somethin' more from their own persecution than how to do the same thing to others."

Susan made me quail, still does. I've never had the energy, or maybe the courage, for her kind of stern, one-track anger. All my emotions are mixed. But we talked for a long time on the telephone that first evening and at the end of the call she asked if I would like to come with her on Monday night to Joni's, a woman-only health spa on Polk that hosted CR sessions three times a week.

CR?

What? I had never heard of Consciousness-Raising? I was going to love it. They were a great group of women and they talked about everything, everything, exploring how their personal dilemmas were politically rooted. There used to be hundreds of such spaces all over this town, but in recent years, she didn't know why, they were closing down, little lights going out.

The spa was in what looked like an old factory building. There was no elevator and we walked up three flights of rickety stairs to be met at the top by a dainty Latina woman, about forty years old, wearing a buttonhole that said: Cunt Power! She hugged Susan and then they both turned to me and she said, "Welcome, Jo, I'm Dolores," and kissed my cheek. Her lips were dry, powdery, and she smelled of something herbal. "Susan has been telling me all about you."

The same smell permeated the lemon-and-lavender-striped corridor they steered me through. "Susan tells me you liked Bridge," Dolores said, taking my arm.

"Yes."

"I'm so glad. It's a really seminal book, I think."

"Shouldn't that be 'ovumnal', sweetheart?" Susan called from behind us.

"Hey, that's a great word," smiled Dolores over our shoulders. "Ovumnal. I love that." She turned back to me. "Have you ever done a naked consciousness-raising before, Jo?"

"Naked?"

"Oh, sorry," said Susan, breaking into peals of laughter behind us. "Did I not mention the naked?"

"Please do not mind her, Jo." Dolores's arm locked mine, propelled me onwards. "It is all very non-threatening. Very gentle and supportive. The idea is we present ourselves to each other in all our vulnerability. We take off our inhibitions with our clothes."

In the spa room, three women were already in the jacuzzi pool. "This is Gloria," said Dolores. "And Zoe. And Arlene. Women, this is Jo."

"Hi, Jo," the three responded, together.

Gloria was fortyish and black, Zoe was my age, white with dreadlocked hair, and Arlene, also white, was much older than the rest. That was all I had time to notice as Dolores led us through to the dressing room. In the time it took me to hang my jacket on the hook and unzip my bag, Susan had her clothes off and was parading around the dressing room, her towel trailing from her fingers. The vast expanse of her body drew me out of my own self-consciousness. Furrows of fat cascaded from beneath the bowls of her breasts. Her girth was frightening, each thigh the size of an average waist. She seemed like a parody of a fat woman, the sort you see in cartoon postcards, with feet that looked too small to support her. Gross and magnificent, she postured around the room.

Meanwhile, I slinked out of my clothes and let her lead the way back to the pool. I held my head up and managed not to use my hands to cover myself. I wasn't normally prudish, but the artificiality of the situation, the weighing of our nakedness with meaning, made me want to grab the nearest towel and run.

One after each other, we slid into the pool. Everyone else's breasts were held above the water line so I let mine do the same. The water bubbled and the underlying drone of the pump was soothing, but my thighs clutched the smooth plastic of the seat, unable to relax. Dolores opened the session by introducing and welcoming me, then outlining the rules of the coming conversation. We must suspend judgement. We must listen with respect, seeking to understand rather than persuade. We must speak freely and with sincerity of what has personal heart and meaning. The topic for today would be our experiences with the medical profession.

"Before we get started," said Arlene, "I just thought y'all might like to know that I did it."

"Way hey, girl!" cackled Susan. "And did you find what you went looking for?"

"Tell us everything, Arlene," says Dolores. "Everything. Did you buy the hand mirror?"

"Uh-huh."

"And you took it to your bedroom?"

"Bathroom."

"Ran a bath?"

"Mmm."

"Lit candles?"

"Yes."

"Good," said Dolores. "Candles are good. Low, gentle light."

"Arlene is — or looks like we can finally say was — a masturbation virgin," Susan explained to me.

"Oh," I said.

Arlene reclaimed the conversation, told how she had also bought — she quivered at her daring — some female erotica. And then she...you know...um...down there...

"Not 'down there', Arlene," said Dolores. "Come on now."

"Touched my...vagina," Arlene whispered.

Dolores clapped her hands. "Well done, Arlene." Gloria and Zoe joined in.

Susan was unimpressed. "Can we be a bit more specific?" she asked, melting Arlene's expression of triumph. "It wasn't your 'vagina' you were aiming at, was it?"

Furrows erupted on Arlene's forehead. She began to bite her lower lip.

"Christ, girl! Ain't you ever going to say cunt?" said Susan.

"I don't want to say that word, I've told you."

"Now, Arlene, we've discussed this," said Dolores. "We have to embrace all the words. We have to reclaim our bodies, especially our sexual organs, from patriarchal disfigurement. We have to own ourselves and love ourselves."

"Well, I can't help it," Arlene said. "I just hate that word."

Dolores reached across, put a hand on her shoulder. "You've been conditioned to hate it, remember? Remember last week, when we talked about the word 'country'?"

Arlene nodded.

"You don't hate that word, do you?"

She shook her head.

"It's only a collection of letters, Arlene. If you hate it, what you're feeling is hatred of women. You have to break that in yourself."

"I used to be the same, Arlene," said Zoe. "But now I'm totally able to say any of 'em. Pussy! Vagina!"

"Labia!" said Gloria, cupping handfuls of water and throwing them in the air. "Vulva!"

"Men have plenty of names for their genitalia, Arlene," Dolores said. "And none of them is vague."

"Too right," said Susan. "No fear of them mixing up their prick and their balls. 'Down there'? I mean, Jesus! It's the 1980s."

"Hold on," said Zoe. "She did say 'vagina'."

"Don't any of you want to hear," Arlene said, pulling herself up into the dignity of her years, "what happened?"

Dolores was contrite. "Of course we do. Come on, everybody, this is Arlene's time to talk."

"But, honey," said Susan, "until she starts naming names, we can't even be sure what she's talking about." She laughed so hard she swallowed some jacuzzi water, while Arlene looked like she might cry.

"It's okay, Arlene," said Gloria. "You take your time. You'll say it in a minute, won't you? When you're ready?"

But she didn't. And afterwards, I found myself beside her in the dressing room while Susan and Dolores were showering. She said to me: "This is your first time here, isn't it?"

I nodded.

"I hope you weren't offended by that talk earlier."

"No." I shook my head. "No, I wasn't offended."

"It's hard at the beginning. After my first time, I was so shocked I stayed away for weeks, but something made me come back."

I dried between my toes.

"I'm still a bit overwhelmed, as you've probably gathered," she went on. "I sometimes have to fight myself not to put my hands over my ears."

"I'm not surprised," I say, with feeling.

"Oh, I'm so glad to hear you say that, I always feel like it's just me."

"Definitely not." I said, smiling back. "Just don't report me to Susan."

"She's formidable, isn't she? But kind too, very kind. I've seen that in her." She zips open her bag, starts to put on her underwear beneath her towel. "But you know, I wish they hadn't gone on about the words again. They didn't give me a chance to tell them how grateful I feel."

"Grateful?"

"To have found it." She beams a smile so beatific you'd think it was God she'd found. "After sixty-three years of being ignored, there it was. And still...still in working order."

We are both smiling now.

"I knew it must be something, from the way you young people are always going on. But, oh my!"

"1923," I find myself saying.

"I beg your pardon?"

"You were born in 1923?"

"Yes, that's right, dear. You must be very good at math."

"No, it's just...You're the same age as my mother."

"Is that so? You must bring her along next time."

"Oh, no," I say and the way she looks at me tells me I've been over-vehement. "I can't. She lives in Ireland."

"That's a pity. But maybe she's more advanced than me?"

"Oh, no," I say again. "She's Irish."

"Then bring her when she comes to visit you. Tell her what happens here. Tell her about me: sixty-three years old and..." She drops her voice to a whisper. "...I can't get enough of myself."

Richard loves this story when I bring it home to him, but he doesn't like much else about the group. Whenever I ever try to get him to acknowledge the links between gays and women, he ostentatiously yawns. "Don't be a bore, Squirrel," he'll say. Or "I've told you before, political is so not your colour."

This is ironic, because in the group I am considered not political enough. Susan, in particular, thinks me hopeless: I wear short skirts, I defuzz my armpits — I teach aerobics, for pity's sake. She wrinkles her nose at all this, and implies that she would probably find it unacceptable in anybody else. Mostly I ignore this unasked-for indulgence — Susan needs her convictions, I am glad to have lost mine.

But I don't like when she starts on Richard. "He's a woman-hater," she says. "Can't you see that?"

"He doesn't hate me. And I am a woman, am I not?"

To him I say, "Susan says I'm a fag hag."

"At least she didn't say fruit fly."

"She says gay men despise women."

"That's her idea of a chat-up line, Squirrel. She thinks you find it seductive."

"No, she doesn't. She knows I'm straight."

Though she thinks I shouldn't be. For Susan, lesbianism is political choice as well as a sexual preference. Men fragment female unity, she says, and heterosex always puts men first. I take her point, but I won't be taking it any further. I shrink from real breasts, smooth faces, soft skin. Men are easily pleased, but don't women always find each other wanting?

So I call my sexual orientation straight and refuse to choose between Susan and Richard. In my new, busy life, I want them both and all the people they bring with them and the other friends I am making in work and other places and the dear companionship of the city itself, its parks full of the rolling beat of bongos, its head shops selling drug paraphernalia, its kaleidoscopic street murals, its pride marches and street demos, the blue theatre of its bay. Still now, three years on, walking across Golden Gate Bridge at sundown thrills me: the glowing, pink-white buildings undulating against the hills down to the sea.

I know as I walk that I am on the "Bridge of Sighs", the "Golden Leap", the best-known suicide site in the Western World, where more than a thousand named people have jumped to their deaths, and countless more have jumped unrecorded, at night or through fog, into the strong current that runs oceanward beneath, into the sharks feeding there and beyond.

I know the homeless in the streets and parks are as broken here as anywhere else, but still. Still, for me, the tourist cliché of this city viewed from the bridge, or this bridge viewed from the city, is a wondrous sight.

But now my sister is coming here to see it. Why do I feel that once she does, its light will dim in me?

1995

*I*t is my week for visitors. At four in the afternoon, I look up from my desk and find Rory's wife is standing at the door looking in at me. A thought jumps into my head: You're too late. Too late by one day.

"I'm sorry to be doing this to you," she says.

Then don't, I think. Don't do it.

Her face is impassive, but I can read embarrassment, though she is not blushing. She doesn't have the complexion for blushing.

"Can I...er, come in?"

I want to say no, but I push my chair back instead, bring her through to the back to sit on the grass where Maeve and I went before. She is better looking than I realised: hair highlighted blonde, body exercised and groomed, good clothes. Not unlike my sister, in fact. For the first time this summer, I feel scruffy in my shorts and T-shirt.

I take Hilde's chair. "Pregnancy privilege," I say, waving at the rug.

"Of course," she agrees, awkwardly folding herself down. "How are you feeling?" A polite enquiry, woman to woman.

"Fine, never better actually. Just tired of looking like a baby elephant."

"What stage are you at?"

"Six months."

"You don't look it at all. That's probably from the jogging, is it?"

"I've no idea."

The conversation dries. After the interval grows too, too awkward, I say: "You better tell me why you're here."

She opens her mouth, falters, takes a deep breath, tries again. When she still can't find the right words, she shakes her head. "I'm beginning to think I shouldn't have come."

You shouldn't, I say in my head. You really shouldn't. What a thing to do to us all.

Eventually she says, "I've come because I want to know the answer to two questions and it seems like you're the only one who can give them to me." But she stops again, trying not to cry.

Well, I'm not going to be the one to speak. I don't have to. I plead fifth amendment.

The silence stretches and stretches until it feels like it's going to snap, then she says in a rush: "What I want to ask you is...Is your baby Rory's?"

"No!" Whatever I'd expected, it wasn't that. "How could it be?"

Her shoulders slump and I see how tension has been holding her rigid.

"I'm almost seven months pregnant. You must know I've only been here since May."

"He was away for a few days in February, on a golf trip. I thought maybe...?"

"The day we met at my mother's funeral was the first time I saw Rory in twenty years."

Things must be bad between them if that's what she thought. And things must have been bad before I came along. A golf trip:

I try not to shudder. She is making me part of something detestable.

"Your other question?" Let's get this over with, let's get her gone.

This one takes even longer to dredge up and out. "Do you want him?"

"Want him?" I echo, foolishly.

"Yes. I need to know. How serious is it? How far has it gone?"

I look at her, aghast. Oh no, my dear, that is a question for your husband, not me. She looks back at me, and whatever she sees makes her face fall into her hands.

"Oh God!" she says through splayed fingers. "It's true."

"Listen, this isn't fair —"

"Are you serious about him?" she asks, in a small and broken voice. "Or is this just a fling for you?"

"Now see here —"

"Please, you must tell me. I need to know. Do you want him for good or do you intend to move on?"

I don't like her categories. To listen to her, you wouldn't know that we existed before she ever came along.

"Rory and I have a history," I say, in a voice that surprises me with its calm.

"I know all about that."

"No," I say, stung by her tone, "What you know is Rory's version of our history. Just like I know his version of your marriage."

She winces and the sick look on her face dissolves my scorn. "I'm sorry, I shouldn't have said that," I say. "He hardly talks about you, to tell the truth."

I am trying to make amends but that doesn't sound much better. I love him, is what I want to scream. I love him. He was mine first. Go away.

"I don't suppose he does." She looks at me and a lighter look, not quite a smile, comes swimming into her misery. "He talks about himself, right?"

That surprises me. I look fully at her for the first time and, in our exchanged expressions, Rory shrinks a little. Suddenly, her questions seem to be for me, as well as her. We both sit quiet, thinking our thoughts, until she says: "I do want him."

"You've got to tell him that, not me. I just —"

She frowns. "I know, I know that. But before talking to him, it would help if I knew your plans. Are you going to stay here?"

"No."

"I don't mean here," she says, indicating the shed. "Obviously you can't go on living here."

"I knew what you meant."

"So you're leaving Ireland?"

"I think so. Probably. Yes."

"When?"

"Soon."

"Before the baby?"

I resent her questions, questions I wouldn't answer from anybody else. So what bond between us makes me answer her?

"No, not until afterwards. It costs a fortune to have a child in the States."

She hangs her head. "If you want him, he'll go with you."

"I wouldn't be so sure."

She nods, her face miserably certain. "I'm too available. I should go off and have an affair myself, shake him up."

That is how she persists in seeing me: the affair. And I suppose that is what I am. She and the children are his base. Having them allows him the luxury of thinking he wants more.

I look away from her resentful face, out to sea. The sun shines and the cloud clusters are light and fleecy, but yesterday's rainstorm changed the weather. It's a few degrees lower today and something in the light says that the best is over for this year. Tonight, it will get dark earlier than last night, and tomorrow earlier again. I gaze, trying to imprint the sea's serenity on my brain, trying to calm the emotions this woman is stirring with her audacity.

"It's nice here," she says, following my eyes. "Sitting here, I can see what attracted you."

"It was what I needed at this time."

"Are you over the worst?"

I look at her, puzzled.

"Your mother's death," she says.

"Yes, I'm over the worst of that," I say.

"It's a pity you didn't get to see her, before she died."

In other circumstances, we might have been able to have a real talk. She has listener's eyes and I'm beginning to see that she is not as insipid as she looks, as she has trained herself to be. But I cannot let us connect. Already we have gone too far.

"I'd better go," she says, realising it too. She stands, pulls her jeans straight. "Look, I'm sorry for coming here...for doing this." She's not able to look at me. "You must think I'm like that desperate woman in that country-and-western song: 'I'm beggin' of you, pleeeez don't take my man.'"

"I don't think that."

"I am that pathetic, I know I am. But —" She breaks off, looks wretched. "He won't talk to me any more. This seemed to be the only way I could find out...anything." Tears rise. "Oh, God, no, I'm sorry." She fumbles in her bag. "I should never have done this. I'm sorry." By the time she's found a tissue, she has got control and no longer needs it. She holds it helplessly, reluctant to leave. "I feel like such a fool."

The sea turns over, wave after wave. Go, I think. Please. Just go.

"We were happy...If we don't...It's the children, more than anything..."

I say, "Talk to him."

She nods into her tissue, blows her nose, then brings her eyes up to mine. "How did you get to be so strong?" she asks.

"Me? Strong?"

"I thought at the beginning, when you came first, that you must be half crazy to be holing yourself up here, like this. But you're not, you..." She lets the words trail off. "Once upon a time I was strong," she says. "It was a word my mother always used to use to describe me."

I look at her jagged face, the fingers grasping at frayed tissue. Maybe, I think, but you are also fragile. As am I. And Rory too.

We are all, all of us, so fragile.

1986

*I*t's September when Maeve comes to stay. The wind blows from the north and the light of the city is so clear that she says she feels her eyes ping whenever she looks out at the shimmery bay. Both she and Donal love San Francisco and are awed by my loft apartment with its grey industrial carpet, its steel racks and track lighting. Relying on Richard, I decide my tactic will be to play up my difference. So I put them sleeping on a futon, feed them sushi and noodles, make little jokes about the Irish way of doing things.

It's petty — and I hate myself while I'm doing it — but I can't help it. I want Maeve to be impressed. I want her to see that there is more than one way to be.

I take them to do all the touristy things I never do: ferries to Alcatraz and Sausalito, sunbathing on China Beach, over-eating in Fisherman's Wharf, snapping Golden Gate Bridge from Marian Green. Richard brings us on a voyeuristic tour of Folsom Street and the Castro. And, at Donal's request, after a book-buying session in City Lights, we go on to an Irish bar so he can have "a decent pint of Guinness."

Another night, I take them to Ice, one of the new café-bars in the Castro. While Donal is ordering drinks, a leering queen gives him the eye. "Don't look now," I smirk, "but I think you've made a conquest." He turns and rebounds in horror off the dissolute, painted face that blows him a kiss.

"Jaysus," he says. "That isn't a woman, is it?"

"Loosen up, darling," Maeve says, delighted to be the cooler one for once.

Maeve decides she'd like to do one of my classes. She has been doing aerobics herself, she says, twice a week in her local hall in Rathfarnam. I bring her to Blues, the premier gym, confident that the best Dublin has to offer will not compete. In our leotards, I see my body is better than hers now, firmer. She still has bigger breasts, and face-wise there's no contest, but the comparison doesn't sting in the old way. She's wrong here. It's not just her clothes and hair, but something in her: the difference between somebody who has lived away from home and somebody who hasn't.

All the way through the class she beams at me, and when we're finished I don't have to ask if she enjoyed it. "It's really different," she says, her face flushed. "Fantastic."

Fantastic is her word for everything San Franciscan, though she's surprised I don't know more Irish people. The 1980s have been tough in Ireland and the Irish are pouring into the States again. There are fifty thousand Irish-Americans in San Francisco, Maeve tells me, and on our trips around the city, she always finds one to talk to. She and Donal get excited when they see the Irish flag hanging from St Patrick's. They buy copies of The Irish Herald. They ask me about the St Patrick's Day parade.

I move away from her chats with these strangers. I don't feel kinship with these immigrants clustering in their pubs or parishes here, any more than I did in London. I don't like that the Irish contribution to American culture is green beer and bigoted parades. I don't like how, since ten IRA prisoners starved themselves to death in Northern Ireland to win political status, an Irish political lobby is growing more vocal in the Bay Area, popping up in bars all over, singing rebel songs and thinking themselves on the cutting edge of The Cause as money for guns and bombs gets dropped in a fund-raising box. And I don't like when another Irish person hears my accent and tries to claim me.

My community is those who think like me, not those who happen to have been born on the same small island. Or in the same small house. I have found people who love me, really love me, not like Maeve — in spite of what I am — but because of it. As I put it recently in a magazine article I wrote, friends are the new family.

But how can I say such a thing to my sister?

To my surprise, Maeve and Richard get on well. He and Gary take us to Troopers, a bisexual club with an indulgent attitude to extra-dancing activities. The four of us spend the night on the dance floor while Donal minds the drinks. As we walk home afterwards, fog swirling white around the streetlights, I link Richard and Gary, and let Maeve and Donal walk on ahead.

"She's fab," Richard says.

"Mutual admiration all round," I say. "She thinks you two are great too."

"You gave her a lousy billing," Gary says.

"She seems different here."

Richard looks at me and I squeeze his arm. "Okay, okay, maybe I see her different here."

"And Hubby coped with Troopers."

"I'd say Maeve spoke to him before we went out."

"I'll never forget his face when Mona gave him the treatment," says Gary. Mona is a butch friend of Gary's who likes to shock: tonight she was wearing nothing but straps around bare breasts under her leather jacket, so she could show off a nipple-ring. She honed in on Donal for the night, as arranged by the guys.

Richard says: "I reckon Hubby would be quite a goer if you could crack the frozen exterior."

"Yeah. Anyone that hung up has got to be repressing like mad," smiles Gary, the psychologist.

Richard nudges him. "Hey, maybe we should see if we can unleash his inner slut."

"Richard!" I warn. "Don't even think about it."

They come back to my apartment for coffee. Donal goes to bed but Maeve stays up, sitting on the chair opposite Richard and Gary, talking about San Francisco's gay culture. I keep the kitchen hatch open, half-listening as I fix coffee. Maeve's feet are curled under her in the chair and her opinions are coming out harder now she's relaxing. As I listen, I decide I prefer her ill at ease. It keeps that damned certainty of hers at bay.

As I put the coffee down in front of them, Gary is telling her that for the past years, five thousand gays a week have been moving to the Bay Area, the greatest influx of immigrants since the gold rush.

"Freedom," he says. "A bigger prize than any precious metal."

"Tell me," Maeve says, with the air of someone breaking a taboo, "why do gays all dress the same and act the same?"

"Do they?" I try to catch her eye as I hand her coffee, stop her in the track I can see she's about to lay.

"It seems that way to me, like there's a uniform of clothes and —"

"Biker gear for the leather-men," I say, trying to head her off. "And crotch-clutching Levi's, flannel shirts and work boots for the rest."

We all laugh because that is what both Richard and Gary are wearing. "The same thing happens in my women's group."

Richard groans. "Oh, no, not the politico-dykes, Squirrel. Not at this hour of the night."

"It does seem to go that way, though," I say, thinking of Susan. "One minute a woman starts making connections between male power and the events of her own life: next thing, she's getting her hair chopped and buying dungarees."

Maeve nods, sagely, and though I don't believe we're on the same side, I go on. "I have wondered about that sometimes, why so many people swap one set of codes and rules for another. Especially people who've been so bruised by rules."

Gary smiles at me. "Not everyone is brave enough to go it alone, hon."

"It's not just clothes, though, is it?" Maeve says. "It's the way they go on."

Richard's eyes narrow. "And how do 'they' go on?"

"Sorry, you know what I mean. I'm not being bad, I just don't understand the obsession with sex all the time. Like that girl, Mona, tonight. It seems so out of proportion."

"Whoa there, Maeve," Gary says, gently. "Don't you think you're generalising a little?"

"What about the keys and hankies and all of that?"

Gay cruising gear. I told her about this the other day, when she asked me about the bandanas she noticed hanging from rear pockets.

When nobody says anything, she goes on. "And the thoughts of those places where you don't even see the person you're having sex with." She shivers. "I'm sorry, it gives me the creeps. I can't help it."

"It's the Roman Catholic in you," Richard says. "You need deprogramming."

Maeve shakes her head, her mouth tightening over her coffee cup. "Personally, I think it's a male thing. Men are afraid of intimacy."

How can she say that, having met Mona? I wish she could have been here for the last Freedom Day Parade and seen the Dykes on Bykes or the Ladies Against Women, carrying their signs — "Recriminalize Hanky Panky" and "Suffering not Suffrage" — or the leather-women strapped and handcuffed to each other in all kinds of bizarre positions, showing the world something that seems to me to be truer and braver than Susan's brand of one-fits-all, earnest lesbianism. Or Maeve's one-fits-all, earnest hetero-ism.

Like so many straights, Maeve thinks she has nothing to learn from the lessons gay people are bringing back from the sexual front line.

I yearn for her to shut up before she says something even worse. The other night she was quizzing me about "the gay cancer" and looked completely dubious when I argued that there wasn't any such thing, that AIDS also afflicted drug addicts and blood-transfusion recipients and Haitian refugees and others. I feel tainted by her ignorance. But I shouldn't. She is not me.

"Are you sure it's not you who's afraid?" Richard asks her.

"Of course I'm not. I'm —"

"Afraid of sex, I mean. Proper sex: the low-down, dirty variety." He runs a look down the length of her body and back up. "Have you ever had it really good, honey? I mean really good?"

My sister blushes and I feel sorry for her, but she asked for it.

"Richard is right, Maeve," I say. "Sex is sex, intimacy is intimacy. It's perfectly possible to have one without the other."

Richard and I have shared a bed, spent nights together on my couch wrapped around each other while we watch TV. I've told him things I haven't told some beloved lovers.

"But the two together," insists my sister. "That's best of all."

"Best for what?" pounces Richard. "Best for who?"

She shrugs, her face red and set, defeated by our unity but unconvinced. Gary, kind Gary, tries to ease the tension. "You know, Maeve, I don't think you're acknowledging the reality of being gay. After years of trying to conform, don't you think it's natural that some of us act like kids let loose in a candy store when we're allowed to be truly ourselves for the first time?"

"Maybe," Maeve says, doubtfully.

"All that guilt and self-alienation has to find an outlet," Gary says.

"Oh, puh-leaze," says Richard. "Spare us the psycho-babble. Sex rocks, is all."

When she's leaving, Maeve packs copies of the Chronicle, Fitness World and Zoe that have articles of mine. "They'll want to see them at home," she says. "Mammy will be delighted. They all will."

Ah, here it comes. I was wondering if we were actually going to get to the end of her visit without it. I'm leaning on her suitcase, while she tries to fasten the clasps. When I make no response, she says, without looking at me: "Have you any message you want me to pass on?"

"Did she send one to me?"

She sighs, shakes her head. "God, but there's a pair of you in it." I make a face at that.

"Look, Jo, I know she wasn't the easiest of mothers, but I find it hard to imagine what she could possibly have said or done to you that you could cut her off completely like this."

"Maeve, don't —"

"To just walk away like that, and never come back...Not even to write..."

I'm not going to have this conversation, because she doesn't really want it; she only thinks she does. Nobody in Ireland wants to look too closely at why so many leave and whether it's really about jobs. Those who can bear living there don't want to know the truth about those who can't. At Christmas, I'm told, they make a great show of welcoming the emigrants "home", Dublin Airport doing itself up with Céad Míle Fáilte signs. "A

Hundred Thousand Welcomes." So long as you're gone again in the new year.

Maeve would like me to be one of those, but she asks too much. It's too lop-sided.

If Gran had written...I'd have done it for Gran. But she made her choice all those years ago and I don't blame her. Mrs D. made it impossible for her to do otherwise.

Perhaps I should tell my sister the truth: I left to have an abortion, Maeve. And I never went back because, well, I couldn't, could I? I couldn't pretend to you and Mrs D. and everyone else that the biggest thing in my life had never happened. And I couldn't tell you the truth, you all made sure of that. So I — like hundreds of thousands of others — came away and stayed away.

"Was it that she broke up your relationship with Rory O'Donovan?" Maeve asks. "Was that it?"

I make my face blank.

She tries again. "I don't know what went on that night you left, Jo, and maybe Mammy did say or do something so terrible that you just can't forgive her. But what I can't understand...what I really can't understand...is why do you never write to Gran? Why do you never ring me back? I often feel if I didn't contact you, I'd never hear from you again."

"Maeve, leave it. Please. Let's not ruin everything on your last day. We've had such a good time."

She sighs again, folds the magazines away in her suitcase. "We have had a good time, haven't we?"

"We have," I say, meaning it. "We really have."

1923

Peg's Diary 12th November: We were hardly out of the beds this morning when Mrs O'Donovan called, sand all over her boots. She'd come the back way up the strand like Norah used to when sneaking down to us. Wariness had her hunched, her black shawl was drawn in around her. The look on her face said she'd rather be anywhere else in the world than at our back door.

"How is she?" the old woman asked, not saying her daughter's name, and I invited her in to see for herself. Both of us were full of the memory of the last time we faced each other like this, when the boot was on the other foot. I was determined to treat her better than she had treated me and felt a need to warn her before she opened the kitchen door. "You'll find her quiet in herself."

"She was always a quiet girl."

"Not like this."

Norah was in the fireside chair that used to be mine, before all the changes to our household. The chair was in the middle of the floor, looking like a raft in the middle of a pale linoleum sea. She had a blanket across her knees and beside her, on a small table, were a blank copybook and a pen. I had provided this: after talking to the doctor about the way she liked to scribble, I thought it might be some comfort to her. So far, however, she hasn't picked up the pen.

Since she arrived, she's done nothing but sit silent in this armchair, either turned towards the fire to look into the flames, or in the opposite direction to look out the window towards the sea. She will come to the table when bidden or do any small chore she is asked to do. Otherwise she sits, still and silent.

She didn't get up, or even turn her head, as we entered.

"Your mother has come to see you, Norah," I said, while Mrs O'Donovan squeezed herself into the chair opposite.

Silence.

"You're looking well," Mrs O'Donovan was half-shouting for some reason, as if it was Norah's ears that were affected.

Silence.

"Looks like they fed you enough anyway."

I marvelled at how still Norah could hold herself, not even the movement of her breath in her chest to be seen. After receiving neither gesture nor reply, Mrs O'Donovan looked across to me.

I knelt in front of Norah, trying to look her in the eye. "Norah, are you not going to talk to your mammy?"

Nothing. Just pale, set eyes in a pale, set face.

Mrs O'Donovan frowned. "Maybe, if you were to leave us on our own?"

I wasn't a bit keen on this idea, but how could I refuse to leave her with her own mother? I looked to Norah. If she objected, wild horses wouldn't drag me from that room, but she gave me nothing to go on. Not a flicker.

So, reluctantly, I moved towards the door. Go easy on her, I wanted to say, but of course I couldn't.

"I'll be outside if you want me," I said instead.

I stood right outside the door, leaning my forehead against

it, but I could hear nothing. I knew how Mrs O'Donovan was feeling. It's hard to see the girl so. My hope is that once the baby comes, things will improve.

The sound of a voice raised came through the door, breaking my thoughts. "Answer me, won't you?"

I went back in. Mrs O'Donovan was standing over Norah like she was a badly behaved child. "Surely to God you'll not let me go without a word? After I coming down here to see you?"

Underneath Norah's bright hair, her face was as washed out as a bleached rag. I knew what a mine of stubbornness lay under that weary surface, so I drew Mrs O'Donovan away, towards the door. "It's not meant personal. She talks to no one at the moment. It's part of her trouble."

She looked at me, like a bewildered animal. "What should I do?"

"Give her time."

"I can't come again."

So we were still forbidden territory. "Let's see how we get on," I said. "Everything should get easier with time."

She drew her shawl tighter in around herself.

"I'm sure Norah is grateful you came. Aren't you, Norah?" I didn't really expect an answer and I didn't get one.

"Grateful, is it?" said Mrs O'Donovan. "Grateful, by God."

She turned to go and noticed for the first time the big black perambulator that I had brought down from the attic the day before. This is the pram that wheeled me about, as a child. And Barney too. It's old-fashioned and a bit battered, but clean and well-polished after the work I put into it, and it's well up to the job. Mrs O'Donovan looked at it like it was a weapon and, without warning, her head dropped into her shawl and she started to cry. I didn't know where to look.

"May God forgive her is all I can say." The shoulders under the shawl were shaking. "May God forgive you, Norah."

Later.

Since her mother left, Norah has been non-stop writing in the copybook I bought her. The doctor in the asylum had told me about her doing this. "It's pure gibberish she writes," he'd said. This was my first time to see her in action. The concentration she brings to the task is ferocious, her whole self gathered up in the physical act of writing. Her face looked clearer as she wrote, more like herself.

All through the day she kept this up in fits and starts. While we were having our meals, she kept the notebook on her lap the whole time and, afterwards, when we were sitting round the fire with Mammy and Daddy, she sat on top of it. Later when Mammy and Daddy had gone off — one to bed, the other to work — I spoke to her about the way she keeps hiding the book.

"You don't have to worry that anybody will read what you write, Norah," I said. "Nobody in this house would go near it." She didn't reply and didn't change her behaviour either, keeping the book close, bringing it with her whenever she went out of the room and upstairs with her at bedtime, no doubt to sleep with it under the pillow.

It does no harm, but I wish she had more trust in me. I, of all people, would never read somebody else's private writing. I know how I'd feel if somebody read mine.

DIARY, 13TH NOVEMBER: Sunday Mass this morning. Norah didn't want to go, and who could blame her? I had explained all to her last night, that we have to face them down from the first — that if we stayed away today, it would be even harder next week and then we'd never be able to go at all, but when I went in to call her, she made as if she didn't know I was there.

I had a jug of hot water with me and I poured it into the basin and then spoke firmly to her, so there could be no mistake.

"Norah," I said, "I'm only going to say this once and after that you can make up your own mind. I think you should go to Mass and not be hiding up here like a criminal. We need God on our side, Norah. If we can't even face a trip to Mass, what will He think of us? I'm going to leave you now. If you come down dressed, I'll know you're coming, and if you stay up here, that's grand. Nobody will say a cross word to you, I promise. I'll just go ahead with Mammy and we'll see you when we get back."

I went down, praying she'd find it in herself to do the right thing. And she did. I was finishing off the drying when she came in, hat and coat on, ready to go. It was hard for her walking down that road, hard for myself too, but she just closed herself off the way she does and greeted nobody. Mammy and I did as we'd planned, smiled and said hello to the staring face of whoever we met along the way, the same smile and hello we'd give if Norah was not with us, then moved on quickly before they had time to act on their curiosity. It was easier than it would have been one time. Between those who won't talk to us because of the war just gone, and those who are afraid to approach us because of Mammy's illness, we don't have so many wanting to chat.

We made it into the chapel without any scene arising and took our seats in the usual place. The O'Donovans were not yet there and we were waiting for them, knowing well that everybody else around us was doing the same. With only a minute to go, they came. I knew without turning round in the pew that they'd arrived by the change of atmosphere in the crowd. The attention of everybody in that chapel was flying between us to them and back again. Mrs O'Donovan and the family sat into the same spot as usual, three seats behind us. The father stayed at the back, with the old boys, the way he always does.

Then Father John came out onto the altar, eyes flickering about the place, on the hunt. When they alighted on Norah, he gave her —and me and Mammy as well — such a look. He held it on us for ages and I have to say I didn't think it was very

Christian behaviour, standing up there like that with his eyes going through us like two bullets for all to see.

Somehow we got through it and, after it was over, we got out as fast as we could without seeming to rush. In the yard, we were headed off by Lil Hayes who came over, and in front of everyone stopped us. "I'm glad to see you back home among friends, Norah," she said, in a big, loud voice.

I was so embarrassed, though of course it was a generous gesture. Lil walked back home with us, giving everybody we passed a look of defiance as if daring them to say a word. The walk from the chapel never felt as long and once we got back inside our front door, we all fell apart.

Lil started us off, doing an imitation of Mrs Sinnott's face. "What's this I see before me, a piece of dirt?" she said, wrinkling up her nose. "My old fella has an eye for every woman, young or old, this side of Waterford, so it's grand for me to have someone else to criticise."

She made us laugh and we all relaxed and started saying, "Did you see the face of this one," or "What about the go-on of that one," and nothing seemed so bad any more.

Norah didn't join in, just sat quiet among us, but her forehead was clear and though I can't say I saw her smile, it felt to me like she felt a bit better too.

Diary 14th November.

I got up early so I could tend to Norah before setting out for school. When I went into her room I found her awake, sitting up in bed with her coat around her shoulders, writing in the notebook again. She looked up as I came in, closed the book over.

"I've told you, Norah," I said. "Nobody will read what you write. You don't have to worry about that."

She held the pen in her hand like an arrow, so tight that the skin of her knuckles stretched white.

"Did you sleep all right?"

No answer.

"Norah, I have to go to school this morning. You'll have to mind yourself until I get home. Mammy's not getting up today, but Tess will be here in a while. She'll get you anything you need."

She lowered her pen onto the cover of her book, drew a small open circle that spiralled into another slightly bigger. Round and round her pen went until the ink ran dry and the nib was scraping the paper.

I said, "Come down for your breakfast whenever you want. There will be tea on the brew. Tess will get the dinner around one. I'll see if I can get a chance to run up during the day but I might not. I take the Feis singers for a practice on a Monday."

The scratching of the pen was annoying me. I took it out of her hand, put it down on the bedside table beside the candle. Her finger and thumb stayed open around the air where it had been.

"You'll be all right, Norah, won't you?"

"I was always a respectable girl," she said, out of nowhere, and I nearly fell out of my stand to hear her speak. Her eyes were properly on me for the first time since she came home, open wide, the same look in them as I once saw in a little tinker child who plucked hold of my sleeve one day in town outside the Mechanics' Institute and pleaded with me. "Please, miss," he'd said, over and over. "Please." I gave him a copper.

What Norah wanted from me now was not so easy to work out.

"We know that, Norah. Don't be troubling yourself about things like that."

"A sin is a sin, says the Lord."

"Don't be torturing yourself about what's done and gone."

"The sin was not mine alone but I was left alone to face it."

I felt hot and ashamed when she said that, I who had encouraged Barney to keep on fighting when he'd wanted to stop and get married and settle down with her. How had I never thought of that from Nora's point of view before? Of course that's how it must feel to her.

"Oh, Norah, that wasn't his intention, I promise. He was going to give up the fight, so he could go and find you and set up with you. I have a letter, sent to me the day before he died. I'll find it for you when I come home from school, show you what he said."

She was blanking off her face again.

"I'd find it for you now only I have to go," I said. "There'll be a roomful of children wild as chimpanzees in a garden if I don't get into school quick. First thing this evening, all right?"

She was pulling back, way back.

"All right then, I'll see if I can put off the singers and try and get home at lunchtime. Would that be better?"

Her fists were clenched and on her face, a film of sweat had appeared. For the first time, I saw what an effort it costs her to keep her shell of stillness intact. I couldn't go and leave her like that, I just couldn't.

"All right so, Norah, I'll get it for you now. You're right, it's more important than anything else. Just wait till you see what he said. He was going to give it all up for you, Norah. To get married to you was all he wanted, all he cared about. Wait a second till I get it from my room."

I found the letter and gave it to her and stayed with her another half hour, making me twenty minutes late leaving the house. As I raced down the road, planning my excuses, I met Jem Fortune, who said the priest was looking for me.

"What do you mean?" I asked.

"What I'm saying. Father John is standing at the school gate, asking everyone if they've seen you."

That put the heart crossways in me and, as I rounded the turn in the road, I could see him, his face as black as his clerical robes.

"This is a grand time to be strolling into school, Miss Parle."

"I'm sorry, Father. We had a bit of situation at home this morning..."

"Did you indeed? And did your 'situation' have anything to do with Norah O'Donovan by any chance?"

I just nodded.

"I thought as much. I would have been up to your house on this matter yesterday," he said, "only I had to talk to the O'Donovan family. They are broken-hearted, as you can imagine, by what you have done to them." He left a gap for me to answer but I gave it the Norah treatment.

"I'm beginning to believe you're a bit unhinged yourself. Is it trying to punish them you are? The O'Donovans?"

I couldn't hold my tongue on that one. "Of course not, Father. I..."

"She has to go back, Peg. The asylum is the place for such cases."

"It may be the right place for some, Father, but it wasn't for her. I saw how it was. No one was caring for her."

He softened a bit then, told me that he understood my intentions were charitable, but that I was misguided. Then he asked me about the baby, said outright that Mrs O'Donovan had told him we intended to bring it to the village and asked if that was so.

I nearly died of embarrassment to hear a priest talk of such things, but I had to get on with it and tell him he was right, which made him shake his head so hard I thought it was going to come off its neck.

"Don't do this, Peg," he said.

"It's done, Father. We've been told we can have her."

"I never heard the like of this in all my born days. I'm very sorry to see you behaving so out of character. All I can think is that the upheavals of the country over the past years have turned your head."

He had to get that dig in, of course.

"What I have to tell you now, young lady, is that if you insist on doing this, we won't be able to keep you at the school."

It was stupid of me but I hadn't expected that.

"We'll have to look for a new mistress."

"If that's how you feel, Father."

He let a small laugh out of him.

"Don't give me that tone, miss. You couldn't seriously think that you could stay on after bringing the evidence of immorality to grow up in your house? You are the mistress in a Catholic school, in case you have forgotten."

I bowed my head. "When do you want me to leave?"

"We might as well make it now."

No chance even to say goodbye to the children.

"Very well." I turned to go.

"Stop," he said. "I have another question for you. Is there a pair of you in it?"

"I don't know what you mean, Father."

"I'm referring to your wedding."

I looked at him, still not understanding.

"The unseemly haste of it."

My face started to flame when I realised what he was insinuating. Even the roots of my hair were blushing.

"No, Father," I said, meek as anything, running off before it was out of my mouth what I thought of him and his small and nasty mind.

As soon as I was out of his sight, I diverted down the strand, while I turned over in my head what I should say to them at home. The thoughts of telling Mammy especially...It had been her own dream as a girl to teach, only her father had matched her in marriage instead. The day I got my teaching certificate was nearly as proud a day for her as the day Barney joined the IRA Volunteers.

Now she has no Barney and I'm no longer a teacher. No

other school will hire me after being let go like this. As it all goes from bad to worse then even worse again, it's hard not to feel that we are being punished by God. If we are, whatever it's for, it's not for having brought Norah back. That much I'm sure of, if nothing else.

1988

"*S*o I like fucking strangers. Call me old-fashioned."

I've heard Richard use this quip before. He still wants to be Mr Entertainment, but he hasn't the energy to think up new lines. He hasn't the energy to do anything much, which is why he is lying here in a hospital bed. George, one of his nurses, is holding his wrist and Frank, another patient, sits on the bed beside his. It's for them that he has delivered his line, though it's addressed to me, and they respond with the requisite laughter. In the AIDS ward, good humour is an imperative.

I put his GQ and Esquire onto his bedside locker and lean low to kiss his forehead. His rash is inflamed, red blazing up his neck and face from beneath his white linen pyjama top.

"You're wearing that look again, Squirrel," he says. "You really must try to be more tactful."

George releases his wrist, makes a mark on his chart and hangs it back on the bed. "Make him rest," he says to me, on his way out.

The nurses know me well. I spend long hours here: because of my schedule I can visit at odd times, when Gary and other friends are at work. I bring in soups and salads, the ones I know he likes. I coax him to sleep, chide him out of self-pity, ensure he takes his medication. Often, I sit silently beside him while he sleeps: more like a mother than a friend.

Today he doesn't want to rest: he has something to tell me. "Marcus was in yesterday after you left."

Marcus is a friend and another PWA, as they are coming to be called. Person. With. AIDS. "How's he doing?" I ask.

"He brought me a present. I kept it to show you. It's in the top drawer."

I open the bedside locker, take it out. It's a book. A Bible.

"Oh-oh," I say.

"I know."

"He meant well, I suppose."

"Meant well, shit."

"Come on, Richard, it's not like you to be so tetchy."

"Tetchy." He giggles. "Tetchy." It's been a long while since my vocabulary tickled him. "I'm tetchy, my dear, because I was looking forward to a real conversation with somebody who knows what this damn thing feels like. Instead, he brings me this born-again booby present and an evening of sermons."

He's not joking, he's offended. Deeply.

"What did you say to him?"

"I sent him packing."

"Poor Marcus."

"He deserved it."

"But, Richard, if it gives him comfort..."

"Comfort? Hasn't he registered that the Bible-brigade has us all down as damned, whether we believe their hooey or not?"

I don't respond.

"Do me a favour," he says, with fury. "Put it in the bin."

I'm surprised at his vehemence. Marcus isn't even that close a friend. "Don't be silly," I say.

"I mean it."

I put it in my backpack, go across to sit beside him.

"He actually asked me to repent. Can you believe it? This guy used to be queen of the pleasure dome and now he's turned into one of those freaks who hawk God from door to door, trying to sell Him." He shudders. "I mean, how insulting is that? Do they really think they're going to curry favour with a God who created this foul and fabulous world by marketing him like a household gizmo?"

"Come on, cut the guy a break. Whatever gets him through the night, and all that?"

He lies back, feeling better for his outburst, closes his eyes. Under the rash, his skin is colourless as water. We've seen two close friends go already, Joe and Lucien, and others we loved a little less. Richard knows what this disease's cocktail of assaults can do.

Will do.

He has faced what's ahead and has no patience with those who console themselves with what he believes to be fantasies.

"The Afterlife..." He shudders. "Ugh."

"Come on, I don't believe in it either, but I can see the attraction."

He opens one eye. "Honey, you'd be miserable there. We both would. With the God Squad in charge of the guest list? And the entertainment? Can you imagine? We'd hate every minute of it, believe me."

Thanks to a US visa amnesty for the Irish, I am no longer an "alien". Instead of teaching aerobics to the public for cash, I now franchise my routines to teams of instructors. Thousands of people now do a Rí Rá workout each week, in gyms and halls and studios across the Bay Area and beyond. I even have a small slice of fame through my exercise video and the fitness features I contribute to newspapers and magazines. The Chronicle has approached me about doing a regular column.

I make a good living now: I have an agent and an assistant, a bank account and health insurance, a down-payment on a two-bedroom apartment in the Haight. I eat at Mani's, buy my clothes at Mary Coles, drive a European car, a Saab. All things that might catch me occasionally with pride if I were free to think, if my friend did not have this disease that is going to kill him. Instead, I find I'm going about like an aged English lady who lost her beau in the Great War, or an American who was a flapper in the 1920s and hungered in the Depression, forever looking back in awe. Oh, that younger me! The way I went about my youthful business, all unknowing! The way I had nothing to worry me but my mind's mindless worries!

It was two years now since the night I called to his apartment to hear the results of his test. As soon as he opened the door, there was my answer, in his eyes, in his face, in the stoop of his shoulders: positive. It was what we had been waiting for; we did not expect good news — how could we, with his night sweats and his weight loss and his history? — but still I looked at him and said those stupid words we always seem to say at moments of crisis: "No. I don't believe it."

As if he were not a promiscuous gay man.

As if we knew nothing about AIDS and its predilections.

I held him hard there in the doorway, held him for far too long, like I'd never be able to let him go. Then we went inside and waited together for Gary, who came home steely, well prepared. I made dinner in the little white kitchen while they had their words and, when the meal was prepared, they made me stay and eat with them. Over the food, we talked ourselves out of disbelief so that by the time coffee came round, Richard was able to look at the man he loved — for once not joking — and say with true, discerning knowledge: "We're all going to die."

AIDS punched a hole in our liberation theories. No wonder some thought initially it was a CIA conspiracy to obliterate the community. Who could believe in a disease that targeted only gay men? Those were the days before we realised it was practices, not populations, that nurtured the virus. Now we knew, and now the front rank of our sexual avant-garde was floundering around the Castro, open-eyed with horror. You bump into somebody you haven't seen for a while and feel a flood of relief that he is still alive, followed by a wave of dread that he might tell you he has it. So many are afflicted that those still testing negative are beginning to suffer survivor's guilt.

The Castro men have become like women, Susan says, now their pleasure comes edged with danger too. Women have always known what it is like to live with worms in the sexual bud: unwanted pregnancy, sexual violence, fatal childbirth... That, she says, is why women are responding so generously to their brothers' cause, though the same brothers were so dismissive or even hostile to them in the Castro's heyday.

Susan daily applies her formidable energies to the crisis, organising fundraisers and aggressively lobbying for political and medical attention. Her indignation is voluble: men like Richard are dying not just because they have a medical condition, but because Ronald Reagan's administration doesn't give a two penny god-damn about a disease that, in the main, kills gays. This homophobia that keeps the government from investing in medical research, that keeps our President from being able even to say the word AIDS: that is what is killing people, every bit as surely as the virus.

And it isn't just AIDS, she storms. You can see the work of the Republican vandals everywhere: in her project for recovering drug addicts, now failing her clients because of axed funds. In the growing herds of homeless people on the streets, shouting half-crazed at phantom enemies, hustling for money, or food, or some other, nameless need that isn't so easily granted.

Through all this activism, she and Richard have reached a tentative liking. At a time when he felt he was losing everything — his job, his insurance, his good-time friends — Susan turned up to visit, and to help, and wouldn't be jibed away. Richard accepts services from her, as from me, that he won't take from Gary: grumbling at our "fussing", but acquiescent. Something in him makes him recoil from such solicitude in his lover. We all know that nicety will have to go with time, that he will have to learn to accept his dependence, but for now we are delighted to indulge him.

The other night, the three of us sat around him, Susan sprawled across the end of his hospital bed, while Gary spoke of how lesbians were so ahead of gay men in so many ways, especially in their sense of cooperation and interdependence. Lots of men are now getting this message, he believed, beginning to look anew at ideas of love and intimacy, beginning to make different choices.

"The party is over," he said. "The 'Me generation' must be replaced by the 'We generation'."

Susan was visibly delighted with this, keen to believe that AIDS might have some redemptive meaning beyond the horrors.

But Richard would have none of it. "Oh, my," he protested, "It'll be the 1950s again. Except now it's going to be gays peddling myths, and getting married for all the wrong reasons."

The Faggot Mystique, he called it, and even Susan had to laugh.

He is out, taking pleasure from things that he wouldn't have noticed before, making me stop to look at a garden crowded with primroses and orange California poppies, or a baby crawling across the grass. Everything is dear because soon he won't be able to see them; the virus is chomping at his retinas. Already the light in his left eye is dimming. He leans on me, so frail I feel no burden.

Back in again, another pneumonia. This afternoon, he is sleeping, or perhaps lying still with his eyes closed. His breaths are short and shallow little sniffs. Beads of sweat crawl like insects down his forehead until I wipe them away. I sit in the chair near the window, reading. Everybody is quiet today. Bill and George are talking to Patrick in the corner bed, acting out for him some bureaucratic drama with hospital administration, trying to cheer him up: he got his results yesterday and the news is the worst.

Steps approaching from the hall make us all look up: something new has arrived. Steps in an AIDS ward are usually tentative, not this stamping tread. Richard opens one eye when he hears the footfalls.

"She's here," he says and he begins to haul himself up his pillow. The doorway of the ward fills with a large middle-aged woman in a red pant-suit. Only North America could have produced her.

Richard's mother. He finally got round to telling her two months ago; now she has finally got round to coming to see him.

Mothers are moving in their droves to San Francisco, to care for dying sons. Our friend Lucien's mother left a disapproving husband and a job in some upstate New York town to move west. She lived in Lucien's apartment until he died, both of them broke, managing to survive only through the kindnesses of friends who kept them supplied with gifts of food outside the door and money through the mailbox.

Richard's is a different type of mother. If I had never heard a word about her, I would see this in the way she holds herself in the threshold of the door, taking in the scene. Her umbrage comes to rest on George and Bill, two nurses, engaged in their camp pantomime with Patrick.

Hurling her eyes heavenwards, she alights on her son's bed. "This is unbelievable, Richard. Beyond belief."

"Hello, Mother."

"Who is responsible? That's what I'd like to know."

"Mother dearest, what are you talking about?"

She puts her handbag down on the bed. Distress contorts her face. "Can we close this curtain?" she says.

"Sure. But first let me introduce you to Jo, one of my very best friends."

I get up from my chair near the window, hold out my hand. She barely takes it, then lets it drop.

"Is she one too?" she asks Richard.

"Excuse me?"

"I think you know what I mean."

"Jesus, Mom!"

"Well, Richard, you're the one who said it's no big deal. If it's no big deal, then what's the problem with asking?" Her double chin is half the size of her face, a cushion on which the rest of her face — her pursed mouth, the hard line of her jaw — reclines.

"Shall I close the curtain for you, Mrs Burke?" I enquire, pulling it across before she has time to answer. I toss Richard a sympathetic face, but he doesn't see me. He is terrified, like an animal on its way to the abattoir. I take my seat a discreet distance away and sit, in case he needs me.

Inside the cubicle, Mrs Burke whispers loudly. "What are those people doing here?"

"Who?"

"I must say, they are the last people I expected to see here."

"Who, Mom? Who?" Richard's voice is lined with pain. I don't know if he is playing dumb or whether she genuinely has him confused. I know that it's George she objects to and Bill: the two nurses who are so obviously gay. "It's a disgrace. They're the last people who should be here. They did this to you."

Light dawns for Richard. He raises his voice, addresses us outside the curtain. "Ladies and gentlemen," he says. "My mother."

"There's no need to get fresh, young man." She scrapes the

curtain open again and steps out. "I don't want you here," she says to George. "Or you," to Bill.

Their faces freeze.

"You needn't stand there smirking. I'm going to see what can be done. I am his mother, you know."

She walks out.

"Oh, God," Richard groans. "Why did I ring her? Squirrel, get in here."

I go into the cubicle, try not to laugh at his crumpled expression. "Poor Richard."

"What did I tell you? See, mine wins."

He means our mother competition. I try to imagine Mrs D. here and find I can't. I don't know how she'd be: lost, I think.

I take a tissue and wipe his forehead.

"I can't do this, Squirrel," he says. "She didn't even say hello."

"She's upset. She'll come round."

"What's she trying to do down there?"

"Shhh, Richard, it's okay. Nobody's going to pay her much attention. They're going to realise she's upset."

He groans. "You have the right idea, Squirrel. Cut off. Don't look back. I should never have rung her. Why did I? Why?"

Dear Jo,

Surprise! I hope you haven't fainted away with amazement to see this letter arrive on your mat. I ran into your sister in Dublin last week and she wrote down your address for me. I'd often wondered where you got to, but didn't know how to go about tracking you down — there wasn't much point in ringing your mother, I knew that much. So it was great to meet Maeve. She had the little one with her, she's lovely. I'm an auntie myself, four times over.

Anyway, what's the crickety crack? Maeve says you have it made out there. Things are the same as ever here i.e. boring as hell. I finally finished my PhD and I've got a job offer from an agricultural research centre. It's a good job, and good jobs are pretty scarce in Ireland these days, as you may or may not know, but the way I feel is that I've had enough of microscopes and white coats and root nodules for a while. I want to take a year off and see a bit of the world before I sign my life away.

My mother is having kittens — after all those years of impoverished studenthood to turn down a good permanent and pensionable job! Her plan after I finished my BSc was that I should do a teaching Dip. Mine was a Master's and a PhD. I won, but not without major ructions. Now I've gone and done this to her. I'll never earn a crust, she says, after all her investment.

I have to say I do feel a bit guilty. As you know, it wasn't easy for her to scrape the money together to send me to college in the first place, not with what Daddy left in the pot after he'd finished in the pub. But (BIG BUT...) it's my life — and the way I see it is, once I start working, that's going to be it until retirement (or maybe maternity leave, but the way the love life is going, retirement looks closer). Mammy doesn't understand where I'm coming from at all, so I've given up trying to explain.

All this is, of course, a roundabout way of inviting myself over to you for a visit. I'd love to see you and "Sin City" too. Is it true they have orgies in the streets over there? If so, I might stay on for a bit.

Anyway, one way or the other, write to me, Jo. I'm dying to hear what you're up to. I've enclosed a couple of pictures so that if I do come, you'll recognise me when I get off the plane!

Love,

Your old pal,

Dee

She stays in my spare room for two months, until she gets a job in the Silver Tassie, and a place of her own in The Mission. Before long, she has amassed a crowd of party-loving people and is always asking me out. Sometimes I go along, but they're a hard-drinking crowd and my orange juice or mineral water keeps me separate. It amazes Dee that I don't drink any more.

"What made you quit?" she wanted to know.

"Aerobics. Alcohol really interferes with your fitness level. I gave up smoking back then too."

"Not even take a glass of wine with a meal?"

"No."

She turned a wide-eyed look on me.

"Really, I can't be bothered any more," I shrugged. "It just doesn't interest me."

She doesn't buy this and I tease her, tell her not to be so Irish. I can't tell her the truth. "Alcoholic" is a word I have never spoken aloud and I certainly can't say it to Dee. To her, it spells her father, her nemesis, who still makes her spit hate when she's had too much to drink herself. It is not a word for people like me.

Or her.

She shies away too from Richard and Gary and their world of other unspeakable words: lymphadenopathy, mycobacterium, pneumocystis, Kaposi's sarcoma. I don't blame her, I'm tired of it all myself.

In a dark corner of my mind I often find myself wishing it were already over for Richard. Because I want to spare him what's ahead? Oh yes, yes I do. But I also want to spare myself.

1923

*T*ipsy couldn't take his eyes off the child. Typical of him, he had given no thought to the reality of her at all, not until she was wriggling and squirming in his arms. After they had done all the paperwork and the nun brought her in and placed her in Peg's lap, he looked set to fall off the chair. Pure astounded. But then she was astounding, the dote, with her dark tight cap of hair and her straight little back and her two big eyes, like blobs of dark ink, staring them out of it. Wondering who they were, probably.

Her nose was full of snuffles and tiny flakes of dried mucus powdered her nostrils. She had a bit of a head cold, Sister Margaret said, but nothing serious. Nothing to worry about.

Peg squirmed at Tipsy's stare, nervous that he was about to say or do something he shouldn't. Any thought that came into his head registered across his face and, as often as not, came hopping out of his mouth. At home, he was easy enough to manage — the poor chap was as aware as anybody else of his shortcomings and her pity usually outweighed her irritation — but it was a mite more embarrassing being out and about with him. Especially in Dublin. Especially here.

You couldn't dislike Tipsy. There was not one ounce of badness in him, but...she felt as if she were a twig caught at water's edge, pulled and pushed and turned over by the waves. The only way for her to keep bobbing back up to the surface was not to look at any of it too close, to stay in the minute and not fret over how she got herself here or what was yet to come. Amends. Amends. This was how she would make amends for the wrong she and Barney had done in the war times.

The baby smiled a gummy smile. "Ah, look," said Peg.

"She's very good," Sister Margaret said, with no trace of anything like a smile cracking her own face. She was a formidable woman, in her black wimple. "Sleeps from seven to seven, or later sometimes. And a good eater. You won't have too much bother from her."

Peg took the baby up in her arms. The little head smelled like something between vanilla and honey.

"It's good you'll have her for the Christmas, anyway," Sister Margaret said, walking them out to the big front door, clearly happy to see another assignment brought to its conclusion. She handed over a bag of baby paraphernalia and waved them off.

"Fierce businesslike, wasn't she?" Peg said to Tipsy, once they were out of hearing range.

"Only short of spitting in her hand."

Christmas again, thought Peg, settling the child over her shoulder for the walk down to the omnibus that would bring them back to the railway station. When Sister Margaret had said that about Christmas, Peg had been shocked. Nearly a year already since they lost Barney. If anyone had told her this time last year that by now she'd be a married woman with a child...well! It was true what people said, you really never do know.

The baby was heavier than you'd think to look at her. Not a peep out of her as they walked along. No sign that she was disturbed by being carried so by a stranger.

How would Norah be, this evening, when they got her home? She was fierce agitated this morning when they'd been setting off. Not that it showed. She'd held herself so quiet on the front step, watching them set off, but the turmoil was written on her, if you knew how to read it. Peg would have to make a special effort when she got back, to make her realise it didn't matter who got the title of mother. They would mother the child between them and then, later on, when Norah was a bit better in herself, she could take over completely if that was what she wanted.

And later again — they'd know when the time was right — the little girl would be told the truth.

The bus took a half-hour to get to the station, and when they arrived the Wexford train was already in place, huffing on its tracks. They settled themselves in, hoping nobody else would join them. The baby's cold made her sleep noisy, punctured it with snuffly snores, but otherwise didn't seem to bother her. She lay in Peg's arms, her little lashes closed, tiny blue veins marbling the skin of her eyelids. The train pulled away. People rocking down the corridor smiled in at them through the window, and Tipsy preened under their attention, delighted with himself.

"Is she all right, d'you think?" he asked. "She's due that feed an hour past."

Peg smiled. "If she was hungry, she'd wake for it, wouldn't she?"

"I suppose."

As if on cue, she began to stir.

"Now look what you've done," Peg chided, but to tell the truth, pleased as well.

Tipsy reached down to the bag at their feet, took out the bottle, held it ready for when it was needed. Sister Margaret had put everything together for them nicely; they wouldn't have thought of half the things themselves. The baby gave a small cry and when Peg handed her the bottle, she latched onto the teat with a strength that would frighten the life out of you. Because of her blocked nose, she had to stop every so often to take a deep breath between sucking.

"Isn't it a grand life you have at that age, all the same?" said Tipsy. "Nothing to do except eat and sleep and be ferried about the place. Isn't it a pity you don't remember it?"

Peg rubbed the baby's head gently. "She's very good, isn't she?"

After the milk disappeared from the bottle, Peg sat her up on her knee. The child looked swollen, stupidly full. Her eyes were enormous, like two planets in her head, as she looked around her, taking it all in. Tipsy offered her his finger and her little hand curled around it. Peg saw a frightened look in him. She could see why: something in the child's look made it seem like she knew everything and they knew nothing. Then she let a big belch and they both laughed.

"She's wet," Peg said. "But I think I'll wait until we're home to change her. I don't fancy doing it here, with the rocking."

"Do you want me to hold her for a while?"

She was surprised by the request, but handed her across. He rested her into the crook of his arm. Already her little eyes were heavy again with sleep. She was calm, happily sated. He put his hand on top of Peg's and when she didn't move it away, he lifted it, took it in his hold. She let him. Then she was sorry because she could see him wishing that somebody else would come along the corridor and take a look in at them. She shifted away from him in the seat, stretched out her legs.

"I'll be glad when we're home," she said, with a small yawn. "D'you know, I never want to see the inside of another institution. Since this thing started, it's been nothing but big houses."

"That's over now, anyway."

"We've a bit to face yet before we can relax."

He turned a puzzled face to her.

"The reaction of the village, I mean."

"I'd say we're over the worst," he said.

"Don't talk soft, it's only starting. And it will be no frolic."

He shrugged, which was irritating. But then maybe it was different for him. He was used to people not thinking a whole lot of him. That could be a strength in this situation. For herself, she was finding it hard. Bringing Norah back was bad, marrying him was worse, but now, adding this child to the mix. They would be full out for her now.

In Mucknamore it didn't matter too much what you did, so long as you managed to keep it hidden. It was going open that got you punished.

And she would have nobody to share the trouble of that. She had to keep a good show up in front of her parents and Norah, and not let poor Tipsy down either. He was the one she failed on most often.

Peg held out her arms for him to give her back the child. As she looked into the little sleeping face, she immediately felt better. The purity of a child's repose would calm any demon. "We'd better put a name on her," she said. "We can't keep calling her 'she'."

"The nun called her Mary, didn't she?"

Peg snorted. "The nuns call them all Mary."

"Not Mary, then?"

"Norah and I were thinking of Maureen?"

"Heh?"

"'Little Máire'. Maureen."

"After your mother, is it?"

"Norah likes the idea. She thinks the world of Mammy. What do you think?"

"Maureen?" He put his head to one side, considering it. "I'd better prefer Josephine."

Josephine? Did he not realise she was only doing him the courtesy of asking? "Where did you get that?"

"It's my own mother's name."

"Is it? I never knew that."

"Do you like it?"

"Em...I think it would be hard on the child. She's already used to Mary, Josephine might be a bit different for her to get used to. Whereas Maureen is like enough."

"Ye have it stitched up between ye, so." He turned back to the window. Outside, it was pure black and he couldn't be looking at anything except raindrops trailing across the window. After a time, he turned back to her. "We'll have to think how we can keep the child away from your mammy." The words tumbled out of him in a rush, giving the impression that he had been waiting to say this to her and had decided he might as well say it now, while she was cross with him anyway.

"What do you mean?"

"She can't be brought too near."

So it had not been her imagination, the way she thought she'd seen him avoiding Máire. How to explain to him that you couldn't let the illness her mother had rule your own life? How to make him understand that there was no accounting for who got struck down? Look at herself, healthy as a sand-boy, after living with it for years. The disease picked its own. And all the precautions were taken, the house kept ventilated and disinfected daily. "She'll be well minded," she said, pulling the blanket tighter round the baby. "You needn't worry yourself about that."

He turned away again. Was she being fair? A child was different, he was right there — a child was more open to every class of sickness. And she didn't like the sharpness she could hear in her own tone.

Amends.

"Would you like to hold her again for a while?" she asked, in a different voice.

He turned back with a smile. The poor chap, it was too easy to be offhand. She'd have to watch herself or she'd end up walking all over him. Considering that none of this was his idea, that just wouldn't be fair. She'd have to pray for God's help on it.

"You don't mind the name, do you?" she said.

He couldn't resist her, of course. "I think it's a grand name," he smiled. "Fine by me."

The train trundled onwards towards Mucknamore.

Back at the house, Máire got up from her place by the fire as they came in, but Norah, who had been sitting opposite, stayed put. Peg could see the questions glowing in her eyes, though she could see too that another person who didn't know her so well would probably notice nothing.

"She's here, Norah," Peg said, looking down at the bundle in her arms. "She's here and she's lovely."

"Come, Norah," said Máire. "Come look."

Norah stood up, but made no move to come forward, so Peg crossed the room to her instead. As she took the blanket from the baby's face, the little girl's eyes opened to her new surroundings.

"Ah, look at her," said Mrs Parle, from a distance. "The little dote."

Norah looked like someone who'd been struck. She took a step backwards and Peg followed her, holding out the child to her. When Norah made no attempt to take her, she plonked her down into her arms.

"We've fixed on Maureen," she said, with a smile for her mother. "Tipsy liked it too."

Norah was holding the child like you'd hold a dead animal: with straight arms, out from her body. The child, feeling the strangeness of the position, or maybe of the person holding her, was beginning to wriggle.

"Pull her in close, Norah, and give her a little rock," Peg sad. "She loved the rocking of the train and of the trap on the way home."

But Norah didn't do anything. She made no soft words or sounds, gave her no hugs or little strokes. The child started to whimper, low first, then gathering air and noise.

"Norah! Hold her closer to you." Peg folded her arms, mimed a rocking motion to show what she meant. "She feels like she is going to fall, I think."

The baby started to scream, her face growing red, her forehead wrinkling up.

"Do you want me to take her from you, Norah? Just hand her over if that's what you want. No? Then pull her into you, give her a hug. Do it now, Norah, because she's getting very upset. You want me to take her? That's all right, that's fine, just put her in my arms. Good girl. That's it. You've plenty of time to get to know each other, don't you? Of course you do. There, there little one. No need to cry. That's your Auntie Norah. Yes, it is. Let's get you out of that wet nappy and then you'll be in a better mood for your auntie. We gave you a fright, didn't we? Silly us. No need to cry, though. No need to cry."

The child's sobbing began to subside. When the storm had eased, Peg laid her down on the small rug in front of the fire where she could watch the flickering of the flames. Her mother heated a small bowl of water with a drop from the kettle, took the new bar of soap and new cloth that was all ready and waiting, and laid them on the floor beside Peg.

The baby was cleaned and changed and bundled into a night-suit. She opened her jaws into a little yawn, stuck her fists into her eyes.

From the far side of the room, Peg's mother was entranced. "Ah, would you look, she's tired out, the creature."

Peg asked Norah if she wanted to try again. She got no answer.

"I think I'll take her on up to bed," Peg said.

"You're right," Máire agreed. "A good night's sleep is what you all need."

"Do you want to come up with me, Norah?"

Norah was at the window now, looking out at the night. Peg exchanged a look with her mother, then went and took her by the arm. "Come on, Norah. It's time to go up." With her hand on Nora's elbow and the baby up on her shoulder, she led the way to the stairs.

It was only later, after she had the two of them in bed, that she remembered Tipsy and wondered whether he was all right, left downstairs with her mother.

PEG'S DIARY 10TH DECEMBER: I'm so agitated I can hardly write, but I have to. I'll try to tell it all, just as it happened. The afternoon started well enough with me managing to escape for a walk on the strand. The weather is so strange these past days, like a thick cloud has sunk to earth. I could hardly see two feet in front of me, the fog was that bad, but it felt good to be out of the house, to be on my own, to breathe. I felt like the fog had been created just for me, to cut me off and aid me in my longing for a bit of time alone.

To find the sea, I had to go right down to the edge of the water. It looked like a frill of lace on a roll of grey. Walking along, I was struck by the impulse to paddle in the water. It was late in the year for such a thing but unseasonably, strangely warm, so I decided to risk it and hitched up my skirt to unfasten my stockings. The fog gave me protection, knowing nobody could see me in my pocket of mist.

It was lovely, but I couldn't stay long. I'd left Norah in charge of Maureen with instructions to Tess and Daddy to keep an eye on both of them. I had a string of jobs waiting for me once I got back: the evening meal to prepare for them all, reading to do for

Mammy and two sheets to be repaired as well as whatever else might present itself. Little Maureen is always at her crankiest in the evenings and Norah would be put out if I stayed away too long. I had my shoes back on and was beginning to walk back across the sand when I heard my father calling me.

This put the heart crossways in me.

"What's wrong? What's wrong?" I shouted back.

"Come quick."

I hurried towards his voice. When we found each other, we were that close that we nearly collided. "What is it?"

"Dan O'Donovan is here."

"Dan?"

"Talking to his sister. I thought I better come get you. I think he's upsetting her."

I ran as best I could through the mist. When I got to the kitchen nobody was there, except the baby all alone, sitting on the floor having pulled anything loose down onto the floor beside her. She looked up at me all guilty as I came crashing in, one of the antimacassars stuffed in her mouth.

"You little divil," I said, bending and scooping her up into my arms, and going through into the bar. Tess was behind the counter. Pat Duggan and a few others were in. I just gave them a nod and retreated; it was obvious that neither Norah nor Dan had been there, they were all too calm.

Back in the kitchen, Daddy was coming in. "They're not here, either of them," I said. "What was going on between them, Daddy? How did he get in?"

"He must have come round by the back. When I came in to check on Norah and the baby, like you asked, I found him here. I asked him what he was doing and he said, 'I've come to see my sister and I want to speak to her in private.' That's when I thought I'd better get you. I'd have called your mother but —" He ran a crabbed hand across his scalp.

My mind was racing, wondering where they might have got

to. Could Norah have agreed to go home with him? Would she just up and off like that? I didn't think so, but if Dan wasn't taking no for an answer...

Daddy said: "The girl was trembling, whatever he was saying to her. He's a right bully, that fellow."

That made up my mind. I planted Maureen into Daddy's arms and told him to mind her until I got back.

"Where are you going?" he asked me.

"I'm going to O'Donovan's to see if he's brought her up there."

"Peg!"

"If he can come down to our place, I can go up to his."

"But —"

"Daddy, I'm not leaving her alone with them. She's not strong enough. Look after Maureen and I'll be back as quick as I can."

The fog that was a comfort to me a short time before now felt like something teasing, on the side of the enemy. I was breathing water instead of air, like I was drowning in my own breath. As I rounded the corner by the side of the house, a shape materialised like a ghost. My hand flew up to my heart.

"You!" I said.

He was startled too, but he composed himself quicker. "Yes, me. I've come to see my sister. That's not a crime, is it?"

"I don't know," I replied. "Has the Free State made it one yet?" I was pretty pleased with that reply and didn't give him a chance to frame an answer. "Where is she?" I demanded. "What have you done to her?"

"She's gone running off. I tried to stop her but I couldn't see a blasted thing in this fog."

"Running off? Where?"

"Not too far, I'd say." Then he spoke in a squeaky voice, imitating what Norah must have said to him: "'This is my home now.'"

"And so it is."

He throws up his eyes. "You're not doing her any favours, Peg, if you think you are."

I snorted. "And you are, I suppose? Why don't you just go on home, Dan, and leave us alone?"

"Ooooh, listen to that! We weren't always so unwelcoming, were we?"

That is what he said to me, I swear it, and he meant it as bad as it sounded. I wanted to dig my nails into his face until they drew blood. I wanted to catch his hair between my fingers and tear it out off his scalp. But I turned on my heel. Norah was the important thing. There was nothing left between me and him anyway.

"Wait a minute!" he called after me. "You might as well know, my family want my sister placed where she can be properly looked after."

I walked back to him. "Return her to the asylum?"

"It's the best place for her."

"You can't do that to her."

"We most certainly can. It's her family's decision, as you well know."

"And what about Norah? Is she to have no say?"

"She's not fit to decide."

"That's not true."

"But it is true, isn't it, Peg? She hasn't been right since she came home, has she? And it's not any better she's getting, is it, but worse?"

"You're only thinking of yourselves, not her —"

"And what sort of concern have you shown her, bringing her into a house with consumption? I suppose you forgot that little detail when you were talking to the asylum bosses. That mother of yours should have been sent to a sanatorium long ago. It's not right that she should be kept here, in a public house. It's not safe."

Even after all he's done to us, I couldn't believe he was being so cruel.

"Oh, yes," I cried, "You'd have her sent away too. You'd like to send all your problems off like they don't exist."

"It's common sense, woman. It's —"

"Get out of here now, Dan. I'm not letting you stay here one moment longer. Go back to your traitor's barracks and let us be."

"I'm not the one going anywhere, Peg."

Something in his voice alerted me. What did he mean?

"No, it's home to Mucknamore I'm coming. I'm getting a transfer to the Civic Guards and, as I'm also getting married, my father has kindly donated a bit of his land to put up a house. It's not me who'll be going anywhere."

So he was to marry Agnes Whitty, the Cumann na Saoirse girl, one of those girls who stood for nothing except her own advancement, and bring her to live in Mucknamore. "Live where you like, with whoever you like," I said. "It's nothing to us so long as you leave us in peace."

"But it's hardly that simple, is it? I can tell you that it is only with the greatest effort that I have kept my father from coming down to this house. He's not happy to let this lie and neither am I. I have no intention of living up the road from it."

I looked at him, the man who killed my brother, the man who was once our friend, and I wondered how he had managed to tuck the knowledge of all he had done away, where it cost him no trouble.

"Look at you," I said, nearly more to myself than him. "Look at what your foul little war has done to you."

"Jesus," he said, bursting into one of his crowing, jeering laughs. "That's a good one. Have you taken a look in the mirror lately?"

We faced each other down, the fog greying the air between us, stared each other out of it for so long that, to our own surprise, our hostility waned. We couldn't hold it up: the understanding we had once shared could not be reduced to single-minded dissension.

I was first to weaken, to take a chance and appeal to the better nature I felt must be there still, somewhere, within him. "Dan, please...Stop this persecution of Norah. Have some feeling..."

"No, you stop, Peg," he said, but more gentle. "Stop fooling yourself that your actions are for my sister when really it's revenge you're after, revenge against me and my family. Revenge for something I never even did."

"I wish I could believe that," I whispered.

"It's the truth, Peg. I've told you. If Barney had come out when called, he'd be alive today. And whoever fired the bullet that killed him, it wasn't me."

I wanted to cry then. I wanted to tell him that I had forgotten nothing, not a single blessed thing that had passed between us.

"The problem with you die-hards is you think people who aren't going round ranting and raving have no feelings at all."

"But Norah..."

"Ah yes, Norah." With that, our moment passed. He changed back to the soldier-in-charge. "I have to tell you, Peg, that Norah is not going to be a pawn in this any longer. The asylum is the proper place for her and the asylum is where she's going."

"Dan..."

He held up his hand. "No more about it. As she won't talk to her own family, you can pass her on a message." Here he paused for effect. "You can tell her that I'll be back to get this sorted and soon. And this time she'd better cooperate."

And with that he took his leave.

It took me a while after he left to get moving, and then I spent nearly half an hour looking for Norah before I found her in the bottling store, hiding among the stacked cases. She wouldn't come out when I called her so I had to get in beside her to coax. No matter what I said, or how I tried, she was dumb. I could get no good out of her until in the end I lost my patience. "Please, Norah," I snapped, "How can anyone help you if you won't let them? Don't be so selfish."

She cried then, the first time I'd seen her cry since she came to us from the asylum, and really and truly, they were tears I was glad to see. They felt more natural than that desperate silence of hers. After a time, as if a blockage flowed away with the weeping, she spoke. "I'll have to go away again."

"No, you won't. Why should you?"

"He'll make me."

"He can't make you. How can he? You have us to protect you now. Come on back to the house and try to forget about it. Everything will turn out all right, you'll see."

So I said, though I couldn't see how myself.

"Things are never as bad as they seem," I said, and it wasn't just her I was trying to convince.

"I can't be here if he's here, Peg."

"I know it's hard, and to tell you the truth, I don't much fancy the thoughts of it myself, but —"

"No, you don't understand. I can't stay if Dan is here." She gripped me by the wrist and turned two wet eyes on me. Something in her words knocked me back.

"What do you mean, Norah?" I asked. "What are you saying to me?"

"I'll have to go away," she said, her fingers so tight on my wrist they were near denting my bones. "He makes everyone do what he wants."

Again I felt it, that there was more in the words than they were able to hold. Something cold and dead slithered across the pit of me. I looked hard at her and she held me in a horrible stare that made me want to look away, but I didn't. I let what I was seeing pierce me. I kept my eyes up and open to her. I let her truth come crawling out, over and under my skin, and realised that one tiny, secret, buried part of me had half-known all along.

When she saw for sure that the knowledge had reached me, she let go of my arm. "You see, Peg, I can't stay in Mucknamore if my brother is living here. I just can't."

a fter Rory's wife has left, I feel raw, like a scab that's been picked too soon. All the anger that eluded me while she was there, in front of me, thrashes through me now. But I have learned, this summer, that I don't have to stay within such feelings, allowing them to throw me about. I can write, or run, or swim, or walk: any of those will change the balance, make me bigger than the emotion, shrink it back to its proper place inside me. Not me inside it.

I check my watch — five hours to sunset — and decide to walk.

I move awkwardly down the small climb onto the beach, the weight of my bump pulling against me. It is one of the things I most look forward to regaining after the baby is born: my own way of walking. Off I set, doing my best to stride. Onlookers glancing as I pass see only a generic pregnant woman, but inside, I am Fury unbound. How dare she! How dare she! And as for him... If I think of him, lying off in my bed after sex, snoring, I want to kill him.

I stamp towards The Causeway, ranting and storming, knowing all the while that really it's my own self making me so angry. I am in a mess of my own making. Why didn't I hold to what I said? "I want us to think about what we expect from each other," I had told him, that day we came out here to Coolanagh for the picnic. "I want us to think about where it might take us." That was the right tack and I should have stuck with it instead of letting myself be swept along, with nothing clear. After all I'd learned and said and written, there I was, still an absolute fool for him.

Snarled in thought but mindful of my balance, I negotiate my way out The Causeway, up and down the rise and fall of the dunes. Ahead lies Coolanagh, fern-green against the summer-blue sea. I am going to walk all the way to the far side, which I've only done twice in my life before. The night before I left here twenty years ago, when I first realised it was going to be me in my life, alone. And the night I thought I was leaving again.

It takes me thirty minutes to get to the Neck, where causeway and island meet. From there I turn right, awkwardly negotiating the shelf that I must climb to get up onto the outer ring path. I find the pathway, bracken-strewn, rising steeply to top the tall cliffs that buttress the southerly side of the island. On this side, Coolanagh is a slow eroder, even to the lash of Atlantic waves. Crags and cliffs, deep caves and extravagant rock formations hold out against the onslaught. A steady climb brings me to the plateau of the southern summit, a high rocky outcrop overlooking a gannet colony. I tiptoe forward, nervously, to the edge. Below me, majestic gannets sweep in and out of home and below them, two hundred feet below, thundering Atlantic waves roar against the base of the cliff. You'd think it a different sea to the one that politely spreads itself across Mucknamore beach.

To the east, arcs of high cliffs curve away, each covered with thousands of birds: guillemots, razorbills, kittiwakes and others I don't know. My attention is drawn by an unusual bird above, soaring on an updraft of air. Black as a raven, but with a longer neck and shorter beak, gliding high and elegant. It is so completely itself, so joyous in its swoops and loops through the air, that my vexing thoughts fall from me to wonder at it.

It's a trigger, taking me out of my head into the moment I am in. I feel the thousands of birds nesting and preening along the cliff face, each one calling its call and feeding its young, is a tiny herald of peace. Deep down, under the tumult of my thoughts, beneath the fury of my feelings, I know what they know.

After a time, I get up and begin to make my way back the way I came. When I come to a turnoff that cuts down the side of the cliffside, I take it, remembering that it leads to a small cove, the only safe place to swim off this side of the island. Somebody — I wonder who? Nobody has lived on this island for a century and a half? — has cut back the ferns and brambles and nettles, making it passable. The evening sun feels warmer down here: the height of the cliff behind me cuts off the breeze.

About now, he is due home from work and she will surely tell him that she has been to see me. What will he do?

"If you want him, he'll go with you," she said. Oh, but I do want him, I might as well admit it, I do. I have only been holding back to protect myself. But is he really prepared to leave her and his two children? Do I really want a man who could do that? If he did, where would we — how would we — live? I couldn't live in Mucknamore and presumably he wouldn't want to be too far away from his two children. I have treaded through these questions many times without ever reaching the finishing line of an answer.

I picture him arriving home today. Parking the car beside hers, putting down his briefcase in the hall, loosening his tie as he walks into the kitchen to find her waiting for him, her eyes swimming with significance. I see her sitting him down, telling him they must talk. And she's right: they must. Didn't I say so myself?

No. Stop. Stop all this thinking, I order myself. Like you did up on the cliff. Feel the fading sun on your eyes and the breeze on your skin. Pull yourself out of your head down into your body, the body that can't be in tomorrow or yesterday but only here, where it is.

This is what I've learned, from reading Gran's diary and Norah's scribblings: that there will always be something to think about, to feel bad about. If it wasn't Rory today, it would be something else. I can let the waves of feeling be, without letting them sweep me away. Underneath the feeling is another part of me, a depth that is tranquil. I can rest back into it.

And I do. In the middle of my trouble, I let it go and experience again that shift in perception that makes the scene before me seem to recompose itself. Everything in my sights — the black juts of rock fingering the waves, the grains of sand being flattened by my feet, the fading light glancing off the water, the gentle evening air stroking my hot cheeks, everything — seems more completely itself than usual, full of its own living presence. And somehow, simultaneously, more connected to everything else.

I kick off my shoes, slip out of my clothes, walk into the sea. My skin is porous, no longer a boundary: I am melting into the water and all the world. Joy surges: the same molecules dance in me and in everything.

By the time I'm back up on the path, the light is being sucked away over the horizon, taking the warmth of the day with it. The breeze sharpens with the advance of darkness, rippling the surface of the sea water and making goose bumps stand to attention all along my arms. Further in, towards the village, the tide has retreated, leaving behind hundreds of tiny sand-pools reflecting the sun, like a scattering of giant, golden coins.

He was due at my shed over an hour ago. Will he come tonight? Maybe she didn't tell him what she did, maybe she will bide her time instead, watch him leave to go to me as he has every other night this summer. Or maybe they talked and he came anyway. Maybe he is still waiting there right now, wondering where I am. Maybe.

About halfway back, I stop near the warning signs, slide down the small dunes to the fencing where I prise apart the two strips of wire and twist myself through, evading the wire barbs that want to claw at my clothes. A further slide down the rest of the slope brings my feet onto flat sand. Coolanagh sand. I am not frightened: here, at the edge, I am safe. The danger is further out and it stays out there; you have to walk out to meet it.

I sit, waiting, watching darkness deepen from blue to indigo to black. No trace of mist or fog on this dry, moonless night, but still I can see almost nothing. I turn on the pocket torch I've brought with me. Beyond its puny shaft of light darkness swells, immense. It would have been the same with an oil lamp, worse in the thick fog that was down that night in 1923.

Walking forward, just a little, I stretch for answers to a different set of questions to the ones that have poked at me all evening. How far out did Dan walk on that fateful night? What if he had refused, overcome her, taken the gun, turned it back on her? He was so much stronger; it could easily have gone that way instead. What if he had decided to make a run for it? Would she really have shot him?

I picture him quick-trudging his way out The Causeway to meet her. In his pocket is the typewritten note that enticed him into the wet night: I need to talk to you, it says, or some such words. Meet me you know where, out The Causeway. Seven o'clock... He walks as smartly as the fog permits, his head down, his shoulders staunch. He can hardly see five steps ahead but he has walked this strip a thousand times. He keeps to the centre and makes steady progress, right-left, right-left, right-left, lieutenant soldier boy to the last.

I see him slow his pace as the light below The Causeway catches his attention. Not in Lover's Hollow, where he expected, but a little further on. He steps down towards it — no barbed wire then to slow his progress — skids down the side through the top, damp layer of sand, not thinking to be fearful. As he comes close to the light, she says his name, hesitantly — "Dan?" — and when he confirms it, she tells him to stop where he is. He does what he is told, halted by surprise. Underneath the glow of the lamp is the barrel of a gun — Barney's gun — pointing his way.

Poor Dan. He thought he was on his way to a tryst with a woman who once loved him: who had, he reckoned, a soft spot for him still. He went to meet her, expecting...what? Not to find a rifle, this rifle, pointing at him, intent on revenge.

Arrogant man.

She blocks his way back to The Causeway and gives him a choice: a close-range shot in the chest or a walk across Coolanagh sands. He picks the chance of unsafe sands over the certainty of a bullet, just as she knew he would. The gun points him in the direction she wants him to go and he goes, walking upright, disdaining to pick his steps. He has taken only a few strides when he feels the ground shift and then collapse.

He is down, sucked by quicksand.

Then he knows fear, oh yes. Freezing, wet, chest-clutching, fear. "Help me," he calls out to her, the lady of the lamp. "Help me...Please."

Oh, sunken, shrunken man: did you really think she would?

Back at my shed I find nothing, no sign of whether he came or not.

I think not. I shine my torch around the door, along my table-desk where I left pen and paper handy if he should want to write. I turn on the lamp to have a closer look, but there is no sign of any visit.

I'm calm, I know what I must do.

Taking my torch, I cross the field, picking my way through builder's mud, to the back door of the house. It's late but there's a light glowing in the kitchen window. Even if they are asleep, I intend to wake them. I need Hilde to make the arrangements tonight.

She will think this odd, but I will insist — it must be tomorrow morning, no later — and odd or not, she will comply, not only because she is so obliging, but because it will suit her and Stefan to get it done, to see me gone. They have been holding off for me.

Next morning, I am up at first light, heading eastwards towards Rathmeelin, stopping only to pick wild daisies to place on the grave.

As I approach it, up the cemetery path, I see it is a mess, covered in rotting bunches of flowers, plastic wrappings still swathing some of the decayed clumps. I can smell them, fetid in the morning air. Among the wilted stalks, a single carnation clings to a faded shade of its former colour, pink. The whole thing looks terrible, like nobody cares. But who is there to tend things like the family graves now Mrs D. is gone?

I check the inscription on the headstone. Maeve wants to know it is precisely right before she pays the stonecutter. It seems to be just as she ordered: Maureen Devereux, née Delaney. Born 25.5.1923. Died 12.5.1995, aged 71. Go nDéanfaidh Dia Trócaire ar a hAnam. The new-chiselled letters, black on the old grey stone, stand out strong and bold, as if Mrs D's death is the one that really matters.

Some of her rotting flowers have slid across onto Auntie Norah's patch. I pick up the rotting stems and they shrink in my hands, oozing slime. Holding the mess away from my body, I carry it down the slope and over the wall, onto the soft sand of the beach. I dump it there, then go back up for another handful. And again until I have cleared it all away. On the beach then, I kneel and dig a hole with my hands, scrabbling like a dog at sand that is soft on top, like pale brown sugar, but darker and damper underneath.

When the hole is big enough, I transfer in the stinking vegetation and cover it over, pat it down. I stand to finish the job, dragging soft sand across with one foot, stamping it flat.

Then I lay the new flowers I've brought.

Back in the shed, it's still only seven a.m. I haul the two suitcases I packed the night before up to Hilde's house. One is light, with the clothes I brought from San Francisco; the other heavy, packed with papers. I sit on the heavy one, beneath her new kitchen window, to wait, emptying my head of thought, knowing I am doing right.

Regiments of cloud are mustering on the horizon, the morning air has an autumnal tang and the sea dances friskily under an offshore breeze. After a time, the hum of a car approaches and slows to a stop out on the road. A door bangs, the engine revs away and one of the workmen comes through the passage at the side of the house. The one with the mermaid tattoos. In his hand, he carries foil-wrapped sandwiches and a flask; under his arm is a tabloid newspaper. He doesn't see me.

A demolition machine sits with its steel ball expectant. He climbs into it, ignites the motor. It coughs into a roar and lumbers across the field like a tank, pulling up beside my shed. He turns off the engine then, evacuating the air of noise. Across the dunes, the sea surf sounds again. Opening his flask, he spreads a newspaper across the steering wheel and takes a sandwich from his pack. He eats and reads. In the distance, a dog barks.

Soon the others are arriving, taking out their tools: sledgehammers and mallets and picks. One of them notices me and nudges another, who says something, then they all turn their heads for a look. I stare back at them, protected by distance. The man in the machine switches the ignition again, diverting their attention. With another spluttering cough, it is primed, ready for action.

The time has come. He hoists the jib on high, tugging the chains and yanking the steel ball from its mooring, so the heavy globe plunges towards the ground. It is stopped, mid-drop, by its chain, and it reels and jerks like a fish at the end of a line, but the chain holds strong and it settles, a solid black orb, level with my shed's windows. The other men stand back and I rise to my feet. We all watch as the steel ball swings clumsily and strikes.

One whack is enough: down she goes, my little shed, my childhood refuge, my summer sanctuary, gusting up puffs of dust. At the centre of the collapsed brick and corrugated iron is the bed I slept in, still creased with the imprint of my body. The second machine closes in, bucket tilted to scoop it, and all the rubble, away.

Two other outhouses are also to be knocked, but I can't watch any more. I pick up my bags and go round the front to rouse Hilde who has made me promise that I won't leave without saying goodbye.

1923

The Wexford Weekly
12th December, 1923

"FREE STATE OFFICER FOUND DEAD AT MUCKNAMORE!"

On Wednesday morning last, fisherman John Colfer of Mucknamore was taking to the sea in commencement of his day's work when his attention was caught by a body trapped on Coolanagh strand. The sands at Coolanagh are deceptive, appearing firm, but in fact being subject to a "quick" condition, and this person appeared to have got into trouble there overnight.

As the deceased was dressed in a Free State Army uniform, Mr Colfer returned to land and proceeded with haste to inform the military barracks at Wexford. The military arrived and, with the aid of planks and ropes attached to the military lorry, proceeded to try to extract the body from the sand, a scene which attracted a great number of people from Mucknamore to observe proceedings. The operation took upwards of two hours and engendered great excitement among a growing crowd.

The deceased was identified as Lieutenant Dan O'Donovan of

Mucknamore, a National Army officer, and the death has caused a sensation in Mucknamore and surrounds.

It is presumed that he inadvertently wandered off the Point out onto Coolanagh sands in the dark. On the night in question, this area was submerged in fog, and there is much speculation as to what would have taken him out on the Point at Mucknamore in such dangerous conditions. While not a native of these parts, Lieutenant O'Donovan had lived here for some years and it is thought unlikely that he would not have known of the dangers associated with Coolanagh strand, notorious as it is throughout south Wexford.

The remains have been transferred to the morgue, awaiting inquest. Pending investigation, further details will be provided.

PART IV
SURGE

1923

*T*he two brown doors of the public house were closed, which was strange, because it was almost twelve o'clock, well beyond opening time. Brigade Police Officer Patrick-Joe Brosnan turned up the collar of his military coat against the rain and banged on the door again with his fist, one last time — thump-thump-thump — no longer expecting an answer. The motor engine was growling behind him and he turned and shrugged his shoulders at Private O'Dwyer, sitting dry at the wheel of the army lorry, enjoying a cigarette. O'Dwyer made a gesture back at him, but the downpour was so thick he couldn't properly see.

He went across and stuck his head in under the car canopy, a small respite. "What are you saying to me?"

"The door of the house, down the far end," he said, pointing. "You might have better luck down there."

It was what Brosnan had intended to do, the obvious thing to try once he'd got no reply in the shop, but he didn't trouble to say so.

He ran back through the rain. Since the fog lifted yesterday, these bitter, gusty squalls had assailed them. Filthy weather. He put out his hand to bang the brass knocker but, as soon as he touched it, the door nudged ajar. From within, he could hear a strange noise, a child's voice it sounded like, and it seemed to be grunting, querulously: eh – eh – eh. He gave a small cough and knocked politely, at which the door swung inwards and two frightened eyes stared back at him from the end of the stairs. They belonged to a young woman, a fine-looking girl in her early twenties, sitting on the bottom step.

She didn't get up, or change her expression, or in any way acknowledge that he was there. Beside her was a baby sitting up in a pram and it was from this small person that the grunts were emanating. Eh – eh – eh: reaching towards her toy that had fallen to the floor, one of those woollen sacks that makes a noise upon shaking.

"I'm sorry to disturb you, Miss." Raindrops falling from the peak of his cap so he took it off. She didn't answer, just stared at him as if his face was a mirror.

"I'm making a visit to all the houses in the area on behalf of the National Army."

Again she made no reply. Then the penny dropped with him. She must be the loony, the dead man's sister. Gallagher had filled him in on the queer set-up in this house. What a tragedy, a looker like her. That pale skin under the red hair was a striking combination.

"May I?" When she made no indication, he stepped in. He felt his best ploy would be to play innocent. "I'm making enquiries about one of our officers, lost to us here yesterday. A local man, Lieutenant Dan O'Donovan. Was he known to you?"

Her stare was unnerving.

"Eh – eh – eh..." continued the child. He'd have thought no woman could ignore those sounds. He felt like going over himself — him, a man, and a stranger to the child — and picking up the thing and handing it to her. He would have, only it didn't seem right. An internal door opened and another young woman came through, about the same age. Dark to the other girl's red, not as pretty in the face. Not today, anyway: her eyes were swollen and her face blotchy, either she had a bad cold or she'd been crying. She stopped dead when she saw him in the hall and affectedly eyed his uniform, up and down, the familiar sneer of the die-hard distorting her face. "What do you think you're doing in here?"

"Sorry to disturb you, miss," he said. "This lady let me in."

"Did you, Norah?"

No answer for her either. The child raised its voice, turning its grunts to a cry. The second girl saw the problem instantly, retrieved the toy from the floor, beamed back at the wet, pink-gummed smile that rewarded her and turned a frown on him, all in one fluid move. To him she said, "I didn't hear the knocker."

"I'm here about the dead officer found in this vicinity yesterday."

"Well, you should never have been let in here so I'll thank you now to leave the way you came."

"I'm afraid I can't do that, miss. I've questions to put to you both, and to the rest of the household too, if I may."

"You may not."

"Look," he said, trying for patience, "a man is —"

She held up her hand. "Save your talk."

"I have to insist —"

"No, I insist. I insist on your respect. My mother died in the room above us one hour ago."

Jesus, what rotten blasted timing. Was he mistaken or was that a smile from the lunatic girl?

"Oh!" he said. "I'm sorry. I didn't know, I..."

"We haven't had time yet to put up the card on the door."

He found his equilibrium. "I'm sorry for your trouble," he said. "May she rest in peace."

"So we won't be receiving any Free State detectives or whatever you are." She ran that disdainful look up and down his uniform again. "Or answering any Stater questions either. Not today."

She was enjoying this. She was upset of course — her mother was dead — but a part of her was enjoying his discomfort. The lunatic girl's face looked impassive but somehow managed to register hostility too.

"I'm sorry for your trouble," he said. "Sincerely."

"You shouldn't have let yourself in without a by-your-leave."

"The door was open...I wasn't to know..." He found himself, somehow, walking backwards, towards the door. "I'll have to come back soon. You do understand that?"

She looked at him like he was a person without morals.

"We have enquiries that won't wait," he said. "When is your funeral?"

"We've hardly had time to think of that."

"I'll see if I can leave it until the day after. As a favour, like."

Instead of being grateful, she looked at him like he was pure poison to her. "Suit yourself," she said. "You will anyway."

She turned to the other girl, put out a hand. "Come on, Norah, let's get you two inside." Her voice for the girl was so different, drenched with kindness. She helped her off the stairs, tucked the blanket in around the baby's legs.

"You can close the door behind you," she said in the tone she had for him, "on your way out."

And with an arm around her unfortunate friend, she steered the perambulator towards the door at the end of the hall.

Outside, O'Dwyer had the engine turned off and was smoking again, warm and dry in his vehicle, unscathed by female hostility. "How did it go?"

"Terrible," he said, climbing in beside him. "They've had a bereavement. The mother of the house has died."

"Ah, Mrs Parle, has she gone? Lord have mercy on her, she's been sick this long time. And she was only a young woman, forty-five at most."

"They were in no mood to answer questions. I said we'd come back."

"Fair enough."

"So where to now?"

"Have you any recommendations?"

"You could try Mrs Mythen in the post office. She's usually good for what's going on."

"All right," Brosnan said. He didn't hold out much hopes of it, but it would give him time to unravel his twisted-up thoughts. How had that interview gone so awry? He shouldn't have let himself be put on the back foot like that, as if he had done something bad to her on purpose. If only he'd known, he'd have done them first, yesterday, instead of spending the day on the men in the barracks and that girl from the pub. Kavanagh, his superior officer, wouldn't be too pleased: the Parles were central witnesses.

"What do you think, O'Dwyer? Do you believe they —" he nodded towards the house — "had anything to do with it?"

"Hmmm. I'd be inclined to say no, but with the state of the country, it's hard to tell which end is up these days."

"They had a motive."

"They wouldn't be alone in that."

"Really? Was O'Donovan not liked? Kavanagh seemed to think he was."

"Not by die-hards, he wasn't."

A pause. Then: "Do you know her, the daughter of the house?"

"Not well. She'd know my sister."

"She's quite a fury."

"Really? I never heard that of her. She was the schoolteacher here for a time. Well respected."

Yes. Kavanagh had filled him in on all that, how she'd lost her job for taking in the lunatic girl and the baby. A rare sort, to do a thing like that. And she was also Cumann na mBan. The country was learning only too well what vixens they could be when roused.

Brosnan sighed again: to think that when he applied to join the Guards, it was to get away from killing. When he was offered this job in Wexford, he'd jumped at it, thinking policing milder than soldiering, and the divide less bitter here than in County Kerry.

After the Ballyseedy affair, he'd have jumped at any offer that took him away from his own county. That whole business sickened and shamed him. Some nights when falling to sleep, he'd find himself trapped in a nightmare watching his colleagues tie those Irregular boys together around a ticking bomb, and seeing it explode them into smithereens. In his dream, he looked through the eyes of the one who had, miraculously, survived intact, who hid watching the body parts of the other eight being divided into nine coffins by the Free State. He didn't want to be part of an army that did such deeds — and then denied them.

But he needed an income. He had a wife, two children, a third on the way.

The Civic Guards had offered him a way out. Some said the Guards were only a tame branch of the army, others that this was not the time for their introduction, but Brosnan believed in the idea of an unarmed force and thought Ireland could not have it soon enough. That was what he wanted to be part of: the force of law, not the law of force.

Yet here he was, somehow, still in the middle of the worst of it. Wexford turned out every bit as embittered as Kerry and he found himself floundering around like a blind man who'd stumbled into the wrong house.

"You have some chance of getting somewhere with them," Kavanagh had said, when he was explaining the job to him. "A local man would be devoured."

It was a strange, closed village, its people full of a strange, closed pride. Most of them wouldn't talk to him at all and those who did had a drawly, dawdly way with their words so that he had to stretch his ears to make sense of what they were saying. Even his army colleagues seemed to be wary of him. A foreigner, he'd heard himself called.

And now this. Brosnan took off his cap, smoothed back his hair, wished himself far from Mucknamore, far from Kerry, far from Ireland altogether.

They'd try this post-office woman, but he hadn't any great hopes of her. People who knew the dead man well were his best hope.

"A good soldier," Kavanagh had said, describing O'Donovan. "Nothing showy, but brave as he was needed to be. Good leadership ability. All qualities that would have stood to him in the Guards. I'd say he'd have made Inspector."

"Could it have been an accident, Sir?"

"It could, I suppose, but I don't believe so. Why would he go out that way by night unless he was forced? Especially the night that was in it. Can you think of any good reason?"

"It's hard to, all right."

"You know the danger good men have been living with. He was shot at before, you know, and his house set fire to this autumn gone out. Mind you, this has a different feel to an Irregular shooting, more underhand."

He had handed him over the file. "Whatever the motive and whoever the cause, we can't have the likes of this going on, Sergeant, or we'll have the English looking to come back, claiming we can't keep control. Over to you. Don't let us down, like a good man."

O'Dwyer looked askance at him. "Are you all right, Sergeant?"

"Have you a spare cig?"

He took it and bent to the light that O'Dwyer struck for him, inhaled the smoke deep. What next? He hadn't the faintest idea. "Right, let's go to the post office, see can we get any good out of them there."

1995

No silence is ever total. Here in this hotel room, the quiet is thicker and the underlying noises more muted than the swoosh of the sea and the whine and whack of building work that was my soundtrack for the summer. Here it's corridor voices, wheels whirring over carpet, tea trays tinkling and, outside the window, the rattle and drone of Dublin traffic, muffled by double glazing. Beneath it all, the subterranean creaks and gurgles of a huge central-heating system. The air here is thicker too than the open air of my shed, lined with lemon polish and carpet dust and a trace, despite the cleaners' best efforts, of other people.

I wonder about them, all the others who have slept in here, the business travellers and holidaymakers, as I lie between my laundered linen sheets, trying to persuade myself to get up. It's four in the afternoon and I've been asleep since two, would be asleep yet, had I not been kicked into waking by you. But it's good that you've roused me; I should already be up.

In less than an hour, Maeve will be sitting in Bewley's Café, a fifteen-minute walk away, waiting for me. I need to shower and dress and turn myself out. I need to plan what I am going to say when she asks me again why I want to "waste good money" on this hotel room. It is expensive, this square beige space with its peach-and-cream curtains, its pallid furnishings, its innocuous matching paintings of flowers from four different angles in their identical wooden frames.

So why, my sister wonders, am I staying here instead of at her house, where she has not one but two spare rooms? Neither she nor anybody else would bother me, if that's what I'm afraid of. I could come and go as I pleased. All this she has already said on the telephone, and I know she will say it again today. She will do her best to persuade me. I will not let myself be persuaded.

She'll also want to know how the writing is progressing and all about hospitals and birthing arrangements and the question of afterwards. The prospect exhausts me, and has me clinging to the mattress. I would ring and cancel our meeting — as I have once already — were it not for her saying at the end of her call yesterday that she had "something" to tell me. Though it seems unlikely, I cannot rid myself of the idea that this something might be to do with Rory.

I seem doomed to repeat every action of my life. Here I am, pregnant again, having made an abrupt exit again, and here he is, again failing to follow me. It wouldn't be difficult for him to track me down; Maeve's name is listed in the telephone book and though it might be mildly awkward for him to have to telephone her and ask if she knows my whereabouts, it's a small test. Tiny.

Is he really going to flunk it? After all that he said, surely he cannot leave it like this?

I throw aside the covers but I can't propel myself out. What I'd like to do is escape into another nap. Since coming to Dublin, that's all I seem to do: drift in and out of sleep between bouts of writing. I no longer run, have to force myself even to walk. Breakfast and dinner come to me via room service because going downstairs to negotiate waiters and other diners feels like too much bother. I'm growing heavier and slower. My face and arms and wrists are swollen now, as well as my belly, and I get short of breath just taking a shower.

It's all your fault, especially the tiredness, not helped by your inability to tell night from day. Whenever the mood takes you, off you go on the move, kicking and nudging and poking me from inside. I have surrendered to your rhythm and spend some of most days asleep and some of most nights awake (last night I worked from two to five a.m., transcribing some of Norah's notes onto my new computer).

So here I am. This is as far as I've got: lying in an anonymous hotel room, teetering on the edge of sleep, feeling what I think is your heel against my rib, convulsed inside my own longing. Longing, longing, longing like a lovesick teenager, pinning my hopes on this meeting with my sister, shrinking from what I suspect will be their disappointment.

I walk in sunshine through the regimented flower-beds of St Stephen's Green to meet Maeve, past ducks that look just like the ones Rory and I used to feed when we were students. People sit on benches and stroll or stride along the paths, but Dublin's short lolling-on-the-grass season is over until next year. The park is busy, though it's mid-afternoon and the after-work crowd has not yet started to pour through. Despite the crowds, I can never believe in Dublin as a real city. It's about the same size as San Francisco, but feels much smaller, and its loudly touted, new-found cosmopolitanism always seems to me unconvincing, like a child rigged out in its mother's high heels. The biggest village in the world, Oscar Wilde called it, and the description still fits.

I negotiate my bulk through the throngs, down Grafton Street and into Bewley's, past the pile-up of pastries at the take-away counter, into the bowels of the cafe. It takes my eyes a time to adjust to the dim light. Maeve is sitting in one of the low red booths at the back, waving at me. She looks haggard, forcing her mouth into a crooked smile. I bend to kiss her cheek and up close I can almost smell the misery from her. I want to turn and run out the door.

Her skin, despite its pallor, is hot under my lips. "You okay?" I ask.

"Sure. Fine. You?"

"Fine."

Our eyes meet and we hover inside a moment of possibility. Disconcerted, I point at her cup. "Would you like another one of those?" There's a ring of cold coffee lining the inside of the half-empty cup in front of her. She must be here a while.

She nods. "Please."

"Black?"

"Lovely. Thanks."

This is ridiculous, I think as I shuffle along the line-up at the counter, waiting to order. She is not fine. I am not fine. So after I return to the table, and hand out the coffee and the spoons, and put away the tray, I ask her straight: "Maeve, what's wrong?"

She shakes her head, takes a slim tin of artificial sweetener from her bag, tips two small, white pills into her coffee. Shrugs. Sighs. Shakes her head again. I wait. Eventually it comes. "Donal's gone."

"Donal?" This is so far from what I expected that I sound like I've never heard of anyone called Donal. "Gone?"

"Yes, Jo." She wipes a hand across her forehead, irritated. "Donal, as in my husband. Gone, as in left me."

So there is nothing of Rory here, thinks selfish, selfish me. "Maeve, that's terrible."

Her mouth wobbles, goes misshapen. "I know. Of all the times...Now...Mother —"

She breaks off. I know what she means, and yet I can see how this, and her way of saying it, even her way of feeling it, could infuriate.

"But is it permanent? What's going on?"

She reaches into her bag again, this time for paper tissues, crinkly in their plastic handipack. "He blames Mother," she says, snapping the pack back into the bag. "While she was sick I had to go down to Mucknamore, a lot. Naturally. But he resented it. And I resented him not supporting me through it." She shrugs. "According to him, in that time we grew too far apart."

"And is he right?"

"If we did, there was no need for it. He always griped about Mother, you've no idea. He could be completely ridiculous about it. It was pathetic: a grown man jealous of an old woman and her needs."

I recall Donal's sarcasm at the funeral and realise as she is talking that I don't know the guy at all, that he has never seemed quite real to me, just Maeve's husband, slotting into his allotted place in her ordered life.

"He never made it easy for me, if I wanted her to come on holiday with us or to go down to Mucknamore for Christmas."

"You went down every year, didn't you?"

"We could hardly have left her on her own for it."

Why not? I ask myself and she catches my face. "You think he was right!" she accuses.

"I haven't a clue, Maeve. It doesn't matter, does it, what I think? I'm hardly an expert on marriage."

"You know more than you pretend to know," she says, blowing her nose. "Well, you and Donal might be happy to pretend you never had a mother, but most people appreciate their parents and look after them when they get on a bit. I was happy to do it; it was the right thing to do." Red-faced, she shrugs. "It's not like we had her with us day and night. She would have liked a lot more attention than she got."

"You were pulled between the two of them."

"I could never see why he had to make such a big deal about it. We always had at least one other family holiday, without her, each year. And as for Christmas...well, it's what you do, isn't it, at Christmas? The family thing."

I grimace, recognising my part in this. "It all fell on you," I say.

"Well, yes. We were the only family she had left after Auntie Norah and Gran were gone. She used to say that, often."

I bet she did. I take a sip of coffee to stop my retort.

"And it's not like I didn't put her off. I did, many times. For him. And felt awful about it. None of that ever counted for anything with him."

"But, Maeve, I don't understand. If Mrs D. was the problem between you, then surely things should be better now that she's...gone?"

Her face closes over like a fist. "This is why I went down to Mucknamore, to you, that day two weeks ago...to tell you...And I should have, I know I should, I felt so wretched driving away. But I was so overcome by your news...Are you really okay, by the way? Have you seen a doctor yet?"

"Maeve, never mind all that. We can discuss that later."

She nods. "You're right, I should have talked that day. Having gone all the way down, to drive back up without...But, Jo, I'm finding it very hard to talk about this. None of my friends know, not one. I can't seem to get it out."

I know that feeling.

"And...our friends...I don't know how I've done it but...none of them...I don't seem to have anybody I can confide in." She screws the rumpled tissue into her eye sockets. "Also, saying it somehow makes it more real, less likely to..." She lets her hopes trail away into silence.

"Where's he staying?" I ask.

"He's rented an apartment. And..." She falters.

"And there's somebody else?"

Two wide eyes expand wider. "How did you know?"

"I was just asking," I say gently.

"She's only twenty-five."

Is she indeed? I didn't think Donal had it in him.

She starts to cry then, weakly, like she's cried so much that she's tired of it, but it's all she knows how to do. With a grimace she says, "Jo, I want to ask you something."

I nod.

"I wanted to ask if you..."

I wait.

"If you would come...and stay with us for a while?"

I turn from her wet eyes, their entreating heat. The stained glass here in Bewley's turns the light blue, making its close, shabby warmth seem cooler, airier than it would otherwise. Above us, four wooden gargoyles, magnificently ugly, jut out from the wall, and all around, at other tables, Irish and continental and American voices talk and laugh and cups clink against their saucers.

"I wouldn't ask, only...Having you there would be a distraction for Ria...She's such a good kid and I...at the moment, I'm...I can't seem to..." She takes a steadying breath, starts again in a stronger voice. "Jo, it's for Ria, really, that I'm asking. It's so awful...She and I...each trying not to crack..."

At the word, tears break in her again. "Ria's heartbroken, you see...She doesn't understand. How can she? I don't understand myself..."

I think lovingly of my beige hotel room, my solitude. Inside me, I am constricting, like somebody is shrink-wrapping my neck in cling film, working their way up towards my face.

"I'm sorry, Jo," she says into her tissue. "I don't know what your plans are. I shouldn't...I don't want to be a..." The bag clicks open again. She takes out a fresh tissue. I find I'm putting my hand on hers. She cries a little longer, sniffles to recovery.

"It's okay," she says then. "I can see you'd rather not."

"No," I say. "It's not that. I —"

"It's okay, Jo, I understand. I know how you value your privacy."

"Maeve, I'm —"

"You don't have to explain, honestly. Really...I shouldn't have asked..."

"Christ, Maeve! Will you stop for a second?"

She stops, looks at me through the dampness of long lashes that I have always envied. I squeeze the hand that is under mine and it feels like I'm squeezing my own heart.

"Of course I'll come," I say. "Of course I will. Of course."

*R*ichard dies on the evening of October 17th, 1989, a date known to every San Franciscan. And when he dies, though I have been told in time to know, I'm not there. Gary has called me. Susan has called me and for days I've known his time is getting close. But that last afternoon, after hanging up the phone on Gary, instead of making my way there immediately, I sit back down to finish the article I was writing when he called.

An article entitled, somewhat ironically, 'Urgency Addiction: Why You're Not As Busy As You Think'.

It is a perfect October afternoon, blue and balmy. I have an orange juice — freshly squeezed — before me. I am wearing my favourite, most comfortable T-shirt, my fastest pen is between my finger and thumb, filling my page with the words and phrases that will keep my editor happy. All is as it should be, except for the awareness of my failure underlying every thought and act.

I haven't been to the hospital for weeks. Weeks. In August, the disease started in on his brain. For the longest time before that, he had seemed to us too fragile to last. Just skin on a shrunken skeleton, everything that made him Richard, including his sense of humour, gone. Just a sick man, full of sickness's self-pity. And after that came the dementia.

I push on with my work. "The stress addict has the same troublesome dependence as any other addict," I write. "Just because your mood-altering drug of choice is the physiological responses of your own body doesn't mean you are safe. Surging epinephrine or glucocorticoids won't get you in trouble with the law or leave you bankrupt, but like any addictive substances they trigger side effects that can wreak havoc with your health and happiness..."

Though I am getting proficient at this writing, learning just the right tone of certitude, part of me despises it, especially magazine-land's breezy conviction that life is eminently fixable, just a matter of tweaking the right buttons. I won't be able to do this forever, I say to myself, not for the first time. As I write, the table begins to vibrate beneath my notebook and I feel — or is it hear? — a subterranean growl, like a deeply buried tummy rumble. The windows rattle, making me look up. Quake?

I set to sit the tremor out, as I always do, but then the earth growls and everything is wobbling, violently. The floor jerks and screams rise from the street outside, flying in through my open window. Could this be the long awaited "Big One"?

So, I think, it may not just be Richard. We may all go together.

The thought leaves me strangely comforted. At the same time, all the facts I have heard about old concrete, new concrete, stress levels, earthquake procedures are flashing through me. There is a low-roaring snarl underfoot, then the world bucks. Books come crashing down off my shelves. A second newsflash from my mind asserts that I don't, in fact, want to die and for the first time since I came to San Francisco, I go to stand in the doorway. The steel L-shape shelving unit that lines one corner of my living room is flapping back and forth violently, trying to tear apart. Crockery is falling, smashing against tiles and more books are tumbling down in heaps. Oddly, my television, atop another shelving unit, doesn't budge.

It goes on for what seems like a long time, though it can only really be seconds, then the world slowly settles to stillness. I wait. Yes, it is still.

It seems to be over.

It seems I am to live.

Now I have a good excuse for not being at the hospital. Crossing the city becomes an impossibility, I give up even pretending that I might go. I stay home, listening to the news reports coming in on my battery-operated radio. A building has collapsed here, a gas-main has flared into fire there. The upper deck of Bay Bridge has collapsed onto the lower, squashing hundreds of cars. Of the inhabited areas, the reclaimed land in the Marina district and parts of the inner Mission are worst hit. Liquification, they call it, when earthquake dissolves reclaimed soil, so that it temporarily acts like quicksand. Those with power still up get to see it all on TV — history's first real-time disaster movie — available on three major networks, thanks to the World Series football game that was in progress when it struck.

Sixty-seven San Franciscans died that day from being in the wrong place, at the flash-points of the quake. In the weeks that follow, the whole city is in mourning, which feels fitting for Richard. But I am not good at grief. I cannot cry and I don't want to. I go about my days, aghast. Stunned by what it is to know that he is dead. His mouth was covered in ulcers and his body, inside and out, in excruciating KS lesions. He was blind in one eye, only barely sighted in the other. He couldn't hold his own coffee cup, his own medicine, his own shit. A time ago, I heard him writhing through the night, pleading with no one: "Please...please..." And it got worse after that. That last day I arrived to the hospital and he screamed at me from the bed about stealing his food, I looked at his face disfigured by KS and rage and thought: you are not Richard.

But who, then, was he, this crazed stranger in Richard's bed and body?

I couldn't bear it. By the end, Susan was going into the hospital more often than me. There: that is how loathsome I am.

Death was a release. That's what I tell others, at the funeral. Not at his family's Episcopalian cremation, but at the memorial held by our friends. Mozart's Requiem. Judy singing 'Somewhere Over the Rainbow'. Gary reading Thom Gunn and Oscar Wilde. Me reading my own poem: "...We thought the laughter would roll on and on / But we were young and we were wrong."

The horror of scanning the room, seeing those who were going to die next and all the other missing faces, those gone already. And afterwards, everybody talking about Richard's enthusiasm for life, his humour, his irrepressibility.

He would have had none of this, I found myself thinking, even as I clung to the compliments. He would have taken pleasure in bursting our burbles of comfort, with his particular brand of starkly honest humour. He would never have let me get away with it the sentence I dole out to all — that his death was a release. It's true, but also so completely insufficient to the truth of his final macabre months and minutes, that it's no consolation at all.

His dying and his death were an offence to nature. An insult to all that is most human. An affront to everything I had come to hold dear. I am outraged, outraged, outraged, by his loss.

Sometimes I dream about him, dreams where he is fleshed out again, his old self. These dreams are usually silent, but once I dreamed that I answered my buzzer and his voice said, "Hello."

When I opened the door, there he was, standing on my step, looking sheepish. "Hi! I'm back!"

"But you're dead," I said to him. He turned his eyes away from me, evasive. "Richard, you're supposed to be dead."

"I went to Ireland."

"No, you didn't. You died. I was at your funeral. You were cremated."

"Hmmm," he said, ambivalently, smiling a maddening, unanswerable smile.

Everyone tries to be kind. Susan goes into motherly mode and I have to pull out of her grasp. Maeve sends a surprisingly thoughtful letter. Dee, too, tries to help, but she's at a loss; Richard was sick before she arrived out here and she never knew him in his heyday. She is getting impatient with me, can't understand why I'm taking it so hard.

I don't fully understand myself. He was my friend. I loved him and I miss him, but why do I feel like it is my own life that has ended?

What Gary finds hardest is that he wasn't there for the end. He rang Richard's mother in Telport to let her know and she thanked him by making him leave when she arrived so that it was she, not Gary, who saw Richard out of this world. The hospital let that happen because she was next of kin. This rule has since been changed, permitting the patient to nominate their own person.

Richard would have wanted the man who had loved him most from the moment they met. Gary wanted — needed — to be there. But, instead, his last sighting of his beloved boy was his face muzzled by the ventilator, and Mrs Burke standing guard over him, arms folded across her chest, an empty fortress of righteousness.

Gary can't shake that image — of Richard's eyes rotating wildly over the plastic cup, unable to see, unable to speak — out of his head.

The two of us spend a lot of time together, sitting in slumped silence or in front of the TV. Is it worse for him?

Everybody says it is, and I suppose it must be, but I cannot imagine how.

I am offered a new job, as an agony aunt. A "sexpert", as Lauren, my new editor likes to call it. She knows just how she wants it to be: my name will be Sue Denim and I'll do four letters per page, one Problem of the Month and three others. The advice will be responsible but worldly, the approach caring but daring.

"Women love the truth," she says. "It's men who are the prudes."

Lauren is evangelical about women's magazines. It incenses her that they are disparaged, not taken seriously by the world. "It's because they're for women," she says. "Baseball and automobiles are important, you know, but what we wear and eat and who and how we love — that's trivial girl's stuff? Yeah, right."

She offers me a sum of money that sounds ludicrous and when, unsure whether I want the job or not, I seem hesitant, she offers me half as much again. I take this offer; I can't afford not to. The aerobics boom is dying off and numbers in the Rí Rá classes are beginning to drop. Aerobics is now an activity like any other, with its own adherents, rather than a craze igniting everyone.

Hearing word of my new job, Dee turns up at my door with a bottle of champagne. "I know you're Miss Healthy America and never let alcohol cross your lips any more, but this is a celebration."

She takes down two champagne glasses from a high cupboard, places them side by side on the table, holds the bottle at arms' length, pops the cork. As the fizzy liquid flows up and out of the glasses, spilling out over the table, she laughs. I take the glass she hands me: it's wet on the outside from the overflow. I put damp fingers to my mouth and lick. The alcohol tastes sharp, but sweet too.

Dee is lifting her glass, smiling across at me. "Sláinte," she says, the Irish salutation.

"Chin-chin," I reply.

We both tilt our heads back and drink.

The column is a success. It's because it's so different, Lauren says. So refreshing. I don't know why it works or what happens when I "become" Sue. That is how I think of it. I even have a ritual for the transformation: I dress in an old loose trousers and smock top, no bra and bare feet; I burn joss sticks and put Mozart on the stereo. That way, it is her perspective, not mine, that pops onto the page. This sounds silly, but left to me, as me, I'd never come up with any answers. Sue believes in sexual liberation, that the heart of freedom lies there, in what we are prepared to do and think and be, sexually. And in part, I agree with her.

In part.

But...

Who is this "I"? What is this "but..."?

Dear Sue,

For most of my life I've lived monogamously with one man after another. At the same time, I've always been bothered by the world's obsession with couples and longed for love of a different kind. I dreamed of a sexual energy that could flow free between me and a variety of people at once, without guilt or shame, games or betrayal, free of the insecurity that demands ownership.

I turned thirty this year and realized that it wasn't going to happen if I didn't make it happen. So I decided to launch an experiment. I had been living with a man for almost a year as part of a two-couple household. One night, after the four of us had consumed a lot of alcohol, I made the suggestion that we should extend our sexual intimacy beyond our two complacent couples. Everybody was willing and excited by the prospect, so I got together with the other guy and agreed to share "my" man with the other woman (none of us was interested in a same-sex encounter).

All seemed to go well for a while. I thought the four of us were growing, setting ourselves free of societal constraints, having the courage of our desires. But now I've found out that while the other man and I were just expanding our relationship, breaking out of nuclear bondage, etc., our respective mates were falling seriously in love with each other.

He told me last week. He loves her and wants to live with her exclusively. Sue, it hurts so much. I have never in my life been so full of rage and jealousy: I fantasize about killing them both in their sleep. The other man is devastated and spends his time either crying on my shoulder or berating me for starting the whole thing. What should I do?

Chastened

Dear Sexual Adventurer,

What should you do, you ask? What can you do, except carry on living through the fruits of your experiment?

Freedom is not safe. But you already know that.

You cannot control how other people will respond. But you already know that.

Emotions pass. In time, when the rage and hurt have subsided, you may recognise your urge to push out your boundaries as something bigger than the transient pain it caused. Or you may come to think of it as a lesson you needed to learn about faith and faithfulness.

Whichever, don't be "chastened." Look deeply at what's happening and accept it, without letting it quash the spirit that makes you so venturesome.

You are a big person, riding the big waves of a big life.

Live on.

My postbag swells and Lauren is delighted. The publishers take note and, before long, the column is being syndicated to magazines in South Africa and Australia as well as the States, and in Britain, which also means Ireland. I even get occasional letters from there; their problems seem no different to anybody else's. Things are changing in Ireland, Maeve tells me over the phone, but when I ask how, she talks about jobs and money, bars and coffee-houses. Racing to jump aboard the globalisation express doesn't sound like much of a change to me –- still acquisitive, still conservative, still aping other, more "advanced" places –- but if life is easier for more people, I guess that's progress.

A politician in Idaho denounces my column as filth. I wish Richard were here to help me enjoy the accolade.

Then comes the day I'm standing in my hallway with the telephone in my hand, listening to Maeve tell me that Gran is dead. I stood at the end of the phone, the radio from the kitchen blaring through the open door into the hall, and asked all the right questions in a voice that didn't sound like mine. Maeve wanted me to go back for the funeral, tried hard to persuade me and a part of me very much wanted to be there, releasing the tides of my tears. But if I was going to go back for Gran, it would have been while she was still alive. We both would have preferred that.

With her gone, I wasn't about to deliver myself up to Mrs D. — who hadn't even asked.

Thirteen weeks later, another phone call. Auntie Norah this time. She couldn't live without Gran, Maeve says during this call. She willed herself to die.

I hate, hate, hate the tone of Maeve's voice as she tells it. This time, I don't even think about going back.

Sue Denim has all the answers, but she's no help to me. I don't even know what my question is.

Richard would know how to make me believe in what I'm doing. I miss the way things were when he was here, when life was exuberant and I had flings and relationships and experiences that gave me pleasure. Pleasure.

It doesn't sound like much — and I do remember sometimes feeling that I wanted more — but it seems like all a person needs, now it's gone.

I used to have lovers; now I have pick-ups. I used to have fun; now I have alcohol. Everything I'm doing is bad for me, I know it. I've done it all before and I know where it leads, to where I swore I'd never go again, but I can't stop myself. I'm a vessel unmoored, with somebody else at the helm. The old me, perhaps? Or maybe somebody from further back, somebody who could have taught me how to navigate, but never did.

1995

"Donal drove me mad the whole time," says Maeve, recalling her visit to San Francisco. "I spent nearly every night after we'd gone to bed calming him down."

"I knew he was a bit fazed by the scene, but I'd no idea he took it so bad."

"Dreadful. He was even afraid to drink out of cups that Richard or Gary had used."

I feel the skin on my face blaze up. I was right to never like him, I think.

"I know, I know," she says. "But you have to remember the times. Afterwards, people came to understand a lot more about AIDS, but then...Well, he was hardly the only one, was he?"

It is Richard's anniversary: six years ago today since he died. Six years. Where did they go? It's so hard not to think of them as wasted. All day, as I went about my business in Dublin, I've been dispirited, struggling against the suck of misery. None of the things that make this year different — writing, pregnancy, being in Ireland — were able to keep me buoyant today. The writing I have been so wedded to seems hollow and useless, a concoction of nothings. I'm getting fearful about the baby and about afterwards, of how we will be together. Together, alone.

Rory still has not come or sent any word, and is unlikely to now.

As for Ireland, the faction fighting goes on, the antagonism that seems more virulent here than anywhere else. Each day, the radio brings belligerent adversaries into Maeve's kitchen and, over breakfast, we listen to them slinging their tirades at each other over Northern Ireland. The IRA has declared a ceasefire, but the gesture is insufficient for the British government and Unionists. They are calling for all Republican guns and bombs to be destroyed before peace talks can begin.

The IRA refuses. Irish Republicans have never handed over their armoury. Not in 1921, during The Truce with Britain. Not in 1923 after the Civil War, when weapons were dumped, not surrendered. And not now.

The second talking point is the scandal of what has come to be called abuse, the slime under the rug of power. Beatings, humiliation, molestation and rape were, and are, endemic in Irish schools, seminaries and institutions — and in that other great Irish institution, the family, too. Every time I hear a priest or politician pontificating on the radio, I am reminded of why I fled this country. It is not that such things don't happen in other places, but the Irish version is too virulent for me.

I have to tell Maeve so repeatedly. She keeps making suggestions about how good it would be for the baby to grow up with an aunt and cousin nearby; how raising a baby all alone is hard work; how, in a few years, Ria will be old enough to baby-sit...Tonight, such is my sense of frailty, that I almost feel I could be persuaded. Almost.

It's her thoughts on Richard that have made me warm to her. I didn't realise until this evening how much she really liked him; she has so many memories of him from her visit to San Francisco, memories we never discussed before. Through dinner, we regaled Ria with some of the more repeatable stories and, since Ria went upstairs to bed, the two of us have been sitting together in front of the sitting-room fire, turning over memories. Maeve occupies the armchair, a whiskey and water in front of her; I recline on the sofa opposite, in the only position that is comfortable for me these days: half lying on a nestle of cushions, my belly protruding upwards like a hill.

"You and Richard never had a thing?" she asks. "Or did you?"

"God, no. You met him, didn't you?" Five minutes with Richard should be enough to locate him at the furthest, gayest end of the sexuality spectrum.

"Mmmmm."

"And what is that sceptical sound supposed to convey?"

"I just find it hard to understand why his death flattened you so."

"He was my friend, Maeve. Simple as that."

"I mean, more than your own mother's! It's unusual, you have to admit."

Oh, no...So long, soft, sisterly feelings. She shrugs her puzzlement and the gesture makes her neck and shoulder bones protrude. Her neck could be held in the grasp of one hand. I have pity for that neck. I also have the urge to choke it.

So far, we have avoided conflict. In the morning, after she and Ria leave for school, I get up and go into the centre to write. I go to the Winding Stair, a rickety old bookshop café on the north bank of The Liffey. Each of its wide windows has its window box of valiant flowers fighting the traffic fumes gasped up from below. There I write, looking down at the floods of shoppers rising and falling over The Liffey's Ha'penny Bridge, under high, complicated Irish skies.

It's a good view of Dublin — almost soothing. I write well there, which is why I take the trouble to travel in each morning, even though this house of Maeve's lies empty all day. I tried writing here, just once, up in the bedroom, but Maeve's years with Donal were in the air, and all those years when I was out of the country clustered in the silence.

Sometimes I return to my hotel room. I like knowing it is there, available to me. I've managed to spend the occasional night there by inventing a friend, somebody I knew in college that I "meet" every so often and, when I do, I call Maeve to say that I am spending the night at her apartment. Then I go to my beige bolthole and breathe free for eight or ten or twelve hours, refreshed enough to return. Maeve suspects the truth, I think, but appreciates the lie.

"Don't take this wrong," she says now, "but it strikes me that being so fixated on Richard allowed you to avoid something else."

"Something else?"

"A relationship of your own."

"You've been seeing too much of that shrink of yours," I say, lightly.

Maeve is attending a counsellor, to try to understand where she and Donal went wrong. Can she hear the menace under my airy tone? If she's not more careful, she will break our truce.

I would like to say it straight to her, tell her that Richard gave me what I should have got from her and Mrs D.: unconditional love, as her therapist would no doubt call it.

Richard's simple acceptance of me won him my undying devotion. Literally undying, staying with me even though he has gone. Maeve, who I suspect has never had a real friendship, still thinks romantic love is the best. That it has recently — and presumably for some years now — let her down, in no way diminishes her belief in it. Though Donal is now refusing to see her at all, asking her to drop Ria outside his apartment block for her custody visits without meeting him. Still, she nurtures hope that he will come back.

And how can I despise this hope when I live with my own version of the same affliction? I want to be gentle with her, I really do, but she makes it so hard. If I can be careful of her, why can't she extend me the same favour? Why always this need of hers to make me face the hard questions? (Like: how small a thing was my devotion to Richard if I couldn't even be with him at his end?)

I want to get up off the sofa and pace the room, but it would take a crane to lift me, so I confine myself to stretching out my swollen legs. The ankles are so puffy, an older, fatter woman's ankles, pooled with blood. New veins, like blue in a Stilton, have surfaced all over my legs. The skin of my abdomen is stretched to transparency: I never imagined skin could stretch so far.

You are so big now that the discomfort is constant: heartburn arrives at regular intervals to sting my oesophagus. You ripple my belly with each movement you make. You too are cramped and uncomfortable. We both want out.

But I am also dreading the labour. After years of suffering no worse physical pain than a small cut or bruise, I am scared.

"It's time to get closure on it, I would have thought," Maeve says, still harping on Richard.

When she starts on like this, I think that maybe I shouldn't be here, that we are not helping each other at all. We disagree on almost everything. Yesterday it was the North. All her patriotism is affixed to the Republic of Ireland. It stops at a border created by the British and she sees no irony in that.

I take up that topic again because, though we differ on it, it will distract her from Richard. "I've been thinking about what you said yesterday, Maeve, about the North, and I wanted to ask you: do you not see what's going on in the North today as a continuation of Granny Peg's 'War of Independence'?"

"Things were different then," she says. "The old IRA were men of honour."

"All of them?" Has she not been reading the manuscript pages I've given her?

"They killed and died for an ideal."

"The ideal hasn't changed, has it? Isn't it the same struggle, the same methods? Just that a bomb kills more people than a gun?"

"But..."

"Don't get me wrong, it's not that I agree with that struggle. I personally think we'd have been better off growing up in an Ireland that had remained part of the UK."

This statement swings things round. Maeve stops in the act of twisting her hair up into a clip, and stares at me with green eyes aghast, wearing the exact expression that Rory wore when I said the same to him. "You can't mean that?" she gasps.

"Why not?"

"You're being provocative. You don't mean it."

"But I do. All the damage done by English colonisation was well done by the time of the so-called War of Independence. What the Irish did to themselves afterwards only made a bad thing worse."

"I completely disagree with you. And why do you say 'so-called' War of Independence? That war did get us our independence."

"Did it?" I ask, thinking of Granny Peg and Mrs D. And me and Rory. And think about those moments that I have felt more frequently this summer, when I found within myself a tranquillity below thought. When I realised that I am something more than a bundle of nationality, or gender, or sexuality, or any other kind of identity I want to throw into the basket called "me". Down in those depths, I am suddenly sure, is where true freedom resides.

I am trying to formulate this insight into words that I can pass to my sister when the doorbell interrupts: Ding-dong, ding-dong.

"Good God," Maeve says. "Who's that? At this hour of the night?"

Ten fifteen. My stomach takes a small flip. The kind of time you'd arrive if you left Wexford at around seven thirty or eight o'clock. After coming home from work at six and having a conversation and packing a hasty suitcase...

"Maybe I won't answer it," Maeve says. "You can't see the lights in here from the front."

"I think you'd better," I say. "You never know."

"I suppose." She gets slowly out of the big armchair, uncurling her legs from under her, giving a small grouchy stretch as she goes, leaving the door ajar. I hear her open the front door and the surprise in her greeting. She says a name, but I cannot catch it. I cannot hear her words, but her tone makes something in my stomach start to ferment.

Then the other voice speaks, muffled, but a male voice. Definitely male.

You give a strong kick. What do you know or sense?

There's the door closing. More suppressed talk. A silence. Footsteps approaching across the tiled hallway. Two sets of footsteps. The door opening. I'm afraid to look up.

"Jo?" Maeve's voice is tentative, a whisper.

Her head is peeping round the door, her face flushed. "He's here, Jo."

"He is?" I get up out of the chair. Blood swishes into my head, probably from standing up so fast. I forgive him, I realise as I wait for the black amoebas before my eyes to vanish. Whatever may lie ahead, I forgive him all. But why is Maeve keeping him out there? Is she afraid that I don't want to see him?

"We'll be in the kitchen," she says.

"Kitchen?"

"Yeah. We need to talk. Obviously."

I give my head a waggle. When I see her again I know what I should have known from the start. A memory rises: Mrs D. and Daddy, the day he came back home to us after leaving us for four years. Maeve is wearing the exact same expression on her face as our mother did back then. Hence, perhaps, the anger I feel, white and hard as bone.

"Well, well," I say. "The prodigal returns." His words to me at Mrs D's funeral. "Why don't you bring him in here?" I manage to say, in a steady voice. "I was ready for bed anyway."

She opens the door wider, flourishing him in.

Ashamed of my pettiness, I jump on top of my anger, wrestle it down, and change the tone of my voice: "Welcome home, Donal."

Donal's return changes everything. Now, I am in the way. Maeve says this is nonsense, but I am. Neither of them want me here, knowing what I know, and I don't want to be here either, witnessing their travails. Things she has told me about him rankle.

Also, I don't want to lose what she and I have so recently gained. Living together is straining our newly-won, tenuous bond.

But she won't let me go. I was good enough to come when she needed me, now I must stay until the baby comes. It wouldn't be right for me to have to go into labour alone, in a hotel room. What about those pains I am having in the night?

It is true that you have started to bear down inside me, that I am assailed by stabbing pains in strange new places, pains that sometimes stop me in my tracks. It is true that I am afraid to face into labour alone. It is close now, very close: a week to the due day. Even if I go over my time, it can be no further away than a fortnight.

Can Maeve and I live in the same house for that long without a breach?

Fingers crossed, I stay.

1923

*S*ergeant Brosnan gave Private O'Dwyer the nod to start the car. A day and a half now they'd spent, questioning witnesses, and the only useful one so far was the bar girl from Ryan's of Rathmeelin, who, as far as he could make out, was the last person to see O'Donovan alive. He had taken a drink there around teatime and left, telling her that he had an appointment in Mucknamore at seven o'clock. At 7.14pm his watch stopped, presumably in the wet sands.

Stuck in sinking sands waiting for the returning tide to take you: what a death. If he was lured, Kavanagh was right in saying it was one evil act.

The car spluttered and coughed into its workaday rumble and they were pulling out onto the road when a man came lumbering up to them and started to wave his two arms like a windmill. He was poorly dressed, two strings of twine where the belt of his coat should be.

"Stop the car!" he shouted and O'Dwyer did.

"Yes?" Brosnan snapped.

"I'm hearing that yez are investigating what went on here the night before last. Would that be so?"

"If you mean the death of Lieutenant O'Donovan, then yes, that is so."

"In that case, I've something of interest to yez."

"Have you indeed?"

"I have."

He stood there, like a child waiting for a pat on the head.

"Well? Go on."

He looked around, over each shoulder. "I'm thinking it would be better if we went somewhere more private. I don't want to be handing it over in front of the entire village."

"Handing what over?"

The fellow tapped a finger to the side of his nose, looked about him again. The street was empty, the little windows appraising.

"Sit into the car," Brosnan said. "If you must."

"I don't know, sir. I don't think that would go down too well with some, to see me voluntarily climbing into this particular vehicle."

Brosnan looked at O'Dwyer, who slid his eyes upwards. "Go on, so, be off with you."

"Don't misunderstand me, sir. Myself, I'd be entirely happy to get in. But these are dangerous times we're living in."

"For Christ's sake, man. What is it you want?"

"It's not so much what I want." He gave a slow, stupid grin. "Sir," he added, belatedly.

"Is this a game?"

"I'm quite disposed to satisfy you. But in order to do so, I have to ask yez to make it look as if I'm being forced."

Forced? The devil. And he probably had nothing at all. But what if he had? So far, not one single lead...

He nodded at O'Dwyer to do it. The blackguard made a convincing — O'Dwyer would probably no doubt say too convincing — attempt at resistance, until the private's hat was knocked askew on his head and Brosnan said, "We've had enough of your nonsense. Get in now or we're going."

The fellow let himself be taken by the scruff of his collar and shoved into the back of the car. "Drive down to...the...back strand," he said, breathless.

O'Dwyer ignored that and took them out the Wexford road. Once outside the village, he pulled to a stop by the ditch.

"Right," Brosnan said, turning round. "Let's be having it, whatever it is."

A sly look. "I don't know how to put this, sir. Is it a Sergeant you are?"

Brosnan nodded, peremptorily.

"Well, Sergeant, I'm supposing that the army would be grateful for information about why Dan O'Donovan went walking The Causeway in the dark that night?"

The fellow still had his teeth, but every one of them was black-rotten in his head. The car was filling up with an unpleasant pong.

"And if so, how would such gratitude be demonstrated?"

So that was it. He should have known from the first. "That would depend."

"On?"

"On the quality of the information," Brosnan said, not looking at him.

"But there would be a...token of your appreciation?"

"Bear in mind, man, that it is your civic duty to help in a...in such an enquiry." He nearly said "murder enquiry", but that wouldn't be right. Despite what was being said abroad, they had no proof of foul play. And he wasn't going to promise this repulsive creature anything. Let's see what the fellow had first.

"I'd need to be sure, Sergeant."

Brosnan could see the future of this village written on this blackguard's face. From here on out, it would become ever more closed and insular. Fright at what they'd shown themselves capable of doing to each other had thinned their souls, souls that were already reduced from hundreds of years under the British yoke. None of them — maybe himself included? — was able to face the true shame of this dirty little war, the wicked whys and wherefores of it. Some would react by making too much of small differences, because otherwise they'd have to admit they'd been killing and dying for nothing. Others would try to pretend the horrors never happened at all. Least said, soonest mended. Whatever you say, say nothing.

Well, he might not think their cause worth killing or dying for, but he wasn't afraid of the truth. He said, "You won't be let down, man. Not if you have something worthwhile to pass on."

Satisfied, the creature reached inside his coat and made a great commotion of taking something from his inside pocket and presenting it with hands aloft. A gun. A Webley rifle. He held the booty under Brosnan's nose. "I found it this morning," he said.

Brosnan nodded. "Go on."

"There I was, after bringing out the cows, walking back up the road towards my house..."

"Which is where?"

"Down by the Tench, Sergeant."

Brosnan shook his head.

"Don't you know the Tench?" He made a show of surprise. "On the other side of the village, down towards what we call the Hole in the Wall." There was that knowingness again, that simple-minded delight at knowing something that Brosnan, an outsider, a stranger — a foreigner! — did not. "The strand exit nearest The Causeway, Sergeant. Which is the way out to Coolanagh, if you get my drift. There I was, strolling along behind the cattle, minding my own, when next thing I spied it, out of the side of my eye. Lying there, half in and half out of the ditch."

"And you think it significant?"

He looked at them with feigned surprise. "You don't? Don't you know what this is? Ser—geant?" He drawled the title with sneering affectation, as if Brosnan was the greatest dunce that ever walked.

"Just keep to the facts, please."

"There was only one rifle of this sort owned around here."

"Go on, man."

"It belonged to Parle." He flashed his sly, conniving grin again. "Yes, Sergeant. Barney Parle. I presume you've heard of him?"

*W*hen the fight comes, it's about Mrs D. We're sitting over the remains of dinner, darkness bulked against the glass walls of Maeve's dining room. Donal has gone to the gym, Ria is in bed, Maeve is finishing a bottle of wine and, since the others left, we have been fixed on the topic of our mother.

"How much of her pain was in her situation," I ask, "and how much in her person? That's what I could never work out. If she didn't have Daddy and all-that-had-been-done-to-her to complain about, I still don't think she'd have been happy."

"She was happy after Daddy died. You didn't know her then."

"I did. Daddy was dead a year, I seem to recall, when she kicked me out of the house."

"She did not kick you out, you walked. And in that first year, she wasn't herself...Naturally. Afterwards, she was very happy. She loved her bowls and her golf and her bridge. She liked her life then."

"The merry widow, eh?"

She shakes her head at me. "You're so hard sometimes, Jo. You know how unhappy he made her."

"What about him? What about his unhappiness?" I appear to be shouting, though nothing in the conversation calls for it.

"Yes, he was unhappy too. And he, too, behaved badly. You never blamed him, though, did you?"

I look down at the debris on the dinner table.

"She was your mother, Jo. Does that count for nothing with you? Now that you're about to be a mother yourself?"

She begins to clear away the plates, scrape off the food. "And look what she gave you — all the family papers, the opportunity to put this book together," she says, in the voice of somebody trying hard to be patient. "Anyone can see what that means to you. Can't you be grateful to her for that?"

"She wanted me to do a glorious history of our glorious family. It was for her, not for me."

"Or maybe she knew exactly what you'd do..."

"Come on, Maeve. Mrs D. wouldn't have passed these papers on if she knew the full story. She said in her letter that she never read Norah's notebooks. And you have to read Norah's stuff, as well as Gran's, to get it. No, she thought the extent of the secret was that she was 'illegitimate'." I put two fingers around the word my mother would have used. "Not that Norah was her mother, rather than her aunt."

"My God, Jo, don't you realise what a big thing it was for Mammy to share that."

"I do. But she did it because she wanted a glorified —"

Maeve cuts me off. "She did it because she wanted to draw you back into the family. And, what's more, she succeeded."

"You know, you don't have to defend her every move, Maeve. She was shitty to you too."

She shakes her head.

"Maeve! Don't pretend she wasn't." I have to stop shouting. How can I break through her denial? "She was. I remember. And I remember the way you'd always go crawling back for more."

"She wasn't easy, Jo, I never claimed she was easy." Her

moderate tones are a deliberate contrast to mine. "And yes, I had my difficulties with...Let's just say that since she died, I...Well, she wasn't easy. I can agree with that. But don't you see, Jo? Nothing that she did or failed to do can alter the plain fact that she was our mother. Denying that hurts you as much as it ever hurt her."

"No, sorry. Mothering is something you do, not just something you are. You do it, with Ria." She does. No matter how tired Maeve is from work and running the house and now all the stress of Donal, she still does the mothering thing. Sometimes I feel jealous of Ria, and sometimes impatient at how she is so careless of that.

"I get it wrong, often," she says. "And I hate when I do. Mammy's failures hurt her. Just as yours hurt you, and mine hurt me."

I want to go on arguing, but I can't think of any words.

"Sometimes, now," Maeve says. "I wonder whether it was because you reminded her of Auntie Norah."

"What?"

"There is a physical resemblance, you know. Your hair: she was a redhead too. And around the eyes..."

"Gee, thanks."

"Come on, Jo, just in certain ways."

Could that be right? At least it gives her a reason. Can Maeve stretch herself to imagine how it might feel to be on the receiving end of that? Can I dare to ask her?

My knees are clenching each other, alarmed at what I am about to say. My voice slides down the decibels, so that this time when I speak it's only a whisper. But I speak: "She couldn't stand me, Maeve."

There: it's out. The shameful truth. The truth I have only ever told Richard before. My own mother didn't love me. She didn't even like me.

"Oh, come on..."

"Please, Maeve. Don't pretend. I know you knew it too."

At last I have silenced her. Will she admit it? She never has before, it makes her — the favourite — feel too guilty. For a long moment, we hover; it feels to me like forever. Then she stands up with the plates, looks down at me.

"Jesus, Jo, for once, just for once, could we drop the self-pity?"

I am on my feet, moving too fast, storming past the corners of the table, the kitchen units, my arms around my belly for protection. Mine or the baby's? I don't know. I can't see. My head is drowning in darkness and I am shouting again. "Fuck off, Maeve. Just fuck off. Just fuck off." Like a child, throwing the words back over my shoulder as I hurtle away, down the hall, up the stairs.

The fight has taken us over, the way it used to when we were children. It's quivering in my arms and legs and making her run after me, shouting: "If you'd come out of that self-obsessed haze of yours for five minutes, you'd know that it isn't even Mammy you're mad at, but Gran."

All those years — tiptoeing phone calls, awkward visits, careful conversations — are ripped away in an instant and here we are, hatred wrenching our faces out of shape, its breath panting in its eagerness to strike, to dive, hard and deep into each other's weakest places.

"Isn't that true, Jo? It was Gran not going to you, Gran 'choosing' Mammy instead of you" — now it's her turn to use two fingers to put quote marks round the word — "in some mad competition that existed only in your head. That's who you're sore at, really. That's what you can't bear to admit."

It's true, it's true, it's true. Why, Gran? Why did you never ring, or write? Why? Maeve had Mrs D. I had no-one but you. You knew that.

I hurry on, away from them all, into the spare room that has been mine while I stayed here, locking the door behind me. I expect Maeve to come bounding up the stairs after me, banging on the door, but she doesn't. I tear clothes from their hangers, stuff anything I can see into my bag, brush everything that's on the dressing table in with one sweep of my arm. I'll sort it out later, in the hotel. My hands are shaking so hard I can't get my toothpaste and toothbrush into the wash bag.

Never trust them, never. I knew, but still I came here, left myself open to this. Never again. Never. Never.

A last glance round the room to make sure that I haven't forgotten anything vital. Out in the hall, I see Ria's door ajar. What did she hear? "Goodbye, Ria," I say, but I get no reply.

Maeve is at the end of the stairs, waiting for me. "Oh, what a surprise," she says. "Jo's packed her bag, Jo's decided to leave. Where to this time, Jo? Aren't you running out of places to go?"

I have to take each stair carefully, my balance unsteady. One – step – at – a – time – then – the – next. There: I've reached the bottom. Maeve is standing off to my left. Ahead is the hall door, waiting for me to open it. All I have to do is cross the hallway.

Cross the hallway.

Open the door.

"Don't stop now, Jo. What are you waiting for?"

You.

You are what is stopping me. As I take the final step of the stair, you go whompf within me, and a stabbing pain shoots through my lower belly. Now I have crumpled.

Now I am folded into sitting on the step and I am crying, my face in my hands.

Now I am saying I am sorry, I don't know why, but that is what I am saying, over and over again: "I'm sorry, Maeve. I'm sorry. I'm sorry."

I say it to her, but really I'm addressing everyone: Richard. Granny Peg and Auntie Norah. Maeve, Ria and Rory. Even Orla, Rory's wife. Oh God, yes, even Mrs D.

Now Maeve has her arms around me, telling me that it's all right, that she is sorry too. I burrow my face into her shoulder, trying to explain that's not what I mean, that I am drowning in a remorse so deep and sore that I think it's going to kill me. "I had to get rid of...It would have been..."

I want to tell her more, tell her properly, but I can't snatch enough breath. The skull of my forehead is grinding against her shoulder bones.

"I know," she says. She begins to stroke my head, my shoulder, my back. "I know."

"No, you don't."

"I do, Jo."

This time, the words reach me. I look up and see in her glistening eyes that she does.

She touches my face, nodding gently, gently.

"It's not that I think..." My sobs won't let me form the words right, my tears are wetting the skin of her neck. "If I had to do it again, I'd do the same...I had to...But..."

"I know, Jo," she says, her voice so soft, so soothing. A voice I've heard her use with Ria sometimes. "It's okay. You did what you had to do." She's stroking my hair. "It's okay now. Let it be. Let it go."

"It's just..."

"I know, I know."

Something about the way she keeps saying that... "How do you know?"

Her eyes pierce into mine. "I know because you weren't the only one."

Can she mean...? Surely, surely not? Not Maeve?

"Yes," she nods. "Different reasons, but yes."

I am without words.

"Why so shocked, Jo? Ten thousand of us take that trip to England, every year."

"But I can't...It's just...Did Mrs D. know?"

"Are you mad? Of course not."

She looks so indignant that I start to laugh. Then she joins in, and we find we can't seem to stop. We sit there, at the end of the stairs, waves of hysterical laughter breaking over us, while all the time I'm looking at her, at her head thrown back, and her wide open mouth, and her shoulders shaking and I'm telling myself, over and over in my head, as if somebody is listening in: this is Maeve. This is my sister, Maeve.

1923

DEAD MUCKNAMORE OFFICER'S INQUEST!
Gun Belonging to Dead Irregular Found!

Mother of Deceased Calls for Murder Trial!

An inquest into the death of Lieutenant Dan O'Donovan, National Army, was arranged by the military and held in the courthouse, Wexford, on Friday evening last. Lieutenant O'Donovan was found dead at Coolanagh, Mucknamore, on the morning of Wednesday December 10th. Brigade Police Officer Jas Brosnan conducted the enquiry.

Evidence of identification was given by Dan O'Donovan Snr, father of the deceased. It appears that Lieutenant O'Donovan was granted a few days' leave by the army and that it was on the first evening of this break that the tragedy occurred.

John Colfer, fisherman, deposed as to how he found the body and immediately notified the military authorities. Next witness, Doctor Matthew Morris, testified to having examined the body. There were no marks of violence, the doctor said, and he was of the opinion that death was due to asphyxia. At this point, the mother of the deceased

*interrupted proceedings, saying her son had been murdered whichever
way you looked at it.*

*Police Officer Brosnan responded by saying to the jury: "I
understand the deceased man's father is here. It is open to him to
cross-examine the witness if he wishes, but he has not done so." Mr
O'Donovan, the father, rose to his feet and heatedly replied, "This
inquest is nothing but a farce to my mind." The Chair informed Mr
and Mrs O'Donovan that they would have to behave themselves. If
they wanted to cross-examine a witness, they could do so in the
ordinary way.*

*Miss Anne Comerford, employed at Ryan's public house,
Rathmeelin, three miles from Mucknamore, testified that the deceased
had called in there the night he died, between the hours of half-past
five and six o'clock. He was wearing a National Army uniform, a cape
and a civilian cap. He only remained in the shop long enough to drink
one bottle of stout, saying he had an appointment in Mucknamore at
seven.*

PO Brosnan: Did he describe the nature of this appointment?

*Miss Comerford: What he said to me was he had to see a man
about a dog.*

*The night was dark and very foggy, according to witness, and the
road was in a bad state, but he went off in good health, sober and
cheerful.*

*Staff Captain Sean Kavanagh, National Army, stated that he was
one of the party that proceeded to Mucknamore on the morning the
body was discovered, on receipt of the report from Mr Colfer. With
some difficulty, they had extracted the body from the sand with the aid
of ropes and an army truck. It was he who identified it as that of Dan
O'Donovan. There was nothing to indicate foul play. The hands had
not been tied.*

*They took the body to the morgue. On his person, they found a
typewritten letter rendered unreadable by the wet sands in which he
had met his end. Also a tobacco pouch with tobacco, a pipe, a book
and a photograph. There was a watch also, stopped at 7.14. "The time*

of the murder," cried Mrs O'Donovan, again interrupting proceedings.

Captain Kavanagh continued, testifying that when O'Donovan left the barracks that evening, that was the last any army personnel had seen of him until they received the emergency call the next morning. The army authorities had recently agreed to transfer O'Donovan to the new police force, the Civic Guards. He was a man with further promotion before him, most reliable, and his death a loss to the army and the country.

Final witness was Miss Margaret (Peg) Parle of Mucknamore. As this witness took the stand, commotion broke out, with much talk among the audience and again, cries of protest from the family of the deceased. After order had been restored, the police officer appealed to the jury to decide if the inquest was being properly conducted. The jury pronounced themselves perfectly satisfied that the case was being conducted in a most excellent manner by Mr Brosnan.

Testimony continued. Miss Parle said she was speaking on behalf of her family, as her father was too unwell following a recent bereavement. She was then questioned about a gun that was found in a ditch between her house and The Point the morning after the night in question. A witness had identified this gun as belonging to her brother, an Irregular killed in action some months ago. Miss Parle said she had no idea how it had turned up where it did.

PO Brosnan: When did you last see it?

Miss Parle: Before my brother was shot, I think. I can't really remember.

PO Brosnan: We've witnesses who say it was seen at your house recently.

Miss Parle: I'd say any such witnesses were only trying to bring us trouble.

PO Brosnan: We also have witnesses who say you blamed the deceased for the death of your brother.

Miss Parle: There's those who say so, I know that.

PO Brosnan: And what do you say?

Miss Parle: I say leave us alone. I say, stop trying to make something out of nothing.

PO Brosnan then asked Miss Parle about her movements and the movements of her family on the night in question and witness gave answers that showed all had alibis for the entire evening.

Therein the evidence ended. Mr O'Donovan rose to his feet again. He wanted to know why others had not been called on to testify. He became very excitable and made a number of allegations and was again ordered to be quiet or to leave the court.

Police Officer Brosnan said that he was as aware as the next man of the horrors dividing the country in two and so he had done everything to procure all the evidence possible. If anything in the nature of foul play had occurred, he had no evidence of it. All the evidence that had been unearthed he had placed before the jury to whom he now left the case.

The jury retired and returned with the verdict that the deceased had died from asphyxiation in sinking sands. There was no evidence to show how he came to be walking in such a treacherous area so late at night. Their verdict was "Death by Misadventure". They extended their sympathy to his relatives.

PART V
CREST

*L*et go, my sister suggested, that night after we calmed down. Let go, the sea waves whispered throughout my summer in Mucknamore. Let go, my own musings on freedom had urged. Then along you come and do it for me.

Nine months you spent dissolving my self from within and then at last you are here, out in the world. At last, I am holding you and knowing that your need, your ferocious, helpless human baby need, will reconstitute a whole new self around you.

From now on, I'll still be me, but I will also be all yours.

What an entrance you make! It begins with small contractions, well spaced, and for hours I cope well, but then I end up on a hospital bed the height and width of an ironing board, under orders not to move. All I want to do is get down on all fours. Maeve is there beside my bed, her cheerleader's face making me snap, pain growling through me. It was a mistake to bring her: I'm not going to be able to do this, I am going to fail at what she did effortlessly.

They put me on an oxytocin drip to speed the labour along: it is now four p.m. and I have been having contractions for fourteen hours. When I came into hospital, after holding out at home with Maeve as long as I dared, I was only two centimetres dilated. I later learn that it is normal for first labours to be lengthy, but my midwife tells me it's a problem. I hold out against her first offer of the oxytocin "to help me along", and her second. But when she tells me if the labour goes on "too" long you may become distressed, I capitulate.

As soon as the drip goes in, the pain becomes intolerable. I feel that the God I have always doubted has my belly in His fist and is intent on proving His power. Before long, I have a drip in my right arm, a blood-pressure monitor on the left, an epidural anaesthetic in my lower spine, a catheter bag to my bladder, a foetal monitor through my cervix onto the baby's head. My limbs tremble.

Every so often a falsely cheerful midwife comes in, snapping on a plastic glove to do another "internal". I hate her, I hate them all, and their steel instruments and unfeeling machines, but it is a machine, the foetal monitor spinning slow scrolls of paper etched with stalagmites and stalactites, your heartbeat, that keeps me from wanting to die.

"Phhhhh."

"And again, push," says Midwife One, looking at the monitor screen. She stands to the left of my bed with one of my legs in her arms, her colleague on my right has the other, and between them is a baby who's refusing to arrive. The epidural means I can't feel my contractions and I only know to push when they check the monitor and tell me.

"Push," says Midwife Two.

"Ph-ph-phhhhhhhhhhh."

I feel no active pain, nothing except a growing nausea in my stomach and a ferocious, dead trembling in my numbed, spreadeagled legs that extends up into my trunk. But Maeve, who's down at the other end, watching, is excited.

"Oh, Jo, there's the head," she says. "Black hair! Black! Thick as a brush. Go again."

"Push," says Midwife One.

"Good girl, push," says Midwife Two.

"Yes, push," says the obstetrician, two of the ten words he has so far exchanged with me in the fifty minutes he's spent fiddling with, and staring into, my nether regions. The others were, "Hello, Mum. How are we doing? Good, good."

Phphhh. Phphhh. Phphhh. Phphhhhhhhhhhhh. Oh God, I'm going to vomit. "I feel sick, I'm going to be —"

I gawk and Midwife One whips a silver-tin bowl from somewhere and sticks it under my chin. My insides contract, hurtling vomit out at one end and at the other squeezing you, like I'm a tube and you are a squidge of paste. You spurt out and the obstetrician and the two midwives all pitch forward to catch you. It is he who succeeds, grasping you with two firm hands, and for the first time I feel gratitude towards him.

"Oh, Jo," Maeve says. "Just look! Oh, the little darling!"

At last you are here. You are pink and purple. Your eyes are open. Your forehead is furrowed under a thatch of black hair and your hands are under your chin as if you're praying. Two fists like unbloomed buds. Four limbs curving close to the trunk, fat knees and elbows bent. A blue-and-cream woven cord attached to the stomach. A pair of distended, swollen testicles.

Testicles?

"You're a BOY?" I shout it out loud, my surprise filling the whole room and flowing out into the corridor.

Maeve laughs. "He's gorgeous, Jo! Oh, he's beautiful. A real beauty."

I want to hold you, but my stomach is taking another heave.

"She's going again," says Midwife Two, putting the tin bowl, still full of vomit, back under my chin. I spew again, trying to look at you at the same time. A second, deeper heave and I gawk —

auggghhhh! – and something else spurts out of me. The placenta.
It too flies through the air, as you did, but this time the medics fail
to catch and, splat, it hits the obstetrician's face like a slap of liver.

"Oh dear," I say. Blood is dripping from his jaw. "I'm sorry."

"It's not your fault," says Midwife One.

I know it isn't. Really, I'm not sorry at all. Their whole way of
doing this was so awful, so heedless of my needs, so careless of
my hopes. It is their fault, not mine, that I am stirred and shaken
to vomiting.

Though later I'll resent them and their hospital procedures
for utterly failing to give this holy moment its due, right now it
doesn't seem to matter, because they are handing you over. Here
you are, in my arms at last. Your skin is smooth, silky new. You
give your arms and legs an awkward jerk, astonished, it seems
to me, to find space where the womb wall used to be. You are
wrapped in an aura of serenity, still attuned to that other place,
wherever it is you came from. I pull you in close. Your first
holding in this new world.

Babies are our chance, I understand, our best stab at heaven.
Life is always offering us the opportunity to give, to help, to
serve, to take the path of the good, the path of the happy, but
most of us only manage it for our children.

And some fail even in that.

What about me? Your new blue eyes are looking up at me
like I'm all you'll ever want and I make a vow into them, to
strive to be enough.

"Do you want to try to feed him?" Maeve suggests.

I look at her and see that her eyes are glittering with
standing tears reflecting the light now coming in the window, as
dawn breaks on what appears to be another shell-grey,
Irish day.

Maeve has brought me in Ria's old swimming ring: without
it, I could not sit. Once the epidural wore off, I felt how I'd torn.
Sixteen stitches in three layers. I walk like a cowboy on hot

coals, but it doesn't matter. Nothing matters, everything zings. I'm still euphoric, higher than an acrobat, higher than an aerobat.

Hormones, Maeve says. She may be right, but that's not how I want to think about it.

She and I can't stop talking, talking, talking, like we've only just met. Last night she stayed late, laid across the end of my bed like I used to lie across Richard's. I'm giving her tips on how to handle Donal, Sue Denim style. She manages to implement about a tenth of the advice, but it's keeping them from settling back into the habits that ran them into trouble. In return, she gives me tips about baby care and mothering, which I intend to implement completely. If I can.

She's practicing freeing up, while I look forward to pinning part of myself — the part that spun loose when Richard died — right back down.

You start to cry and Maeve picks you up and hands you over. I am struck again by how beautiful you are, much, much more beautiful than any of the other babies in the ward. Maeve has told me that when researchers gave new mothers T-shirts worn by their own and other babies, all the women were able to smell out the one their own baby had had on. It's the kind of thing I wouldn't have believed before, but that now makes perfect sense. Now touch and smell and taste have the solidity of sight. I run my nose along the sweetness of your skin between earlobe and chin, then follow the trail with a line of kisses, while Maeve watches, smiling bounteously on us both.

The door opens. A massive bunch of flowers comes in, and behind it is Rory. He looks around the bouquet, hesitating in the doorway. Nervous. As well he might be.

Maeve gets up. "I think it's time I was off," she says, awkwardly. "Ria will be home from piano practice."

She bends to kiss my cheek, while squeezing my biceps tight

enough to bruise, and whispering in my ear: "Treat 'em mean to keep 'em keen."

What I said to her earlier about Donal. I manage to keep a deadpan face as I wave her away with a "See you tomorrow."

"I'm sorry," Rory says, once she's gone. "I know it shouldn't have taken me so long to get here."

"Damn right it shouldn't."

His hair has got longer; he has it tucked behind his ears. "I couldn't come until I was certain, Jo."

His eyes are close to mine, shining bright. And though I'd prefer if I could be angry with him, I know that if I were to look in a mirror, I'd see mine are their twin reflection.

Rory puts the flowers on the table under the window, the briefcase he's carrying on the floor beside the bed, and sits down beside me. "Congratulations," he says, easing back the blanket that wraps the bundle in my arms. He smiles at the sight. "Did everything go okay?"

His voice quavers. He is nervous, but I am calm. Already blooded.

"Fine," I smile, lying the mother's lie, discounting the barbarity of the process, the three layers of stitches, the nipple that's beginning to crack.

"Do you have a name?"

"Richard," I say, smiling.

"It's not —"

"A boy? Yes."

He laughs.

"I know," I say. "So sure and so wrong."

"You don't mind, do you?"

"Mind? No, not at all. It wasn't that I particularly wanted a girl."

He looks back in at the little sleeping face. "Richard, eh?" He tries it out. "Richard."

He takes a chair and we relax a little and I tell him about the birth, the drip and the vomit and the hurtling afterbirth. I make a good story out of it and when I reach the part about the placenta going all over the obstetrician's face, he throws back his head in a laugh, the way he does.

"And then," I continue, keeping up the entertainment, 'when it was all over, they handed him to me and I was brought face to face with these two enormous purple balls."

Why didn't somebody tell me about that in advance? I thought there was something wrong with you: such an angry colour and so huge, like an accusation.

"It was the same with Daragh," he says. 'Orla and I were shocked."

Daragh? Orla? Is this how it is to be?

"But they're shrinking now, right?" he says to you, putting out a gentle hand, stoking your black hair flat across your head. Watching his palm passing over that dip in your scalp makes my insides clench. "Get used to it, son," he says. "It'll be the story of your life."

You stir at the touch, then settle back down.

"How's the writing going?" Rory asks. "I suppose it's on hold now?"

"No, I'm still managing to take some time with it. It won't let me go."

"You're nearly finished, then?"

"Near enough."

He reaches down to the floor for his briefcase, clicks it open. "In that case, I've something for you."

"What? You're not serious? More from Mrs D.?"

"Your final delivery. You were only to get this if you fulfilled the request made in the first one and produced a family history.

I reckon you've done that." He hands me a mail-bag envelope, padded and very full.

"What's in here?"

"More letters, I believe."

"Really? Whose? Why were they kept separate from the rest?"

"I don't know. I was just..."

"...Following orders."

"Yes."

Yes. Mrs D.'s yes man, keeping this from me all summer. Is this why he is here? Nothing to do with us at all?

He hands me a white envelope, just as he did back in May, after her funeral. This time I open it immediately and read it in front of him.

The same salutation: Dear Siobhán.

Dear Siobhán,

Mistakes! My life, like everyone else's, is full of them. As I draw near to meeting my Maker, I am trying to put mine right.

Because you have appreciated the other papers and photographs I left you, I now give you these letters too. They will come as a bit of a surprise, I don't doubt — then again, you're surely getting used to the surprises by now.

You'll see there's a lot of letters, going back a long way, to just after the time when Maeve first got your address in England. From that day forward, your Gran wrote you a letter on the last day of each month and give it to me to stamp and send with the rest of the post. Only I never did. Each month, I'd put the letter in the secret drawer at the back of the bureau instead.

Now I know you'll think the worst of me for this, so let me say a few words in my defence. Your grandmother blamed herself for your leaving and staying away, a version of events which was all wrong — I'm sure you'll agree with that much. That woman was forever putting herself in the wrong and the older she got, the worse she became on that front. It was my strong belief that she should have some sign of interest from you before running after you with letters and attention.

I also thought, for a long time, that in giving them over to me, she was leaving the decision in my hands. That although we pretended the letters were sent, she was content that they wouldn't be, unless I was happy to send them. We had those kinds of understandings around a lot of things, no need for words.

By the time I realised that wasn't how it was in this case, that she only gave them to me because it was me who handled all the post for the house and the shop, it was too late. I couldn't start sending them off to you suddenly, out of the blue. You'd surely have told her. So I had no choice but to continue doing what I'd always done.

And so it went on to a few weeks before she died. Around that time, she spoke of you, said that if I ever saw you again, I was to tell you she was sorry. I told her I wouldn't, that she of all people had nothing to be sorry for, she was entirely misguided, etc. etc., but she became quite fixed and agitated on the matter and made me promise.

Now, by your actions, you have shown you care enough to know, so now I can tell you that.

And allow you the letters of that good woman. And as I do I think that perhaps it all turned out for the best, for I believe you will be a lot more open to them at this point than you would have been back when they were sent.

This is the last of it, Siobhán. No more communications from me, no more surprises. And I do hope that you will see my gesture for what it is.

I'm not one for the words, as you know — and those who don't write themselves get forgotten. I've accepted that. The only other thing I have to say is that your grandmother was the best person I ever met. None of us measured up to her. We can but try.

Which is why, as I go towards God, I want you to know that I, too, forgive all.

Your loving Mammy.

I take a quick look at the letters, conscious of Rory's eyes on me. Enough to see that they are lovely, simple and straightforward, each one passing on the doings of the days that had passed since the last.

Auntie Nora's health and Mrs D.'s golf scores and Maeve's teaching triumphs. News from the village and stories from the pub. Her work for Fianna Fáil. Helping to set up a credit union and a running-water scheme. And, at the end of each one, the same two sentences: "Know that we think of you and pray for you every single day, Jo. God bless you and keep you safe, Your loving Gran."

So of course I begin to cry, with Rory watching, unable to help myself. I look for the anger with Mrs D. that I expect to be there and find only confusion.

I'm saved by you, starting to stir, and I realise, from the snuffling you begin, that you are due a feed. Rory sits on, looking, as I lay down the letter and open my nightdress and nursing bra and distract myself from tears by fastening you on. We both watch your ears, moving as you suck.

Rory says, "Hungry little beggar, isn't he?"

I smile, stroke the little head that he stroked a few moments ago, feel the throb of the pulse beneath the membrane and the answering thud in myself.

"Motherhood suits you," Rory says after a long silence.

"Don't sound so surprised," I say, though I'm surprised myself.

"Where did you stay before you came in?"

"Maeve's."

"How was that?"

"Yeah. Fine. She's been very good to me."

You have fallen asleep now, mid-sip. Blissed out. Your lips — lined with milk — lie open round my nipple.

"So," Rory says. "What are the plans now?"

I look up at him, suddenly afraid, and begin to fix up my clothing to get a moment of time. I need to be in order for this.

"I'm going home." I use the word consciously.

"Home?"

"Back to San Francisco."

"I see. You've booked a flight?"

"Not yet. But I expect to leave in a week or ten days. As soon as we get the all clear from the doctors."

"So...?"

So...? Is that all he has to say? What does "So...?" mean? So...can I come with you? So...don't go? So...I've left my wife? So...what, Rory? What?

He drops his eyes. "I'm sorry about Orla coming to see you that day in Mucknamore," he says. "I had no idea."

"It's all right. We got on quite well, actually."

"That's what she said." And he frowns, as if that idea doesn't quite appeal to him.

"Are you two going to be okay?"

He narrows his eyes, as if refocusing. "Is that what you want? Me and Orla to be okay?"

"What do you want, Rory? Isn't that what we need to know?"

He moves his head in something between a nod and a shake. "I'm still so confused...I wish I could be sure of the right thing to do," he says.

And, in that moment, I find that it's okay. He doesn't need to be sure, because, finally, I am. I sit perfectly still then, letting him bring it up, all he has to say that I somehow know before him.

"I feel I need to go away from here," he says. "And I want it to be with you. I like myself so much more when I'm with you. I feel young again, and free, when I'm with you."

He's just the same, he'll always be the same. The younger me

262 | BEFORE THE FALL

was right. She did what she had to do. But I can't resent him. I know how he feels, like he is splitting in two...

"But that's not how it's going to be," I whisper. "Is it?"

"Oh, God, Jo. I really do want to be with you."

"I know you do, Rory. I know."

"Then let's."

"But it's not just you and me, is it?"

"You mean the baby?"

"And your kids. And Orla."

"But people do it, people get over all that."

I shake my head.

"You don't want to," he says, stunned. Part of him thought all he had to do was ask. Neither of us has forgotten just how fiercely I once loved him.

I reach for his hand, hold it. His fingers curl up inside mine.

"Loving you ruined me for love," I say, wanting to give him something. "I never loved properly again."

"But now you will," he says, miserably.

"I don't think that's what I'm looking for at the moment."

"You will."

He sounds so glum that I laugh, and he frowns at me, offended. He wants to keep us in love-story land, but that's not how it is for me, not any more.

I look down at your sleeping eyes. "Loving this little fellow properly will be quite enough for me for now.'"

He opens his mouth to say something, closes it again. We sit for a long time, the three of us, in the quiet of the room, hospital noises outside.

After a long time, he says: "You never told me the end of the story."

"I'll send you a copy of the manuscript," I say.

"Jo, you promised..."

In the middle of our loss, he is still avid for narrative resolution, his questing eyes full of its hold. What happened?

Who did it? Was it really Peg? Tell me, tell. Of course, it's not just a story to him, any more than it was to me. He wants the ending that was our beginning.

"I'm almost finished," I say. "And the book will tell it better than I can."

He shakes his head at me, resigned.

I slip from the bed to lay the baby down in his cot beneath the window and Rory comes to stand beside me, looking in as I wrap the blanket tight around him. The little hands are curled into fists, one on either side of his closed eyes. We stand looking at him for a long time. Then Rory says, "So this is goodbye?"

I'm afraid to look up at him while the feelings that goodbye always bring on are welling into my throat. I think of the aeroplane I will take next week, that will wing me and my son — my son! — westwards, towards yesterday.

"You'll come back again to Mucknamore, won't you?" Rory says. "For a visit?"

"Sure," I say, what I said to Hilde. But then I remember it's him. "Actually, I don't think so, Rory. Not soon, anyway. You come and see me instead."

"I will. I definitely will." He is fervent, like it's a vow.

"I'd like that," I say.

"And you'll send me that manuscript?"

"I promise."

He reaches for me then and we turn to hold each other. With my bump gone I feel, for the first time this summer, the full length of him, with nothing between us. We hold each other, hard. Then our lips search the other's out and we kiss. One kiss, firm and long and deep, with eyes clenched tight. One kiss with everything in it.

Then we let each other go.

PART VI
SPILL

PLASH: NORAH

1932

*C*hild made her Confirmation yesterday, all glowing in white. Like a shiny little angel, but with the devil's eyes when she looks at Norah. Norah would have liked to go to the Confirmation, to see the bishop on his throne, his hat half the height of himself, and the white flowers and the prayers, but the devil eyes that didn't want her made her stay at home.

Peg thinks Child is so good and Child wants to keep it that way. "Isn't little Maureen such a good girl?" says Peg, never knowing it's only like that while she's around, that behind her back it's the nasty looks and faces, and the cold hard words for Norah.

Yesterday, when the two of us were on our own in the kitchen, Child told me I was to stop looking at her. I have the eye of a jackdaw, she said, always following her around, gawping at her, whatever she's doing. Like the eye of a dirty old crow.

"Is Mrs Duggan against Fianna Fáil?" Child asked Peg.

Fianna Fáil is Mr de Valera's latest big idea, the new political party that got him back the power.

"No, Mrs Duggan is not against Fianna Fáil," said Peg. "She's got her eye too much on the next world to care what goes on in this one. Why do you ask?"

Child told her what wee Willie said, that his mother, the praying woman, told him to keep away. From her, from us, from all Parles. Why? Child wanted to know, and out it all came, pouring, all the people who say all the bad things.

Miss O'Neill who is always looking at her with a frown on, as if she has done something wrong, when she's doing nothing at all.

Young Cissie Cummins who said she was surprised that Child was allowed to do a Confirmation at all. Surprised she was even let go to Mass. And Rita Breen, trying to be kind, saying: You shut up, Cissie Cummins, hasn't she as much right as anyone else?

And Mr White, who the other day was going to pat her on the head, but pulled himself back at the last minute.

And most especially Father John, who's always picking her out on his visits to the school, saying to Miss O'Neill that there was more joy in Heaven over one lost lamb than all the rest, looking at her when he said it.

Why is she a lost lamb? Child wants know of Peg. Why is he always telling her to keep up with her prayers? Why doesn't he say that to the others? Why is it only to her?

And Cissie Cummins again, when they were talking in the schoolyard about the plaque going up to her Uncle Barney, said: Uncle, how are you!

What did she mean by that, Mammy?

Poor Peg, her face pulled tight, didn't know what to be saying. The Child was close to crying with all her questions and Peg gathered her in so tight it must have hurt her back.

"You're not to mind that Cummins one," Peg said into Child's hair, her voice all cracked. "Do you hear me? Pay no attention whatever to the likes of her."

"But what did she mean, Mammy?"

"Lord above knows, child. How could anyone know what's going on in a head like that? You're not to mind her, d'you hear me? You're not to mind any of them."

Child came out of her hug and saw Peg's face and put one hand up to touch it.

"It's all right, Mammy," she said. "I won't mind any more."

Now Child goes sneaking round the house, her ear pressed to doors to see what she can hear. Or through the shivery darkness after everyone's in bed, to read the diaries that Peg thinks she's kept under lock and key. Oh, Child, Child, you'd want to watch out. You're going to find more than you want to find...

Coolanagh. The word hurts me too.

Write it down, Peg says. Don't try to forget.

Don't shy away, is what she means, don't be afraid.

Never wondering if maybe she's too brave for her own good.

What I want to write is the real wrong of it, which was mostly in what came after. The way he would look at me, eyes twisted up whenever they had to turn my way, as if he believed his own made-up story.

That was the worst wrong of all. What is that made him do that? That's the only question I'm left with, and all the answer I'll ever have.

We went together, Peg and I, the two of us peering into the fog. Double-blindfolded, once by dark and twice by fuddling mist. Six days we'd had of it by then and the feeling that it would never again move off. Small and careful our steps, because under our feet was a road of slush, and ahead of us who knew what?

It's hopeless, Peg said. We can't see a thing.

But we couldn't go back to the house to sit by the fire, nerves scraping, so we kept on going and we were glad we did. For it wasn't hopeless. We found what we went looking for.

They all think it was Peg who did the deed and they all go shrinking silent round.

As if. Our kindly Peg? The country might have turned itself upside down, but some things are set. The sun comes up of a morning. The sea pulls in and out with the tides. Peg Parle could not kill my brother; she had too much love for him.

And anyway, what she did to unknown Free State solders was a matter of enough remorse to her. The desire to atone for that drives her goodness to all — and always will, for all her living days

No, it wasn't Peg who killed Dan, only Peg's old talk. Too much talking, she did, up there in the sickroom with the door well closed. I didn't know she was doing that: saying those things to her mammy. Things I never said to her. Things I never thought anyone would say.

Mrs Parle did it for me, Peg says, but I was never asked. If I was, I'd have told her...

But Mrs Parle wasn't a woman for asking.

It was I who saw her first, through the fog. Like a pile of rags she looked, all in a heap by the ditch. I nudged Peg and pulled her over.

"Mammy!" Peg cried, a muffled cry, for who knew what might be beyond the next layer of mist. "Mammy, is it you?"

Mrs Parle was lying still, a lump of black in the dimness. Peg went over to her, tried to lift her, and her mother roused. "Peg?"

"Oh, Mammy, yes. Yes, I'm here."

"I...fell..."

But was it on the way to do the deed, the thing she had said to Peg she would do, if she only had the strength? Like a woman possessed she had been above in her room, Peg said. Her eyes glittering and her mouth saying all sorts of unspeakables. Was she on her way there, or on the way back?

"Didn't..."

"It's all right, Mammy. Don't talk. We're going to get you home."

"Didn't..." She was bad for breath, very bad. "Not shot..."

"Oh, thank God, Mammy. Thank God."

"Yes, God. I let...God...decide..." She dribbled a bit and flopped on us, seemed to go.

"Merciful Jesus," Peg said. "Is she . . . ?"

But she wasn't, only passed out.

We took her up between us, our shoulders under her arms. She was heavy, though dwindled with her sickness, and her bones felt thin, like they were almost about to snap.

"What did she mean?" Peg asked me. "What did she mean, 'I let God decide'?"

Between us, we hauled her home, careful at first, but after a while too muscle-sore and frightened of being found out to be gentle. In the end, we were pulling her along between us, her boots dragging behind. In the house, the light felt bright. Child was still asleep in her pram where we left her.

Now Peg could see the state of what we had brought in: her mother, so reduced you'd want to howl, but we had no time for tears.

"Lie her down," Peg said. "We'll have to take her up the stairs on the flat. Hurry, before Daddy comes in."

Peg took the weight of her shoulders and chest, and I took the legs. It wasn't easy getting her round the twist in the stairs. In the bedroom, we took off the nightdress Mrs Parle had on under her coat, all mudded up and sandy at the bottom, to make her clean and dry. In the middle of it, Peg's father called up the stairs and I was left alone with the mother and the two pinpoints of red on her chalky face, like a bee stung her — once, twice — on the bones of her cheeks.

She let God decide, she said. Decide what? The question was a scourge to us. We never thought of Coolanagh, not then, not until next morning when John Colfer came back in his boat.

"She could do with Dr Lavin," Peg said, coming back into the room. "But I'm afraid to call him. What if he notices her wet hair?"

She took a towel and lifted her mother's insensible head off the pillow to slip it under, and then she broke. With the worst danger past, the full knowledge of what her mother had set out to do flooded *through her, and she dropped her head into her hands. I thought she was going to cry, but it was more of a wail that she let out.*

And then a vow. "I swear this, Norah. Whatever's been done this night, that child below won't suffer. No more tit-for-tat. Whatever happened dies in this room."

Dear Peg. As if she had the giving of what flows and what will be stopped. A strange notion, inherited from her mother.

Her mother — who did what she did for me, according to Peg — trying to pull something sweet-smelling from the mire. But I never asked for that. My brother did me wrong, the way he put it all over onto me, but I never would have wanted that.

For what Peg and Mrs Parle and Dan himself could overlook, I never could: he was my brother. He did me wrong, but he was my brother.

THE END

IN THE HOUR

THE SEQUEL TO BEFORE THE FALL

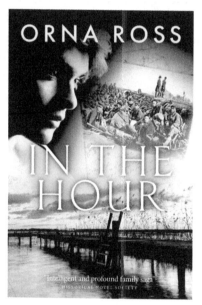

| Coming Soon

In the final book of the trilogy *In The Hour,* again set in San
Francisco, California and Wexford, Ireland, it is now 2010 and

Jo Devereux is a single mother, living with her son Richard, the baby who was born at the end of *Before The Fall*.

Richard ("Don't call me Ritchie!") has a secret, which Jo knows about but they never discuss, but that–and Jo's enduring loneliness–aside, they have been as happy as a mother and son can be. But now, as Richard enters his teens, life is growing fraught.

As he sets about breaking free and becoming his own person, Jo begins to question her long-held narrative about her own coming of age. When he starts his own investigation into his father and his grandparents, new secrets come tumbling out. Jo realizes that there were questions she never even thought to ask.

In the Hour finds that scouring through family history is a process greatly helped by the Internet. Richard has no need to travel to Ireland as Jo did back in 1995 and when he finds Rory online, and now a widower, Jo's carefully constructed life begins to fall apart again.

You can find In the Hour here.

CONNECT

LIKE TO BE A READER MEMBER?

YOU'LL RECEIVE A FREE BOOK AND OTHER BONUSES

MEMBERSHIP includes a free book, advance review copies

And my monthly "HISTORIES & MYSTERIES" newsletter

Subscribe here: ornaross.com/readers

I'D LOVE YOUR FEEDBACK

If you enjoyed this book, would you consider leaving a brief review online on your favorite online bookstore that takes reviews: Amazon, Apple, Barnes and Noble or Goodreads?

A good review is very important to authors these days as it helps other readers know this is a book worth their time.

It doesn't have to be long. Just a sentence saying what you enjoyed and a star-rating is all that's needed. Many thanks.

ALSO BY ORNA ROSS

MORE BOOKS: FICTION

My novels are family murder mysteries, stories of lies, secrets and the ties that bind, across centuries and continents

—The Irish Trilogy—

An epic trilogy that follows five generations of women as they move through the momentous dramas of the 20th century.

—The Yeats Trilogy—

A famous poet, his revolutionary muse, and her confused daughter. What is true and what can only be imagined?

—Blue Mercy—

A heart-breaking, mother and daughter mystery, with a patricide at its heart.

You can buy my novels directly from me on my website, or on your favorite online store

MORE BOOKS: POETRY

My poetry aims to inspire. It doesn't deny doubt, damage or despair but seeks that secret space where we can also transact with the truth of beauty.

—Chapbooks—

Chapbooks of inspirational poetry: Ten poems at a time.

—Themed Poetry Selections—

Here is Where: A Book of Remembrance Poetry

Allowing Now: A Book of Mindfulness Poetry

Nightlight as it Rises: A Book of Love Poetry

—Occasional Poetry Selections—

Poetry for Christmas

Poetry for Mother's Day

AND MORE

POETRY BOOKS:

You can buy my poetry books directly from me on my website, or on your favorite online store

BECOME A POETRY PATRON:

You can become a patron of my poetry on Patreon.com/OrnaRoss.

My Patreon page is supported by a band of poetry lovers and indie poets who receive exclusives and bonuses from me. It's also where I feature the work of other indie poets through

#indiepoetryplease

PUBLICATION NOTE

he early parts of this trilogy were first published in 2006 by Penguin Ireland as Lovers Hollow, and subsequently republished by me in 2011, and further developed into a trilogy. This allowed me to give the books the title and treatment I had first envisaged when writing the books.

The joy of that self-publishing experience, and the experience of selling more books than Penguin, made me a passionate advocate for indie authors and led to the formation of the Alliance of Independent Authors.

ACKNOWLEDGMENTS

My thanks to Jane Dixon Smith for cover design, to Margaret Hunter of Daisy Editorial for editing and proofreading and to Sarah Begley and the Book Whisperer team, especially Emily Volpe, for assistance with editorial and formatting. As in *After the Rising* I wish to pay tribute to Wexford's talented and devoted local historians. I am greatly indebted to their work, particularly that which acknowledges the lives of women.

MY PODCAST

FAMILY HISTORIES & LIFE MYSTERIES

Follow my "Histories & Mysteries"
podcast for more poems, stories and
behind-the-books news

ebook: 978-1-913588-53-3
Paperback: 978-1-913588-54-0
Large Print: 978-1-913588-55-7
HB: 978-1-913588-56-4
Audio: 978-1-913588-57-1

FontPublications

FONT PUBLICATIONS IS THE PUBLISHING IMPRINT FOR ORNA ROSS FICTION AND POETRY, THE GO
CREATIVE! BOOKS AND THE ALLIANCE OF INDEPENDENT AUTHORS AUTHOR PUBLISHING GUIDES.
ALL ENQUIRIES: INFO@ORNAROSS.COM

Made in the USA
Middletown, DE
27 August 2022

72421896R00166